THE MANKILLER

There are several beautiful women in ex-footballer
Wayne Shakespeare's life. Perhaps one too many...

THE MANKILLER

There are several beautiful women in ex-footballer
Wayne Shakespeare's life. Perhaps one too many...

MEREO
Cirencester

Mereo Books

1A The Wool Market Dyer Street Cirencester Gloucestershire GL7 2PR
An imprint of Memoirs Publishing www.mereobooks.com

THE MANKILLER: 978-1-86151-611-4

First published in Great Britain in 2016
by Mereo Books, an imprint of Memoirs Publishing

Copyright ©2016

T A WARD has asserted his right under the Copyright Designs and Patents Act
1988 to be identified as the author of this work.

The address for Memoirs Publishing Group Limited can be found at
www.memoirspublishing.com

The Memoirs Publishing Group Ltd Reg. No. 7834348

The Memoirs Publishing Group supports both The Forest Stewardship Council®
(FSC®) and the PEFC® leading international forest-certification organisations. Our
books carrying both the FSC label and the PEFC® and are printed on FSC®-certified
paper. FSC® is the only forest-certification scheme supported by the leading
environmental organisations including Greenpeace. Our paper procurement policy
can be found at www.memoirspublishing.com/environment

Typeset in 10/15pt Century Schoolbook
by Wiltshire Associates Publisher Services Ltd. Printed and bound in Great Britain
by Printondemand-Worldwide, Peterborough PE2 6XD

ONE

Sex is seldom as it seems. Gentle sex may bruise the soul. Casual sex might maim a lover. A new affair could be ending the last.

These were the thoughts the black-haired woman was having while she waited outside the house of a man she planned to kill. Waiting, waiting, waiting. That was what she remembered most about their relationship. Waiting for him while he lived his life in a rush. Meals on the hoof. Talk on the trot. Sex by the clock. He made love like she was a microwave oven set on three minutes. Sex on the run could be fun sometimes, exciting, breathless, explosive, but not when you became too involved with the runner.

She had often felt like another window in his diary. *You love your diary more than you love me*, she'd told him at the end, throwing his mobile phone at him, adding, *you might as well shag your watch, you look at that more than you look at me.* Then she'd walked out of the door. Only later did she think about the possessions she'd left behind.

That was months ago. Now she was waiting for him again. Waiting to collect her belongings. Planning sex on the run. Waiting to kill him. It was 1.20 on a Wednesday afternoon, and he was twenty minutes late.

She felt more energetic than she had for a while. Her body was lightweight and far too slim, but the depression had abated. She wore a flared dress, black suspender belt, black stockings and nothing else except jewellery. She had worn this outfit for him in the past and it had given her more sexual power. Would he notice that she was thinner and the dress was now too large? Probably not.

His car screeched down the road, swung into the driveway and came to a halt.

She got out of her car and smoothed her clothes. Put on her best smile.

He was gruff and monosyllabic. No time in his diary for an apology. He unlocked the door and ushered her inside.

'They're on the chair,' he said, pointing to a pile of clothes, CDs and DVDs. She darted across the room, picked up what was hers and sat down on the large easy chair without being asked. She slumped into the seat, flashing her thigh and maybe more.

'I'd better check these are all mine and not someone else's,' she said, smiling.

She went through them quickly. Each held a memory of their relationship. She should never have fallen in love with him. His disturbed and restless sleep, his persistent lateness. He had everything in the wrong order – cart before horse, matter before mind, orgasms before foreplay. But here she was again. One final entry in his diary.

She looked up quickly and caught him studying her legs as if they were last week's sales figures. I can still do it for him, she thought.

'I always liked this chair,' she told him. 'Do you remember having me here on your birthday? Wasn't I wearing similar clothes?'

He stared at her.

'That was wonderful,' she said, smiling, squirming a little in the chair.

'Of course I remember,' he said.

'A real turn-on,' she said, starting to stroke her own thigh. 'Wow. I can get wet just thinking about it.' She saw the hypnotic look in his eyes. She smiled to herself when he took a crafty glance at his watch before gazing again at her legs.

He took a slight step towards her and she could hear him breathing heavily.

'Come on,' she said. 'Come on. Quickly.'

Then she felt his hands, rough and urgent, run up her stockings, past the naked promise at the top and into her pubic hair. She heard him gasp, or maybe she was hearing herself. She sensed him fumbling with his belt, his trousers dropping away with a clatter of keys as they hit the floor. She slid her pelvis forward in the chair, her torso further back, and rested one thigh on the arm. With the speed of a man who was late for his next appointment, he came into her quickly and deeply, at an angle that she particularly enjoyed. Come on, she thought, have an orgasm, have a *petite mort*, or even a *grande mort*.

Her body moulded with the chair as he found his rhythm. Such a comfortable easy chair, so comfortable, except for the aches in her joints.

'Hhh . . . huh,' he said. 'Hore . . . whoo . . .'

Maybe he'll have a heart attack, she thought. Save him from the death she had planned.

'Come on,' she said again.

'Hoooorre,' he grunted. 'Huh, huh, hooree . . . Yeah . . . Yeah.'

'Come on,' she repeated.

So he came on, with a shudder and a grunt and a powerful plunge that nearly toppled the chair. And she watched him travel a thousand miles away on his journey of selfishness, and then return very slowly. That did the trick, she thought. She smiled at him.

He smiled back.

'Wow,' he said.

'Wow,' she said.

She arranged her clothing and waited for the moment that used to hurt her so much, the moment that would now make her laugh. Yes, there it was. He was looking at his watch again.

'I'm going to be late,' he said.

'Mustn't be late,' she said.

In the old days she might have felt guilty and grubby. Today she felt good. If her plan went well, he really would be short of time.

They walked out together and she took one look back. This time all she'd left behind was the smell of sudden sex and the impact of contact. She laughed aloud as he got in his car. It was the first time she'd laughed aloud for months. It was the first time she'd made love with hatred.

Sex is seldom as it seems.

Kate Park was a tall, elegant woman in her mid-thirties. She had a PhD from studying sexual relationships but would never call herself *Doctor* Kate Park, especially now that she was working as a nurse. Hospitals had enough doctors already.

'Were you with him when he died?' Kate's friend Deborah asked as they sat inside Kate's temporary home, a canal boat called *Commuter's Fantasy* moored near the centre of Oxford. They were talking about the death of Kate's long-term lover, an American sexologist called Theodore Merlin.

'Yes, I was there at the end,' said Kate. 'They say it's a good thing, but I'm not so sure. It was such a haunting image. I thought I could handle it because I've seen others die, but . . .'

'It's different when it's your own,' said Deborah. 'He was everything to you.'

'Yes,' Kate agreed. 'Teddy was my soul-mate, my lover and my mentor. He schooled me in his work and I promised him I would take it forward. I don't know if I can live up to that promise. I am not sure I could think rationally about sex for a long time.'

Kate reached for tissues. She recalled holding Teddy Merlin's hand during his last moments. They were two connected people, but only one had any energy. Aware that hearing was often the last sense to fail, Kate had talked to Teddy quietly while stroking his arm. She told him how much she had appreciated his love and wisdom over the years, and how much he'd meant to her. She told him that he'd taught her well. She spoke about how she was looking forward to taking his work forward and calling herself a sexologist.

'It was so strange, when he died,' Kate told Deborah. 'He gave out a few last gasps and then he died and there was a real calm. Then I felt something surge through my hand and into my body. It was as if some deserving part of him was coursing through me.'

'You will feel his energy and drive. It will carry you through. Widows tell me that it does get better.'

'I know. But I've got his *Sex and Sexuality* book to update and I can't face it.'

'You gave him a wonderful send-off, Kate. Being with someone you love while they are dying is the best thing you can do. You were devoted. You hardly went out of the house for weeks. You gave him understanding, practical nursing and all-encompassing love.'

'I was so unprofessional, Deb,' Kate said. 'When he died I collapsed on his chest and cried. I don't know how long I was there.' She looked directly at Deborah. 'I forgot to note the exact time of death.'

'I think you can be forgiven,' Deborah said.

Kate looked at her friend. They had met a few years ago on a training course. Deborah was now working as a sex therapist.

'How are you, Deb?' Kate said. 'Is your business still skewed to non-orgasmic women?'

'Nice switch, Kate,' Deborah said. 'But it doesn't work with me. Let's go back to where you were alone with Teddy's body.'

Kate nodded.

'After he died I told myself that the grieving could wait,' Kate said. 'I wanted to lay him out myself, wash the body and wrap him in a sheet. I needed to phone the undertaker, contact his doctor, tell his daughters, deal with his ex-wife, register the death, arrange the funeral, phone his friends, clear the house, look for somewhere to live, find a way of earning money.'

'It's a lot for you.'

'Too much change,' Kate echoed. 'And now I'm living on a canal boat.'

'Who owns this boat?' asked Deborah.

'She's called Caprice. She lives in a dream world, but that's good because it takes me out of myself.'

'Is she the one with a first in English Literature?'

'Probably a double first.'

'Is there enough room for you here?' Deborah asked, looking up at the low ceiling.

'Not really. I hit my head four times a day, and the sofa-bed's too small. Caprice has been wonderful, but I feel cramped and constrained. I can barely breathe for grief. I'm pleased you came to see me on the boat. I was scared of breaking down if we met in public.'

'Are you sleeping?'

Kate scrunched up her face.

'Not really,' she said. 'I'm scared to sleep because of the dreams. Last night I dreamt Teddy was still alive. In my dream he'd recovered from his terminal illness, it was all a misdiagnosis and we were getting on with life again. Then I woke up and Teddy was indisputably dead. I wanted to scream.'

'Could you not have stayed in his house?'

'I couldn't afford it on my own. Even if I was working full-time.'

'Please tell me that Teddy was a rich man and has left it all to you.'

'Not at all. He died with some debts, but he owned a house in the States. His estate goes to his daughters and ex-wife.'

'What about you?'

'My sole inheritance is the proceeds of his major textbook.' Kate laughed. 'I have to finish off the next edition to earn some money from that, and I can't face it.'

Kate stopped talking and cried some more. She could smell Teddy Merlin on the sweater she was wearing. The watch on her wrist had belonged to him, and she was haunted by Teddy Merlin's last spell of arrhythmic breathing.

'I can still hear his last gasps,' Kate Park told her friend. 'Everything revolves around breathing, doesn't it? Birth, death and orgasm. They all come from the same family of noise and peace.'

Wayne Shakespeare was mulling over Tracey Holroyd's plan to kidnap a professional sports star. He was also trying to decide whether Tracey Holroyd's eyes were green or grey. The eyes stared back like two investigative journalists.

It was mid-afternoon that same Wednesday. Wayne had known Tracey for fifteen minutes and was captivated by the coolness of her manner and the casual way she concealed her natural beauty. Her reddish hair was tied back in a blue rubber-band. A few loose strands straggled past her ginger eyebrows and pale cheeks.

'What do you think?' Tracey asked Wayne.

'I think it will carry on raining,' Wayne said. Through the café window he could see water bouncing in the gutters of Oxford's High Street. 'It might be worth checking the time of the next lifeboat.'

'What do you think about the plan?' asked Tracey Holroyd, her eyes greying with anger.

Wayne guessed her to be mid-twenties. She wore a grey shirt and grey jeans, and Wayne wondered how she would look in expensive clothes with her hair down.

'It's a good plan,' he said. 'I can add a few details.'

He'd been surprised by her professionalism. She'd outlined the scheme in a strong, soft voice that didn't carry to the next table.

'Tell me the details,' she said. Her pen was poised over her notebook. Her eyes – definitely grey – were brazen and calculating. Wayne was familiar with plenty of women, but he knew that Tracey Holroyd could bring him new insight and experience.

'I can talk to the assistant manager for you,' Wayne said. 'He's a mate of mine from my playing days. I'll happily talk to the goalkeeper too. He's an awkward lad and not easy to handle but I may be able to get through to him.'

'I know. That's why I've come to you.'

Wayne thought back to when his football career had been at its peak and his security business just a hobby.

'The plan,' Tracey Holroyd reminded him.

'I can't guarantee I can persuade him,' Wayne said.

'I have a foolproof way, as long as we go through you.'

'Have you got a writer for your press releases?'

'Yeah, the editor of the student magazine.'

'Use any trick you can to hit the public on the morning of the match. Maybe you could cut one of his hands off.'

Tracey looked up from her notebook.

'You can stage anything with photographs these days,' Wayne added.

'Will we get the money we want?'

'I think you've got a good chance. Normally with a kidnapping the money comes from one source. Here you are looking for it from everyone and anyone. You need arrangements for collecting the money, and for counting and banking it safely. You need plenty of locked cans and security for the money in transit.'

'When will you speak with our goalkeeper?' Tracey asked.

'*Our* goalkeeper?' Wayne said, smiling. 'He's not yours until you kidnap him.'

Her eyes changed to the colour of steel. Wayne doubted that a man could find any softness in her eyes.

'I'll catch him after training tomorrow,' Wayne said.

'When you speak to him, tell him The Cat will be there too.'

Her voice carried real authority.

'The Cat?' he asked. 'Is that another goalkeeper?'

Tracey Holroyd looked puzzled.

'It's a common nickname,' Wayne added. 'Goalkeepers are often called The Cat because of their reactions.'

'Oh.'

'Some are called it because they are always in a flap,' Wayne added. 'Others because they give their defenders kittens. Or sometimes it's because they're called Tom . . .'

'Spare me the jokes, please.'

'That's strange. I thought you were into finding good jokes.'

She looked at Wayne like he didn't understand anything outside his front door. Wayne stared back. She had the competitive eyes of a self-sufficient woman. She collected jokes as business products.

'You'd make this work with or without me, wouldn't you?' he asked.

'Of course. Once we had the idea, it was forward all the way.'

'Ah, the simple paradox of life – we have to live our lives forwards but we can only understand them backwards.'

Tracey Holroyd's eyes showed personal curiosity for the first time.

'Kierkegaard,' Wayne said. He'd overheard the quotation in the café while he was waiting for her. The eavesdropping in Oxford was impressive.

'I didn't know you were a philosopher,' said Tracey Holroyd. 'I thought you were an ex-footballer who had his own security business.'

'There's more to security than checking the toilets every hour.'

'You work for Richard Bromage?'

'Yes. We call him Mister Richard.'

Richard Bromage was the owner of many companies, including a London football club.

'And you do security at the university?' asked Tracey Holroyd.

'Sorry?'

Wayne's mind had drifted. He was thinking about Richard Bromage and his daughter Juliet. Especially Juliet.

'You work at the university?' Tracey repeated.

Wayne nodded.

Tracey Holroyd shifted the shoulder-strap of her bag and prepared for departure.

'I'd like to ask you more about that, but I have to work now,' she said, putting her notebook in her shoulder-bag.

'Thanks for your help. Ring me on my mobile when you've made contact with Buck Hanson.'

'Aye aye, Boss,' Wayne said softly, but Tracey Holroyd was already halfway to the door. He watched her grey jeans as they blended into the grey day and the High Street hustle.

Wayne sat with the dregs of his drink and smiled at the prospects ahead. He would look forward to sparring with a goalkeeper he disliked called Buck Hanson, and he'd meet with his old mate Bob Blazer, assistant manager of a London football club.

That afternoon the kidnapping seemed like the best stunt Wayne had ever heard. He could see why Tracey Holroyd was in charge of the Rag Committee. She was older than most students and very businesslike. She was in charge of the Rag Magazine joke-book and it was her

idea to kidnap a top-class goalkeeper and ask supporters
to pay the ransom money.

A stunt for charity.

Free the Number One.

What a ruse.

TWO

'I need to move soon,' Kate Park told Caprice, as they sat across a small table on Caprice's boat. 'You've been wonderful to me, but I need my own space.'

At times Kate felt completely lost without Theodore Merlin. Adrenaline had carried her through the funeral period. She had cleared out the rented house and put her books and files in store. Now she had slumped.

'Imagine that you are on a favourite beach,' Caprice said. 'The sun is a pleasant temperature and your room stretches to the horizon.'

'Thank you, Caprice,' said Kate, thinking her surrealist friend wasn't always helpful.

'The place is in your head,' said Caprice.

'I was thinking more in terms of practical ideas, like where to look for a room.'

'Imagine an advertisement with your favourite

wording,' said Caprice. 'Gorgeous specimen of manly landlord requires tall female lodger.'

Kate sighed. This canal-boat arrangement was always going to be temporary.

'Perfect host for a bereaved woman,' Caprice continued. 'A confidential listening ear.'

'Very low rent,' Kate added, giving in to Caprice's game.

'Cooking and cleaning provided. Free massage to the first thousand applicants.'

'Oh sure.'

'Wayne Shakespeare,' said Caprice.

'Pardon?'

'Wayne Shakespeare. I was once his lodger, oft his lover.' Caprice picked up her mobile phone. 'His number is begot in the ventricle of memory. Preferment goes by cellphone and affection.'

Kate had given up trying to make sense of Caprice's mind. She let Caprice take her by the hand and lead her on to the roof of the boat, the only place where Caprice could get mobile phone reception.

Caprice dabbed her mobile a few times and handed it to Kate.

'What if I am disturbing him while he's driving?' Kate said.

'He'll tell you what he's doing when he answers the phone.'

'I don't know this man,' Kate said.

'I'm not on the train,' a male voice told Kate.

Kate looked at Caprice and rolled her eyes.

'Er, Wayne Shakespeare?' asked Kate.

'In person on the telephone,' Wayne said. 'You're not Caprice.'

'No.'

'I know what's happened,' said Wayne. 'You've found Caprice's phone and now you're dialing the last name on her contacts list to see whose phone it is.'

'No, my name is Kate Park,' she said. 'Caprice has given me her phone to call you. She told me you sometimes have a room for rent in your house.'

'I do have a spare room,' Wayne said. 'Would you like to see it?'

'May I ask a few questions first?'

'Ask away.'

'What size is the room?'

'Oh, big enough for a desk, a double bed, a chest of drawers and a small cupboard . . .'

'Is it warm?'

'The cupboard?'

'No, the room.'

You fell for that, Kate told herself.

'There's central heating,' Wayne said. 'Use it as much as you'd like. It works well.'

'And quiet?'

'Reasonably. The whole area shakes when a heavy goods train goes by but everyone gets used to that. In fact it's more fun than a . . .'

'Just you in the house?'

'Yes.'

'I see. Are you a smoker?'

'No. I'm also quiet and don't drink very much. I can

give you references if you wish.'

'I already have one.'

'Who's interviewing who here?' Wayne said. He laughed.

'How much is the rent?' Kate asked.

'It depends on what you can afford, and whether it works out between us.'

'How do you mean?'

'What do you do for a living?'

'I have a whole collection of jobs. I still do some bank nursing . . .'

'And?' Wayne prompted.

'I teach a module at one of the universities, I edit a reference book . . .'

'What's the book?'

'It's called *Sex and Sexuality*.'

'The room's very cheap,' Wayne said. 'You sound really interesting.'

Kate hesitated again. She looked across at Caprice, who was enjoying herself immensely.

'May I come and look at it?' Kate asked.

'Whenever it's convenient for you.'

'About an hour.'

'Perfect. Just time to redecorate the whole house. Do you know where it is?'

'I can ask Caprice.'

'See you then.'

They disconnected.

'You see,' said Caprice. 'It will come if you dream it. Did he tell you that he plays the drums?'

'No,' said Kate, looking shocked.

'That's good. If Wayne didn't like the sound of you he would say he was learning the drums.'

Wayne Shakespeare and Kate Park met at the front door of Wayne's house.

'Come in,' Wayne said. 'Welcome to your potential residence. This place has great potential but it's had it for twenty years. It's the first room on the right.'

Kate walked into the room and assessed it with big brown eyes.

'I allow people their privacy,' Wayne said. 'If the door's ajar, I'm allowed to knock. If the door's shut, I push messages under the door.'

'I need somewhere for a short time,' Kate said. 'Then I may leave Oxford. Is that a problem?'

'Not at all.'

He wandered out of the room and Kate followed.

'This is the lounge,' he said, waving his right arm towards the cushions on the floor. 'There's a television in the study upstairs.'

'Minimalist,' Kate said.

'I was raised by a man who taught me to be sensible with money. He taught me to buy furniture that was experienced and cheap.'

'Your father?'

'No,' Wayne said. 'My grandfather.'

Kate looked at the dog.

'He's never bitten anyone yet,' Wayne told her.

'I'm not surprised.'

'Papier-mâché,' Wayne said. 'Doesn't need walking but listens to all your troubles and scares burglars.'

'Cheap on dog food, too,' Kate said.

'He's a cross between a Weimaraner and a bad artist's impression of one.'

'Does he have a name?'

'Rover.'

'Is that because he stays still?'

'Exactly. Let me show you the kitchen and dining area.'

She followed him.

'Ah, you do have some chairs,' she said.

'Yes, this is a good table to work on.'

Wayne watched Kate curiously as her eyes scanned the kitchen.

'I'll get a firm of industrial cleaners in,' Wayne said. 'Some potpourri in the room, a few flowers, make up the bed.'

'Have you been here long?'

'I bought the house fifteen years ago. I could afford a hefty deposit with money I'd saved from my football career. It's boomed in price since then. It hardly costs me anything now.'

'I can see,' Kate said.

'I'll let you look at the bathroom and toilet yourself. The bathroom is a little small, but it's great practice for getting through a turnstile without paying.'

She was gone a couple of minutes. Wayne used the time to do some hasty clearing up. He suddenly wanted the place to look better for Kate Park.

When Kate returned she stood still and stared past Wayne, as if she was debating with herself.

'Please say what you need to say,' Wayne said.

Kate held her gaze on the wall.

'Yes,' she said. 'Thank you. I have to tell you more about what I'm doing because I will bring some strange books into the house.'

'What sort of strange books?' he asked.

'I'm studying what the Americans know as sexology. I'm someone who studies sexual behaviour from all disciplines. I had a mentor who died recently. I've taken over editing his classic text-book on sexuality. It's a big responsibility. A lot of work.' She looked out of the window.

'It's a very important job,' he said. 'As important as it comes.'

'I'm glad you agree,' she said. 'But I don't like sexual innuendo.'

Wayne thought about it.

'Ah,' he said.

'Sorry,' said Kate, smiling slightly. 'I get lots of smart remarks.'

Wayne looked at her. This could be really interesting, he thought. I want you to live in my house.

'I'm sure what you do is very important,' Wayne said. 'What's in your book?'

'Everything from abortion to zygotes.'

'What you hear here, what you see here, let it stay here.'

'I've heard that you can keep a secret.'

'Do you need to know more about me?' Wayne asked.

'I don't think so. I know about the work you do. I know you're still dealing with a difficult relationship.' Her brown-eyed gaze went off towards the wall again. 'I'm used to hearing people's personal stories. I keep them confidential wherever possible. I'll be here for a few weeks and then I'll disappear, maybe to the United States. I'll listen if you want to talk. If you don't want to talk then that's all right too.'

'Fair enough.'

'And one other thing, I work with sex a lot of the time, so I can't take chances in my personal life. Especially not at the moment. I'm very raw. I'm fragile. The love of my life died only a few weeks ago and I don't want to have to deal with advances or complications.'

'OK,' he said. He felt very safe with her. 'I'll do my best to support you. I won't intrude but I can listen if you need me to.'

'Thank you. I'd appreciate that.'

'The room's yours, whenever you want it.'

'Is tomorrow too soon?'

'No. Let me give you a set of keys.'

Three minutes later Wayne, standing at the front door, watched Kate Park cycle away from her new home.

Wayne cut the pack of cards and Mackie started to deal.

'I knew I wouldn't be able to sleep, Mackie,' Wayne said. 'I was thinking about Juliet Bromage.'

Mackie nodded. Mackie was one of Wayne's security staff, an efficient ex-footballer. They were sitting in the security office at the Bromage building at eleven o'clock at night. After a quick tour of the building, they had started a game of cribbage. Mackie stole glances at the monitors. He was the duty officer.

'I have to accept that it's over with Juliet,' Wayne

continued. 'She's been seeing someone else. I have to move on.'

Wayne was thinking about how his relationship with the boss's daughter had contained too much sex and not enough friendship. Wayne's problem was that he only trusted Juliet when she was naked. When she was clothed, designer-labelled, she was a chief executive and the daughter of a multi-millionaire.

Mackie pointed to the cards.

'I'm seeing Buck Hanson tomorrow,' Wayne said.

Mackie stopped playing and looked at Wayne Shakespeare. Wayne saw something in Mackie's eyes.

'Aw, no,' Wayne said. 'It wasn't him, was it? When I asked you to follow Juliet that time? When I sensed that she was seeing someone else?'

Mackie nodded very slowly. He shrugged. Mackie's way of saying sorry.

'It's all right,' said Wayne. 'I didn't ask you who it was – I just asked if there was someone.'

Mackie nodded again.

'Aw, shit,' Wayne said. 'I didn't know it was Hanson. Or maybe I didn't want to know. How am I going to handle Hanson tomorrow? I'm supposed to be doing a charity stunt with him. How could Juliet go for a nasty piece of work like him?'

Mackie shook his head.

'Married, too,' Wayne said. 'Hanson's married.'

Mackie nodded and played a card.

'That's Juliet's way of coping,' Wayne said. 'Finding someone else when a relationship founders. She's been adrift since she finished with Robin Hookes.'

Mackie nodded.

Wayne looked at his hand.

'I've almost forgotten how to play this game,' Wayne said. The two men had played cribbage on football trips, and Wayne had always felt very comfortable around Mackie.

'I suppose there's always more pebbles on the beach,' Wayne said suddenly. 'Lots more fish in the sea.'

Mackie nodded.

'Plenty more needles in the haystack,' Wayne added.

Mackie laughed.

'More cheques in the post,' Wayne added.

They played some cards and checked a few monitor images. They knew that the early hours of the morning were vulnerable for office buildings, especially at weekends, because all the police were downtown.

'I'm getting a new lodger,' Wayne told Mackie, who nodded approvingly. 'Kate Park. She has a soothing voice. She sounds like a relaxed disc jockey who can cure insomnia at midnight.' Mackie and Wayne both looked at the clock. It was nearly midnight. 'She's got brown eyes. Her eyes are a bit scary. I think she can see through walls.'

Mackie smiled.

'I need to do something about my house, Mackie,' Wayne said.

Mackie nodded like a counsellor.

'The house is so backdated that it makes you think Manchester United are still called Newton Heath,' Wayne continued.

Mackie nodded, smiling.

'Well, there's no need to agree with me,' Wayne said.

Mackie laughed. He had a good laugh. It always made Wayne feel better.

'Do you know something, Mackie?' Wayne asked. 'You could be a big star if silent movies ever came back. I played football with you for two years and the longest speech I can remember you giving was "My ball, Wayne".'

Mackie laughed and pointed to the cards.

They played on.

Wednesday became Thursday.

THREE

Inside the football club's training-ground canteen, Wayne helped himself to a cup of tea and sat next to Bob Blazer, the assistant manager. A camera crew sat nearby, also waiting.

Bob Blazer introduced Wayne to one of the club's other coaches.

'I remember Wayne when he was a 16-year-old kid as thin as a slice of Mother's Pride,' Blazer told the coach. 'And look at him now. Built like a baguette.'

'With a choice of fillings,' Wayne said. 'You look good, Bob.'

'I feel good, Wayne,' Blazer said.

'Still single?' Wayne asked Blazer.

'Still single,' Blazer replied.

Wayne turned to the other coach.

'Bob could be next England manager but for the stories I could tell about his personal life,' Wayne said.

'I learned it all from Wayne,' Blazer added. 'He stopped being a libero to become a gigolo.'

'Bob could charm the socks off women, and a few other items of clothing,' Wayne said.

'Wayne was the one who taught us how to speak

proper-like,' Blazer said. 'Ain't that right, Wayne?'

Wayne laughed at the memory.

'I've heard that story,' the coach said, mildly amused, 'but never from the well-educated horse's mouth.' He pointed to Wayne.

'Bob was my gaffer then,' said Wayne, taking his cue. 'He couldn't work me out. One day he was approached for a fly-on-the-wall documentary. The club's directors agreed to do the film, and Bob came to me for advice. He said I was the best-educated player he'd ever met, and he wanted a crash course in public-relations phrases.'

'Wayne taught me a few words,' Blazer said.

'Aye. Words like abject, though he pronounced it to rhyme with shit.'

'He still uses that,' the coach said, referring to Blazer. 'Tells them they're a load of fuckin' abjitt shit. Or abjite shite.'

Wayne shook his head.

'We worked on finding alternatives to his swear words,' Wayne said.

'No luck, huh?' said the coach.

'I should go back to that, Wayne,' said Blazer. '*You stupid twerp.*'

'I remember that one, said Wayne. '*That friggin' Stanley Matthews statue could make better runs off the ball, you stupid twerp.*'

'*Anthole,*' said Blazer. '*That's bollards.*'

'*Holy ship, Moggsy, I've seen livelier people in friggin' nursing-homes,*' said Wayne.

'Holy ship, Wayne,' said Blazer, smiling.

'When he started off, it gave the players a good laugh,'

Wayne said. 'Then he made a few mistakes and I was the only one laughing.'

The coach smiled and excused himself, leaving Wayne alone with Bob Blazer.

'Still doing our stadium security, I see,' Bob Blazer said to Wayne. 'Still with Richard Bromage.'

'And a university or two,' Wayne added. 'I wanted a word with you about a university rag stunt. I have a favour to ask.'

'I could do with a distraction.'

'Is your job safe?'

'Jobs are always on the line,' Blazer said, shrugging. 'Maybe you could put in a good word for us with the chairman's daughter.'

'I don't think I have much influence there now.'

'Sorry, mate.'

Wayne looked at Blazer, but thought about Juliet and Hanson.

'Never mind, Bob, if you get sacked you'll be able to play regularly for Mackie's charity team,' Wayne said.

'Wayne, your glass is always ten per cent full.' Blazer's eyes were smiling. 'Mackie was in touch about the next charity match.'

'Mackie's silence is threatening. I'll be there.'

'You keeping fit?'

'Yeah, a few laps of the kitchen table.'

'Chase a few women around the house?' Then Bob Blazer held up his hand. 'Sorry, mate, sore point, eh?'

He knows about Juliet and me, Wayne thought. He probably knows about Juliet and Hanson.

Kate Park fidgeted uneasily as a solicitor called Jeremy Spooner explained about Theodore Merlin's estate.

'As Teddy's literary beneficiary you will earn money from royalties in the long term,' said Spooner, sitting in an office in central Oxford. 'As his executor I may be able to advance some money, but not until we have assessed his debts. That will be after the sale of his house in New Jersey.'

'I thought about doing the probate myself but everyone told me not to,' Kate said.

'I've seen a lot come to us when it gets too much for them.'

'I could handle the technical side if I kept phoning the help-line, but I would find the emotional side difficult – dealing with Teddy's family. I could imagine his ex-wife and kids challenging everything.'

'We can deal with them.'

Even though it will cost a lot more money, Kate thought.

'Thank you,' Kate told Jeremy Spooner.

Kate's financial position was precarious and she had hoped for some respite. She would have to work on the next edition of Teddy's book without any immediate reward.

'I have to go to America and sell the house,' said Kate.

'I can pay someone over there to do that,' said Spooner. 'But I can pay you expenses if you want to do it yourself.'

Kate felt relieved.

'The house is occupied at the moment but Teddy wanted me to go through all his personal possessions that are locked in the basement,' she said. 'And rescue some of the books.'

Spooner nodded.

'I *can* offer you some other work too,' Spooner said. He was a man in his mid-forties, confident and handsome in a rugged way. He wore a pin-striped suit and Kate felt underdressed, even though she had put on her black funeral skirt and a dark jacket.

'Some work?' Kate asked.

'I need help with a case.'

'What sort of case?'

'It would have been Merlin's expertise, and he told me you could take on his work. I'm happy to look for cases that can use your knowledge. Other solicitors tend to turn down jobs that involve sex.'

'Thank you,' Kate said again.

'What was that word Merlin used – sexologist?'

Kate nodded.

'Sexology is the general study of all matters to do with sex and sexuality,' Kate said.

'Good.'

Jeremy Spooner started searching on his desk.

'Let me tell you about this criminal case,' he said.

'What's the favour you need?' Bob Blazer asked.

'The university Rag Committee would like to stage a mock kidnapping of one of your players to raise money for charity.'

'Great, take Browny – he's playing abjite shite. I wish someone had kidnapped him before last Saturday's match. Would have saved us waiting till half-time to take him off.'

'They'd prefer the goalkeeper.'

'The crazy man?'

Yes, the crazy man who's chasing Juliet, Wayne thought.

'I have a way of setting it up so that it won't disturb his pre-match routine,' Wayne said, 'and it won't affect the other players.'

Bob Blazer liked the idea. He made a quick phone call to get permission and then called across the canteen to a film crew who were waiting to do another interview. Blazer told them they could break the story at the weekend. The crew filmed the segment indoors, upstairs in a lecture room, so that the weather would not spoil the continuity. Wayne went with them while they did the shoot. Blazer did a classic speech to camera.

This football club desperately needs this player for our game today. I'm putting ten pounds of my own money towards this cause and I hope you will join with me. Otherwise our opponents today will have more empty goals in one match than I've seen in my whole career.

It made for a superb clip.

'Put that in the can and use it Saturday lunchtime,' Blazer told the film crew, putting the ten-pound note back in his wallet. 'I'm not saying any more now.'

'What about the tenner?' Wayne said, smiling.

'Bollards, Wayne,' Blazer said. 'Tell the lad he's got to do it. Catch him in the canteen.'

'Thanks.'

Wayne made his way back to the canteen, got himself another cup of tea, took out a book called *Campus*

Security and settled down to wait for Buck Hanson.

'It's an open-and-shut case and I can't work out a way of earning my money,' said Jeremy Spooner.

Well, that's unusual for a lawyer, Kate thought. She could almost hear Teddy Merlin saying the same thing.

'How can I help?' Kate said.

'I'll give you the file to peruse. Take it next door after we finish and give it the once-over. Then leave it at reception when you go. Basically there are two charges – one of rape and one of sex with a minor.'

Kate had learned some forensic sexology from Teddy.

'I'd like to find a way of getting the rape charge dropped and settling for the other,' Spooner continued. Then he laughed. 'But I have a real problem.'

'What's the problem?' Kate asked.

'My client wants to plead guilty on both charges,' Spooner said.

'Presumably because he is guilty?'

'He's as guilty as hell. It's a rock-solid case against him. The girl's mother caught him in bed with her daughter and called the police. She virtually secured the scene. The man put up no resistance. He confessed to the police. All the physical evidence was there. The girl and the mother gave condemning statements. The man's mortified at what he's done.'

'How old is this man?'

'Forty-two.'

'Any history of young girls?'

'No previous.'

'What would you like me to do?'

'Two things. The first is to read the file. The second is to come with me when I go to see him where it happened – at his home. I'd like you to give me a woman's viewpoint.'

'I can give you a Kate Park viewpoint.'

'That'll be good enough for me. I reckon it will be two hours' work and the time it takes you to write a one-page report.'

'I can't give you an expert witness report like Teddy could.'

'I know. This is just for our benefit. If you can recommend any expert witnesses that might help us, put that in the report. Teddy used to do that for us too.'

Spooner smiled again and then found a sympathetic look.

'You must miss Teddy a lot,' he said.

'Every minute of every day.'

'You were a great comfort to each other.'

He smiled and Kate had a nasty feeling.

'What do you mean?' she asked.

'I was just building up to saying that if there's anything I can help with, just say the word.'

'I hope you're not giving me this job out of kindness.'

'No no. Not at all.'

It suddenly dawned on Kate that now that she was alone in life she would attract predatory men waiting to take advantage of her vulnerability. Men like Wayne Shakespeare and Jeremy Spooner.

'That's kind of you,' she said.

Kate fidgeted with her pen and notebook.

'Our client is out on bail at the moment,' Spooner

said. 'I'll ring him for an appointment.'

Spooner found a number for his client and hit the buttons.

'We're scheduled for Oxford Crown Court in a month's time,' he told Kate, as he waited for the call to connect.

Kate started thinking of all she had to do today. She was booked for a night shift at the hospital, but her next task was to move house. That meant transporting three bags of clothes from Caprice's canal boat, plus several boxes of sexology books and Teddy's old filing-cabinet from storage. She had booked a man with a van, and knew that she might not sleep for over twenty-four hours.

'Kate,' she heard Spooner say. 'Seven o'clock tomorrow night, Friday night.'

'Oh, yes,' Kate said. She took out her diary.

When she looked up, Spooner was still talking on the phone. He caught her eye and winked.

Kate was confused. Some widows might try to fill their void with another man. Others would be fiercely celibate. Kate Park predicted that she would be in the celibate category for at least two years. But nothing was ever certain.

The training-ground canteen had nearly cleared of people when Buck Hanson come in and ordered fish, pasta and peas. It seemed like Hanson wanted every pea cooked differently. The canteen staff, hitherto great company, turned a little sour. But they knew their job and went about satisfying a finickety footballer.

Hanson carried his plate over to Wayne's table. Wayne felt anger wrestling inside his chest and down his arms.

'All right, Shakes,' Hanson said. 'Bob Blazer says I should do something for you. What's the dosh?'

'It's for charity.'

'Aw fuck.'

Hanson stabbed a few peas with his fork.

'Let me tell you about it,' Wayne said. He counted to three and then decided not to tip the table over Hanson. 'We take you away on the Friday night and we lay on everything you want – card games, videos, massage, anything you want.'

Buck Hanson looked up at Wayne.

'Keep talking,' he said.

'We set you up for your normal routine before the match. Food, drink, anything. You tell us and we'll lay it on. Then we get you to the ground at your normal time. You'll have a driver.'

'What about girls?'

Wayne studied Hanson for a few moments.

'Tell me what you want,' Wayne said, speaking slowly.

'One on Friday night and one on Saturday morning. Ones who'll keep mum about it and say nowt to the papers.' He laughed. 'Nah, forget it, Shakes. You wouldn't know how to go about it anyway.'

That riled Wayne. But now he suspected that Hanson didn't know about Juliet's other men. Juliet compartmentalised her relationships.

'Tell me what you want,' Wayne repeated.

'Nah, it wouldn't work. Why should I put myself out with no dosh?'

'You'll have to do it, Buck,' Wayne said. 'Bob Blazer's already paid me some money on film. He did a clip for the television people to use on Saturday morning.'

'Aw, fuckin' stupid twat.' He looked around him. 'Don't tell him I said that.'

'No.'

Wayne thought about the red-haired student called Tracey Holroyd. He would rather be facing Tracey's competitive drive than Buck Hanson's aggression.

'You work for the Bromages?' Hanson asked Wayne.

'I do.'

'My agent's getting me a condom deal. You know about that?'

'Sort of.' Wayne waited for a moment. He didn't want to talk to Hanson about this, but he decided to continue. 'Yeah, they're putting together a promotion campaign for a condom manufacturer. They are looking for sports people who wear protective equipment – wicket-keeping gloves, scrum caps, show-jumping helmets, shin pads, goalkeeping gloves . . .'

'Big names like me promoting condoms,' Hanson continued. 'Old Bucket Hands.' He grinned and held up his huge hands. 'You know, everything in proportion. It's for that Jules Bromage.'

Wayne groaned inwardly when he heard *Jules*.

'Let's come back to the charity gig,' Wayne said.

'Fix me up with a shag tomorrow night, Shakes, and I'll do it for you.'

Wayne groaned audibly this time and counted towards ten. Buck Hanson was too busy with his food and his fantasies to notice Wayne's discomfort. When he reached 'six' Wayne tried a different tack.

'The Cat will be there on Friday night,' he said. He could hear a tremor in his own voice.

Buck Hanson looked up and smirked.

'Now you're talking,' he said. 'Why didn't you tell me that earlier?'

Because I didn't know that would have such an impact, Wayne thought.

'So you're on?' Wayne asked.

'Yeah, yeah. It'll get me away from the wife for a Friday evening.'

'Good.' Then Wayne paused as Hanson finished off his fish. 'You'll have to be a bit careful with Jules,' Wayne said. 'They say she's looking for a father for a child. Someone who's athletic and fit. Biological clock ticking away and all that.'

Hanson looked at Wayne.

'She's looked a bit different lately,' Wayne added. 'I assume you used condoms with her.'

'What?'

'Condoms. Sort of rubber things with a little teat. Goes over . . .'

'I know what a fuckin' condom is, I'm gonna fuckin' promote them. I thought she was looking after that.'

'Looking after what?'

'You know, taking the pill,' said Hanson. 'She said she was taking the pill.'

'*Said?* Ooh, Buck, I hope that's not your condom-advertising chance gone.' Wayne knew that one more misplaced comment could lead to a fight, so he backtracked. 'I'm winding you up,' he said. 'Let's arrange how you want to be collected on Friday night.'

'I'll get my agent to do all that.'

'Hey, we're trying to keep this quiet. Tell your agent and the world will know. It'll spoil the impact if it gets out before Saturday morning.'

Another few minutes and the kidnapping had been planned. The victim had agreed. Wayne somehow stopped himself from attacking Buck Hanson, and left without saying goodbye.

Kate sat in a meeting room reading the evidence against Bruce Venn. According to Fiona Coates' statement, she had met Venn through an internet dating site. They had emailed each other for a couple of weeks. They both lived in Oxfordshire – Coates near Bicester, Venn in Abingdon – so they met for lunch in Oxford. After lunch they wandered around Oxford together.

Their second meeting was for lunch at the Perch, a riverside pub on the north side of Oxford. This time they had an afternoon walk along the river. They hugged when they said goodbye. Fiona Coates thought Venn was an honest and sensitive man. He had his own business and seemed successful. He looked like a good catch.

They met a third time to see a film. This time, when they parted, he kissed her on the lips and invited her to stay for a weekend. Fiona brought her fifteen-year-old daughter Olivia, known as Olly, and they arrived in Abingdon on a Saturday morning and had a good day out. Bruce Venn cooked them a meal that night and they played board games before Olly went to bed. The two adults stayed up a little longer. The three of them slept in separate beds.

Fiona Coates had a double bedroom at the end of the upstairs corridor. She was woken up by a strange noise around two o'clock and went to investigate. Her daughter had been given a single bedroom between Fiona's room and Bruce Venn's master bedroom. When Fiona got to her daughter's room she found the door was open. She looked through the doorway and saw Venn's last few thrusts before orgasm. He was on top of her daughter.

'I screamed and shouted "What's going on?" or something like that,' Fiona Coates told the police. 'I asked Olly if she'd been attacked, and she said she had. She said, "I was fast asleep, Mum, he just came in and jumped on top of me. He wouldn't let me out."'

Fiona Coates turned to Venn and said, 'You bastard, you'll pay for this' and a few other choice words. Then she phoned the police. A special squad answered the call and went through the procedure correctly.

Olly's statement did not add much. She said Venn was a strong man. She called him a pervert and said he had woken her and the assault had happened before she was fully awake.

Bruce Venn confessed to the crime. He apologised for what he had done and awaited his punishment. The case was cut and dried, open and shut, done and dusted.

In a way Kate was glad. She didn't like rape cases. Her own sister had been a rape victim. She knew what the impact could be for individuals and their families.

Her sympathy was with the young girl and the mother, as long as their accounts were truthful.

Kate Park sat back and looked at the story. She didn't have a real sense of the interviews. There was no feel for how the story had been told. Normally, in a rape case, there are tell-tale signs in the way the narrative is constructed by the story-teller. Kate wanted to start from scratch and talk to all the participants. She doubted she would get the chance.

First, though, Kate had to move into Wayne Shakespeare's house. She would spend an hour settling into Wayne's spare room, and then she would need a nap before her night shift at the hospital.

She returned Bruce Venn's file to the desk and left the solicitors' office. She walked to Caprice's boat, wondering if she really wanted to work for Jeremy Spooner. Not if they were all rape cases. Not if they reminded her of her sister's pain.

FOUR

Kate Park returned to Wayne Shakespeare's house at nine o'clock on Friday morning. She took off her coat and revealed a white nurse's uniform speckled with blood.

'You look dramatic and beautiful,' Wayne told Kate. He was sitting at the kitchen table.

'Hardly,' Kate said. 'I feel I've been awake for weeks.'

Wayne made her a cup of tea, and Kate told him a tale about a woman who had been haemorrhaging for most of the night.

'When are you working again?' Wayne asked.

'I'm doing an early tomorrow, but I need to do some other work today.'

'What do you know about the condom business?' he asked.

Kate felt shocked. This was the last thing she needed after working all night.

'In what way?' she asked.

'I've been talking to a star footballer. He told me that the Bromages are going into the condom business.'

'That's interesting,' Kate said. She tested her tea. It was too hot, but it gave her something to look forward to in life.

'Would you like breakfast?' Wayne asked. 'There's some croissants.'

'Please. I'll get out of my uniform.'

Kate went to her room and changed. Her bed was very tempting, but so were food, drink, a shower and the opportunity to unwind. She came out of her room wearing baggy blue jeans, a T-shirt and a man's light jacket.

Wayne served warm croissants with a selection of preserves.

'Do you have family?' Kate asked.

'No.'

'No one?'

'No. My grandfather died a few years ago. He was my family. He raised me virtually single-handedly after my parents died. He was angry with me for a while, but we got on well towards the end of his life.'

'Why was he angry with you?'

'For getting out of professional football. He thought I should have had a great career. Later he understood how much I enjoyed life after leaving football.'

'Football doesn't mean much to me.'

'No, it doesn't mean much to me any more. But there's never a day goes by without me thinking of my granddad,' Wayne said. He looked at Kate. 'He used to say that a good pair of legs ran in our family.'

Kate nodded solemnly.

'I think I understand the genetics of bad jokes,' she said. Then she picked up on Wayne's earlier question. 'Most condom companies are big corporations which also deal in rubber gloves, drugs, footwear or whatever, with condoms more of a sideline. Some companies specialise in charity and government contracts for condoms. Some have contracts for private labels.'

'Private labels?'

'Making them for, say, a drugstore chain. Then the drugstore chain puts its name put on the label.'

'Are there lots of new companies?' Wayne asked.

'I don't think so. I could look up some details.'

'I made a phone call after I'd learned about it,' Wayne said. 'Apparently it's Richard Bromage's idea to market condoms and Juliet's idea to use sportsmen to promote safe sex. She wants them from all over the world – a soccer goalkeeper, a cricket wicket-keeper, a baseball catcher and so on. Her subliminal premise is that athletic bodies need protection – gloves, pads, helmets and condoms. *Safe bodies, safe sex.* I think Juliet wants to meet lots of athletes with safe hands. A goalkeeper called Buck Hanson is on her list.'

'Safety first, sex second,' Kate said. 'I hope Juliet has good advice on how to promote condoms. There are European standards and regulations, and restrictions on advertising.'

They ate in silence for half a minute.

'You knew I'd just broken up with Juliet, didn't you?' Wayne said. 'How did you know that? Did Caprice tell you?'

'Yes.'

'She woke up one morning at my house and said, "I'm now called Caprice."'

'I guessed it wasn't her given name.'

'She once wanted to buy a car because she liked the number plate.'

'Can Caprice drive?'

'No. But she liked the number plate,' said Wayne.

Kate found herself giggling, against her will.

'Hey, I made you laugh,' Wayne said.

'No, not you. It was Caprice who made me laugh. She said you helped her to buy the boat.'

'No, she did it herself. She earned money by cutting hair, making pots, delivering coal to barges. We made a plan so she could somehow cobble together enough resources to buy a narrowboat.' Wayne looked at Kate. 'What else did Caprice tell you about me?'

'She said you liked lodgers who were friendly to visitors. She said you weren't worried about rent as long as the lodger was being fair and honest, and using their time well. And the biggest house crime is to run out of toilet rolls.'

'All credit to Caprice.'

'She also said that you had a great dog.'

'She and Rover always got on well.'

Kate still felt too wired to sleep.

'Tell me about Juliet,' she said.

'Ah, Juliet Bromage,' Wayne started. 'Daughter of Richard Bromage, the multi-millionaire businessman. She's in her early thirties. Divorced. There's a lot happening in her life at the moment. A lot of endings and several potential beginnings. She's tense and irritable, but she's the type of person who moves on quickly.'

'Moves on?'

'I'm sure she has been seeing someone else. Someone besides me. A footballer called Buck Hanson. But I'm having him kidnapped later today.'

'Be serious.'

'It's true.'

Kate looked at Wayne oddly. He looked serious enough.

'It's only a rag stunt,' Wayne said.

'Oh.'

'I think Juliet has two types of men,' Wayne added. 'There are the young, rugged athletic types like Hanson and the older Oxbridge intellectuals like the man she married – Robin Hookes. Maybe one day she'll find both types in the same person. She tries hard enough.'

'Spoken from the broken heart,' Kate said.

'Life is never straightforward,' Wayne moaned.

'Anyone who knows Caprice knows that,' said Kate.

'You suddenly look very tired.'

'Yes,' said Kate. 'My bed is calling loudly.'

'Heed the call.'

Kate dragged herself upstairs. Please, sleep, she told herself. Please, sleep.

Wayne walked into the Bromage Building foyer at ten o'clock that Friday morning. Mackie's eyes were scanning CCTV screens like they were opponents in a penalty area.

'Saw Bob Blazer yesterday,' Wayne whispered to

Mackie. 'He'll probably play in the charity match.' Mackie nodded.

Wayne scanned the visitors' book. The football club manager and his assistant, Bob Blazer, were both in the building. Wayne took the stairs to the third floor, the hub of the empire, where Richard Bromage ('Mister Richard') had a suite of rooms and Jim Bailey, Mister Richard's right-hand man, had an office and bedroom. And, of course, there was Juliet Bromage, Mister Richard's daughter.

The fourth person in the area was Mary Curtis, the receptionist, administrator and general factotum. She was a tense, efficient woman in her early forties who had worked at Bromage's football club before being lured to his business empire.

'Good morning, Mr Shakespeare,' said Mary Curtis. 'Mr Bailey is in with Mister Richard and the football club manager. I've buzzed him.'

'Thank you, Miss Curtis.'

She looked at him oddly. Wayne had known her for a long time and yet he knew her no better now than when he had first met her.

'Is the manager's job safe?' Wayne asked.

Mary stared uncertainly. She didn't speak.

'Is Juliet in her office?' Wayne asked. He could sense Juliet's presence somewhere nearby. His nervousness gave it away.

'No.'

'She's in with the others?'

Mary nodded. Wayne wondered how much she knew about Juliet.

Wayne sat on a plush couch in the third-floor waiting area and thumbed through newspapers he hadn't seen.

Richard Bromage will give his football-club manager an ultimatum today – one more bad result and you're sacked.

Despite his team's poor run, the manager's job is as safe as any.

On hearing a door open, Wayne tossed the paper down and stood up. He preferred to keep on the same level as Jim Bailey, whose 6ft 4in height could be intimidating, even if Jim's manner was generally hospitable.

'Come through, Wayne,' Bailey said.

Wayne went into Jim Bailey's office and looked at the view.

'They've nearly finished in there,' Jim said, nodding towards Richard Bromage's office. 'Sit down, Wayne.'

Wayne sat down.

'What I'm going to tell you is very hush-hush,' Bailey said. 'I know I say that a lot, but this is the most important time I've said it. There's millions resting on this one.'

'OK,' Wayne said. 'Just you and me.'

'There may be a few changes coming up. Richard is not very well. He's been advised to wind down his work. If he goes, I shall probably retire. My wife wants us to do more cruises while we still can, and I need to listen to her advice.'

Wayne felt stunned. 'Thanks for telling me that,' he said.

'There's reasons for telling you. We want you to keep

your ears open for what competitors are saying about us.'

'I'll do my best.'

'Juliet will eventually take over.'

'Of course.'

'I don't know what that will mean for you.'

'I know what you're saying.'

Wayne was immediately thinking about other markets for his security business. More universities? Health organisations? Shopping precincts? Most of the contracts were tied up.

'Don't indicate to Juliet that you know this,' Bailey said.

'But she knows about her father?'

'She knows.'

'Do you think I'll keep the football stadium work?'

Jim Bailey thought about it. He looked out of the window at the view.

'I don't know,' he said. 'Juliet and Richard are assessing data about the future of the club. Juliet is trying to decide whether to be involved. I think they should unload it . . . if they can. But it's a terrible climate.'

Wayne nodded.

They were interrupted by Mary Curtis buzzing through.

'I think they are just finishing, Mr Bailey,' she said in a soft voice that could only just be heard.

Wayne followed Jim Bailey part way and stood in the doorway to Richard Bromage's office. His eyes were drawn to Juliet Bromage as she stood near her father and Bob Blazer. For a moment Wayne wondered if the club manager had been sacked and Blazer promoted from assistant manager to manager, but then he saw the manager looking cheerful and walking towards Jim Bailey.

Juliet was smiling. It was a lopsided, almost insincere smile, but attractive nevertheless. It highlighted her cheekbones, but it also ran from collar-bone to collar-bone because most of her shoulders were exposed, as they often were. She had set up the smile by flicking her long brown hair away from her shoulders. She did this often enough to keep attention focused on her low-cut tops. Wayne thought she wore her clothes as if she wanted someone to help her out of them.

Next Wayne studied Richard Bromage. He looked grey-faced and thin. His trousers hung loosely on him. Yes, someday Juliet would take over this business. Someday soon.

Wayne caught a slight nod from Richard Bromage, so he walked over to him. Bromage leaned close to Wayne's ear.

'Did Jim have a chat?'

'Yeah. Thanks for that. I'm really sorry to hear about your troubles.'

Another slight nod from Bromage and the meeting was over.

Bob Blazer was still talking to Juliet. Wayne went across and joined them. They stopped talking as he approached. Wayne looked at Juliet's eyes and saw a spark of sexual thrill. Her eyes were her most unusual feature. They were freckled, with droplets of beige stardust sparkling amidst the background green. Wayne thought they were best viewed from six inches away.

But there was something even more unusual about the eyes. She had warned Wayne about it when she first slept with him, and he had stayed awake to confirm the truth. Twenty minutes after falling asleep her eyes slowly opened. Then she continued to sleep . . . with her eyes open wide. But she had never needed a long night's sleep. Like father like daughter.

'Wayne was a scintillating acquisition as a player,' Blazer told Juliet.

'A scintillating acquisition?' Wayne queried, raising his eyebrows.

'He added a certain *je ne sais quoi* to my team,' Blazer added.

'*Je ne sais quoi?*' Wayne repeated.

'That's your trouble, Wayne,' said Blazer. He laughed, and Juliet laughed with him. Juliet put one hand on Blazer's forearm, and Wayne looked at her with love and hate.

Richard Bromage called Blazer over for a final word and Juliet and Wayne were left alone.

'You look ravishing,' Wayne said, but she ignored him and watched Bob Blazer.

'He seems really intelligent for a football man,' Juliet said. 'He uses words like abject and vitriolic and ubiquitous.'

'Yeah, I taught him all he knows.'

Juliet looked at Wayne with angry eyes.

'God, you're so arrogant, Wayne,' she said, before tripping away to speak with Jim Bailey.

But I did, Wayne said to himself.

Mid-morning Friday. Wayne sat in sunshine on a wall outside St Mary's Church, eyeing the people of Radcliffe Square while holding his copy of *Campus Security*. He had brought the book in case Tracey Holroyd wanted to discuss the subject.

He spotted her forty yards away and enjoyed viewing her muscular athleticism as she walked towards him. A sleeveless top highlighted well-developed biceps. Wayne wondered which gym she used.

'Thanks for the phone messages,' Tracey Holroyd said, when she sat next to him. 'Thanks for talking to Hanson and the club. Thanks for sorting it.'

'No problem. It was easy once I'd said the Cat would be there.'

As he spoke he watched her closely. Her body language showed no reaction to the news.

'The assistant manager did an impromptu interview for television,' Wayne continued. 'The cameras just happened to be there when I was. I think you'll like the piece. He pleads for the public to give generously and pulls out a £10 note. They'll use it on Friday night and Saturday lunchtime when they realise what it's about. You never know, it might make the nationals.'

She stared at Wayne for a moment.

'Whatever,' she said, reluctantly.

'Is everything in place?'

She looked down at her notes.

'I've set up thirty locked collection boxes and allocated people to different parts of the stadium,' she replied.

'And you checked with the stadium manager?' Wayne

said. 'Their schedule for collections?'

'I've done that. There was a charity listed for that Saturday but I cleared it with them. We've agreed they'll benefit from our collection. I convinced them they would do better that way.'

'OK,' Wayne said.

'We've set up a safe point for counting the money and I've arranged a way to deposit it in the bank tomorrow afternoon.'

'Can I help provide a safe cash transit?'

'I've fixed that with two people I know who work in security.'

'Well done. You seem to have thought of everything.' Her eyes flashed.

'I gave Bob Blazer my word that we wouldn't interfere with the lad's pre-match routine,' Wayne continued. 'Footballers are creatures of habit and superstition. When we pick him up we'll have to ask him if he's got all his lucky charms. I'll collect him by taxi and bring him to you.'

'We already have that covered,' she said. 'It's in our plans.'

'The two security men?'

'Yeah.'

'I feel it's my responsibility to taxi him to the ground well before two o'clock. These people prepare meticulously for a game.'

'We'll see to it. We've got good advice.'

'OK,' Wayne said. 'And can you keep him out of sight on the Friday night? No public places. Even drinking orange juice in a pub is bad public relations. He'd be considered blind drunk if a man called Rumour saw him.'

'I'll keep him occupied indoors,' she said, without smiling.

'The Hanson lad has to follow his routine. It's his livelihood. What if he got injured and something was wrong with his preparations? He'd probably sue us. He's a temperamental lad. He can be nasty.'

'I can handle him. Intelligence is thinking ahead.'

Tracey Holroyd pointed to Wayne's copy of *Campus Security*.

'Have you learned anything?' she asked.

'I've learned how big the task can be. Murder. Rape. Bomb threats if there's animal experiments on campus. Robbery. Assault. Vehicle theft. Computer crime. Cults that target vulnerable students. Property theft. Plagiarism. But it is hard convincing the powers-that-be of the need for 24-hour coverage of campus.'

'What are you going to do?' Tracey said.

'My first task is to collect better statistics so I can get the university to spend more money on security. I'll recommend student dissertation projects – analysing the cost of crime on campus, and collecting better figures on students who have been robbed and attacked, especially on the unreported incidents.'

'Last Saturday a girl was drinking in the college bar,' said Tracey Holroyd. 'She met a man and they set off to her place. He raped her on a dark lane. It was dope rape. He must have given her something in her drink in the bar. It must have been another student who did it because they check your card in the bar. The girl didn't press charges because there was no sign of a struggle and she'd slept with the guy a few weeks back.'

'I take your point,' Wayne said.

'We need to stop that sort of thing at source. I think good lighting and good emergency communication are important, but it needs education in the curriculum. Harvard University has a course in which students learn how to communicate clearly about sexual issues. Another college has a course called *Silence Doesn't Mean "Yes"*. I can give you details of that one.'

'OK.'

'And we need plenty of classes for women,' said Tracey.

'They have plenty of classes.'

'Judo. Ju-jitsu. Karate. Kick-boxing. Boxercise. Kung Fu.'

'Oh.'

She stood up and walked away. Wayne watched her muscles ripple.

Kate Park didn't own a car and didn't like going in cars. Her fears were confirmed early that Friday evening when a car-driver dangerously overtook Jeremy Spooner's car on their journey to Abingdon. The journey was only about six miles, but an extra mile was added when they lost their way on a housing estate.

'The house looks pretty good,' Jeremy Spooner said, as they walked up the path to Bruce Venn's front door. 'Four-bedroom detached? He might be willing to pay me out of his own pocket. Be nice if it went to trial.'

Then they stopped walking and looked at the graffiti on Venn's garage door.

PEEDIFILE

The paint jury had already delivered their verdict.

Bruce Venn was a slim and athletic-looking man who came to the door furtively and ushered them inside quickly. He offered them a cup of tea and a slice of his freshly baked bread. The three of them sat down over the kitchen table. Kate made sure she was on the opposite side of the table to Venn. She wanted to see his face.

'We've entered not guilty pleas to the two charges,' Spooner reminded Venn. 'That was to give us some more time, so we could have a meeting like this. As it stands, to be honest, I don't think you've got the slightest defence. We would have to put in guilty pleas because the sentences could be astronomical if it went to trial and we had no defence. I'd like to get the rape charge dropped and then bargain for a year or two on the other charge. What I need is some reason why the girl and her mother might not want to go to trial. Or some reason why we can say that you thought there was consent.'

'I can't think of any reason,' Venn said.

'Have you remembered any more about that night?' Spooner asked.

'No. I think I was in a state of shock once Fiona came in and found me with her daughter. It's all very hazy. I remember sitting on the bed with no clothes on, and the room looked like a den of iniquity. And it was clearly my fault.'

Kate watched Venn grow more and more embarrassed. He had a fell-runner's build and Kate sensed he had determination and energy. His kindly face had reddened now.

'Had the daughter come on to you during the day?' Spooner asked.

'No, not really. Her mother was my date.' He paused. He looked close to tears. 'Sorry, I find this difficult to talk about.'

Spooner sighed.

'I understand that,' the solicitor said. 'But we have to make an effort.'

'I really don't know what came over me. I must have had a brainstorm to surprise Olivia like that. It was no wonder she hit me.'

'The daughter hit you?' Spooner said, more animated.

'No, Fiona. She told me to get off her daughter and then she slapped my face.' Venn paused with more embarrassment. 'Well, it's not surprising. I deserved it.'

Spooner looked across at Kate.

'What do you wear in bed, Mr Venn?' Kate asked.

Spooner looked surprised at Kate's question and Venn paused.

'Nothing these days,' Venn said.

'And Olivia. Did she have clothes on when you went in her room?'

'I think she was nude too.'

Jeremy Spooner interrupted Kate's plan.

'So she was expecting you,' Spooner told Venn.

'I don't think so.'

'Was she a virgin?' Spooner asked.

'I doubt it. No, her mother had talked to me about that. She said that Olly had had a boyfriend for a few months and now she was starting to play the field. She was worried about Olly. That was why she brought her.

She didn't want her to stay with friends while she was away. But I guess she would have been safer left on her own.'

'You're not much help, Bruce,' Spooner said, exasperated.

'Could you describe Olivia's body for me, please,' Kate asked Venn.

'She was slim, about five foot four, I would guess . . .'

'That'll do, Kate,' Spooner interrupted, looking as embarrassed as Venn. 'Let's look at the upstairs. See where it happened.'

They walked upstairs. They saw the single bedroom at the top of the stairs. The crime scene. They looked at the other two bedrooms.

Kate returned to the single room where Olivia had slept on the night in question. Kate lay down on the bed, then bounced up and down.

'Could you do that for me, please, Jeremy,' Kate said, 'while I go and listen from the other bedroom?'

'Simulation, eh?' Spooner replied. He took off his suit jacket.

Kate went to the room where Fiona Coates had stayed on the night of the crime. The noise barely carried. It had to travel through a bathroom and along a corridor. Kate shut the door. She could no longer hear the bed noises. Maybe she would hear human cries, but she wasn't going to ask Jeremy Spooner or Bruce Venn to simulate the sounds of orgasm.

Kate went into the mind of Fiona Coates. Sleeping in a strange bed. Hearing a strange noise. Going to investigate. Or maybe even deciding to go to the toilet while she was awake and seeing her daughter's room ajar on the way. That might have been how it happened.

She walked back to the others.

'It's still a mystery to me why I did it,' Venn said.

Yes, it's a mystery, Kate decided. Trauma can travel two ways, she thought. Accused to victim and victim to accused.

FIVE

The black-hair woman walked into the jeweller's shop at 5.20pm on Saturday. She had dressed up for her new man. Tight, tailored navy trousers, a white shirt and a navy jacket. She wore a necklace, three rings and long earrings. She had borrowed the jewellery from a rich friend in the group, and it was designed to impress. She looked like she belonged to money. She felt like a woman to die for. She felt like a real mankiller. She would poison him with her body.

'Did everything go well with Hanson?' Wayne asked Tracey Holroyd.

It was 5.20pm on Saturday. Wayne was speaking on his mobile phone at the football stadium during a lull in the security operations. Outside broadcast vehicles lined the streets – even a catering van – and the yellow-coated stewards had debriefed. The crowd had drifted away after an early kick-off and an early finish.

'Couldn't have been better,' Tracey replied.

'Did Hanson behave?'

'I gave him everything he wanted.'

'I won't ask.'

'He wanted to stay another night.'

'You got him to the stadium all right, I see.'

'Our plan was perfect.'

'Anything I can do?'

'No thanks. You've done enough.'

'OK.'

Wayne disconnected, checked for messages, and went back to work.

At 5.25pm that Saturday, Kate Park was resting on her bed after completing an early shift. The ward had been one nurse short, it'd been hard work and she'd stayed late. She was trying not to fall asleep too early. But avoiding sleep was hard work too. She got up and walked around the empty house.

'Good afternoon, Rover,' she told the papier-mâché dog.

I'm as mad as Wayne, Kate thought.

The black-haired woman guessed the shop owner was in his early fifties. He showed her some necklaces and she puffed herself up. Her body was incredibly slim, too thin perhaps, but that made her breasts more prominent. The line of her bra was perfect and she had opened one button more than was necessary on her shirt.

'What a gorgeous shop,' she said, looking the man in the eye. 'I'm in heaven.'

The man was sidetracked by his assistant.

'It's five twenty-five,' the assistant said. 'Shall I start to lock up?'

'Yes, of course,' the owner said. 'I shall stay on while I am still serving.'

At 5.30pm, Wayne Shakespeare was feeling pleased with himself. The day had gone well. The stewards had got on with their jobs, and all the confiscated items had been returned. Two people had asked for application forms to work as stewards and Wayne was always glad to have a waiting list.

By 5.35pm, two jewellery shop assistants had left, the store was locked, the shutters were down, the velvet curtains were drawn closed, and the black-haired woman was confident that the owner was watching her every move.

'This shop is such a turn-on,' she said. 'I'm like a kid in a sweet shop. Thank you for staying on. I hope I'm not keeping you from your wife or your lover.'

'No, not at all. We must find something beautiful for such a beautiful woman.'

'Something that will draw me to a man,' she said. 'I'm going hot all over, looking at these rings.'

'Very beautiful,' he said.

'I'm bewitched and bedazzled,' she said, looking at him again, smiling. In fact, she felt nauseous and fatigued. 'Women must roll over for you in a shop like this.'

She looked at him, smiled, and turned back to the top of the showcase. Waited for him to make a move.

'What do you think of this necklace?' she asked, taking off her jacket and then wrapping it around the hanger he offered. She put the necklace on. 'Does it suit me?'

'It looks very beautiful on you.'

She walked over to a mirror. Stood up straight. Smiled at him through the mirror. He walked up behind her. Looking at her from behind. She stretched her arms high. Her shirt rode up.

'I feel so free,' she said. 'So feminine. So fantastic.'

Then she felt a hand on her right buttock. That was what she had expected at some time. This was how it had been described to her. She nestled her bum into his hand, as if giving him permission to go on. He pressed harder, fondled her, felt her tiny, muscular bum, pressed his hip against her.

Next came his other hand, reaching round her front, holding her left breast. She moaned like a bad actress.

'Let me take off my shirt,' she said, and turned round to tease him while working with the buttons. He dimmed the lighting.

From there it all happened quickly.

Their clothes scattered across the burgundy carpet.

'It's all right, I'm on the pill,' she said at one point.

She lay on her back on the floor and opened her body for him. He came inside her and she stared past his head at the sparkling goods and empty gift-boxes. He took his time. He seemed to want it to last. She was happy with that. They were safely cocooned. The shop was locked and no one could see in.

As he moved her around the carpet she caught a glimpse of the full-length mirror on the wall. She closed her eyes and enjoyed his strength and her own power for a few minutes. Then she opened her eyes again and saw a reflection of their bare flesh in an adjustable mirror on a display cabinet.

An orgasm crept up on her, surprised her. She held him close, delighting in his body more than she had expected. Maybe it was the thrill of the kill. Maybe he was just a good lover. Maybe he does this all the time. Maybe nine out of ten women slap his face, but he ends up on the floor with the other one.

He carried on carrying on. One of the clocks started to chime six o'clock and the other clocks joined in. The man came powerfully and his excitement thrilled her again.

This was a perfect experience. She had seduced the man, enjoyed it herself, and her period was starting. She might have killed him. She couldn't wait to tell the others what she had done. Oh my God, she thought, I could be a serial killer.

At eight o'clock that evening, after an Indian takeaway with Wayne, Kate went to her room with a book called *What Wild Ecstasy* and various research papers. Sitting on the bed, she stared at everything with contempt. She was almost defunct of energy, in debt, collecting more new problems than solving old ones. But she knew she shouldn't make major decisions soon after being bereaved.

Jeremy Spooner's little job had seemed a simple project at the outset – do a few interviews, type up the tapes and plan a hopeless law case – but now it presented quandaries. Would she have to spurn Jeremy's advances without offending him? Would she have to work hard to help Bruce Venn tell his story? Was the story more complicated than it seemed?

Where are you, Teddy, when I need your advice, when I need the security and protection of our relationship?

She sighed loudly.

Kate flicked through Teddy Merlin's address book. Teddy had made little notes to explain who each person was, as if he wanted to communicate with her from the dead. Kate came across Claire Stanworth's name. Teddy had helped Claire with her undergraduate dissertation about prostitution in Oxford, and Claire was also interested in women's refuges and the safety of women on campus. Kate vividly remembered Teddy talking about Claire's work. Claire had observed what had happened to prostitutes on the streets, and she had worked as a room-service escort herself; her high-class escort work had helped finance her MSc in psychology.

Then Kate put two things together about her own life – she needed money and maybe Jeremy Spooner needed sex with her. A third thing came to mind. Maybe this was a time in her life when she was unable to feel anything through sex. She was numb.

In a spontaneous move, she reached for the phone and dialed Claire Stanworth's number and introduced herself.

'Yes,' Claire said. 'Teddy told me all about you.'

'Can I come and see you?'

'Of course.'

They arranged a time.

As she disconnected, Kate had another shudder at the panic inside her. Solve one panic and you create another. The new one felt even worse.

After Wayne had finished washing up dishes, he stayed in the kitchen listening to sports news on the radio. He was disappointed that Kate had gone back to her room to read. Part of him wanted his house back to himself and part of him loved watching Kate work. Most of him wondered what Juliet Bromage was doing this Saturday night.

He had been listening to the radio for some time when he heard a familiar voice.

'I'd like to thank again all those who contributed to the ransom fund,' said Tracey Holroyd. 'The money will be invested in various charitable projects to benefit the old and the young. The fans got to see Buck Hanson, who has been magnificent throughout this whole kidnapping episode.'

Tracey Holroyd was skilled and articulate.

'And what about you, Buck?' asked the reporter. 'How were you treated? Any complaints?'

'Oh, not bad. They brought me food and water, and they played games with me on Friday night. I was quite relaxed for the match.'

'And you got a draw. A bit disappointed?'

'Yeah, we got two ahead, and we felt confident really. It's the best we've played for a month. Then we gave away two bad goals in the second half and came under a lot of pressure.'

'And two great saves from Buck Hanson late in the game.'

'Yeah, it's what I'm paid for. The lads give me great protection for most of the game, but you always expect to earn your keep in a game like that.'

'And the manager resigned after the game?'

'Yeah, obviously all the lads were disappointed to see him go. And Bob Blazer too. But they're both good coaches. They'll be back.'

'After your good game today, Buck, I presume you'll be getting kidnapped before every match?'

Buck Hanson laughed.

'I'll see if I can arrange it,' he said.

'Thanks very much, Buck Hanson,' said the reporter. 'And thanks to Tracey Holroyd, whose university rag students kidnapped the goalkeeper last night.'

'Thanks, Jim,' said the studio host. 'Good to know that Bucket Hands is safe.'

And that seemed like the end of the stunt.

But it wasn't.

SIX

'Sunday morning,' Wayne said, when his mobile phone rang.

'Get over here,' Buck Hanson told Wayne on the telephone.

'What's happened?' Wayne asked.

'Some fucker's taken my wife.' He paused. 'Have you set me up?'

'What's your address?'

Hanson told Wayne his address and then disconnected.

Wayne planned a rapid journey from Oxford to a village south of Birmingham. He didn't own a car – car accidents had disrupted his life too much – but there were times when a car was essential. Every year he paid a friend, a single parent, a proportion of her vehicle overheads in return for the occasional emergency use of her car. If she needed a car while hers was away she rented one and Wayne paid her twice the rental cost. He made arrangements and within twenty minutes he was doing a steady seventy on the M40. He was thinking about the kidnapping of footballers' close relatives. It happened in South America, didn't it?

'As I said on phone, I'd like to do a proper interview with you,' Kate Park told Bruce Venn. They were sitting in Venn's Abingdon house. Kate had cycled to the rail station, taken her bicycle on the train to Radley and cycled to Abingdon. She hadn't told Jeremy Spooner what she was doing.

'Fire ahead,' Venn said. 'I don't see what good it will do.'

'You seem resigned to your fate,' Kate said, sitting back in her chair.

'I am. I'm preparing for prison and I deserve to be there. It's just a matter of getting my affairs in order. It's going to be awful in prison, but it would be here too.'

'I saw the graffiti,' said Kate.

'There's other nasty stuff, too.'

'What's going to happen about your business?'

'I'm trying to hire someone. It's strange really. Part of me is relieved that my worry about the business is over for a while. I might get some reading done.'

Kate wondered if Venn really knew what lay in store for him. Would he be branded a paedophile? If so, was he really a paedophile? Teddy Merlin always thought the term should apply only to people whose dominant sexual longings were towards prepubescent children. Teddy thought it should exclude men who were occasionally attracted to young teenagers. But Teddy agreed that sex with girls under sixteen should be a criminal offence, as the girl's mental and physical maturity was not yet ripe enough for sexual intercourse. Men weren't strictly paedophiles if they had no adult partner and took advantage of a young girl who they thought was over age. Those men were simply criminals.

'I'm trying to get someone to rent the house,' Venn said. 'It might be tricky, but I'm still hopeful.'

'Good luck,' Kate said.

The preliminaries were over and Kate became an interviewer. She wanted to find out how this recent incident fitted into Venn's sexual history. There were scientific ways of doing that. Teddy Merlin had taught her to respect Alfred Kinsey, who set the template for sex research. Interviewers needed to establish confidentiality and rapport, slowly working towards sensitive areas as the subject grew more at ease.

The *Manual for Sexual Health Advisers* also listed sensible guidelines for conducting an interview. It was best to make sure the room was soundproofed, shielded and free from interruptions. It was also important to exclude third parties, such as Jeremy Spooner, who might inhibit the discussion. Kate was willing to do that, even though it meant she was spending Sunday morning alone with a man facing a rape charge.

Buck Hanson lived in a detached house on an estate so new that the roads weren't finished. It was a typical setting for a well-off professional footballer.

At the front door, Hanson was waiting for Wayne like a goalkeeper at a corner-kick. Hopping from one foot to another. Eyes not missing a movement. Fists clenched.

'Watch those hands, Buck,' Wayne said, as he stepped over the threshold. 'They may only be insured for a million.'

'Fuck that.'

Wayne was hardly inside the kitchen before Hanson went for him. Wayne tried to elbow away Hanson's hands but the goalkeeper's muscles were strong. One finger poked Wayne's eye and two others grabbed an ear, so Wayne kicked Hanson in the groin and that broke the grip. Then the two men got in close again and wrestled for a while. Wayne was probably more worried about Hanson's 'bucket hands' than Hanson himself. Eventually Wayne broke free and was about to hit Hanson when he imagined Bob Blazer's voice saying, *Julius Caesar, Wayne, I do you a flippin' favour and you make a bollards of it.*

Then Wayne remembered that Blazer had lost his job.

'Don't make me break your fingers, Buck,' Wayne said.

Wayne took a few backward steps. They were both panting heavily. Hanson's eyes bulged and he looked set to come at Wayne again. Then Hanson sighed.

'Make us a fuckin' cup of coffee, Shakes,' Hanson said.

'Milk and sugar?'

'Yeah. Two spoons.'

Wayne made the coffee in silence and gave it to Hanson.

'This is the first I know of this,' Wayne said. 'Tell me what's happened.'

'She's not here. She's supposed to be here. She's my wife.'

'When did she go?'

'Dunno.'

'When did you first miss her?'

'When I got back.'

'When you got back from the match last night?'

'Fuck off, Shakes.'

He was snappy again. Wayne thought he was ready for more fighting. Instead he looked at Wayne and explained.

'I got back this morning,' he said. 'Awright?'

'So the lads stayed over?'

'Yeah,' Hanson said. He was lying.

'And the last time you saw her was Friday?'

'Yeah. They picked me up.'

'What's your wife's name?'

'Rachel.'

Wayne envisaged a scene: Tracey Holroyd's security man knocks on the door; Buck shouts that he'll be out in a minute; and then Buck kisses his beautiful wife Rachel goodbye.

'Did you phone her over the weekend?' Wayne asked now.

'I tried her mobile this morning. It's not switched on.'

'Did you phone her on Friday night?'

'Nah. Why would I do that? You know what it's like,' Hanson said, looking calmer. 'You've got the match to think about. She knows that. The last thing you want to know is that the fuckin' central heating's broke down.' He paused again. 'She's probably at her mother's.'

'Did you phone there?'

'Yeah.'

'Was she there?'

'They said not.'

Somehow Wayne felt responsible for this. He'd arranged for Buck Hanson to be away on Friday night and that had triggered something.

'What does she normally do on a Friday night when you're away?' Wayne asked.

'Stays here on her own. Or stops with one of the other wives.'

'Have you phoned them?'

'Course I've fuckin' phoned.'

'And she wasn't there?'

Hanson's face turned angry.

'She better not be playing away,' he said. 'I'll kill her if she is. She should be here.'

Wayne watched Hanson pace the room.

'You've no kids?' Wayne asked.

'Nah.'

'Let's phone the police.'

'Nah, I can't phone the police, Wayne.'

'Why not?'

'They'll find out where I was last night, and it'll get in the papers. I stayed over somewhere. Left a message for her saying I had to stick with the kidnapping for another night. Do some interviews, give some stories. I just needed another night away.'

'Was the message still on the answerphone when you

got back?'

'Yeah.'

'Could she have listened to the message and saved it?'

'It was a new message.'

'When did you leave that message?'

'About seven o'clock last night.'

'And she didn't answer the phone at seven o'clock?'

'Nah.'

'OK, Buck. I suppose that's a start.'

But not much of one, Wayne thought.

It took Kate an hour to lead Bruce Venn to the most important part of the interview. On the way she had built up a picture of Venn's early sexual life. His relationships were intermittent during his twenties and none had lasted more than two years. But Kate gleaned no inkling of a history of trouble, no regular attraction to fifteen-year-olds, except, of course, when Venn was fifteen himself.

'So tell me about your marriage, Mr Venn?'

'Yes, as I say, we'd gone out for a time when I was thirty or thirty-one. Then we met again when I was, oh, about thirty-five.'

'How did you meet the second time around?'

'I bumped into her in town. We went for coffee and she poured out her troubles. I listened. At least I hope I listened. She came round that evening and we ended up in bed together.'

'How long were you formally married?'

'Actually, we're still married. We were together for

about a year, then we got married, and then she moved out about three years after that.'

'When did she move out?'

'About two years ago. Actually I should tell her about this and we should try to rush the divorce through so that she's not implicated in any way.'

'Do you know where she is? I may wish to talk to her.'

Venn looked surprised.

'Yes, I have her address,' Venn said.

'I think it could really help you for me to speak with her. She is certain to hear about your plight.'

'I'll give you her address.'

'Thank you.'

'I'll get it now,' Venn said.

Kate stayed seated until he returned with the address.

'So tell me about your sexual relationship with your wife in the last year you lived together,' Kate said. 'Were you still sexually active with each other?'

'Yes. That side of it was all right.'

'How often did you make love?'

'I would say about once a week, sometimes twice.'

'And you both had orgasms?'

'Yes.'

'Which of you would come first?'

'Usually she would come first. I would stimulate her manually or orally.'

'Would she come during intercourse too?'

'Usually. Not always.'

The setting was now very relaxed. Kate felt she could ask anything that was pertinent.

'So it wasn't because of sex that the relationship broke down?'

'No. That was the thing that kept it going for me. I was very tied up with work. We hardly saw each other. Basically I ignored her at a time when she needed support. It was my fault.'

'Did it surprise you when she left?'

'Not really. This sounds really strange but it gave me one less thing to worry about. I was so focused and driven at that time.'

'Did you still see each other after she left the house?'

'We'd meet for sex. During the day or late at night. But she would get mad because I wouldn't talk about us. I'd listen to her and offer advice. About other things. But we never really solved what was happening between us. I just found her too demanding. Well, she wasn't demanding really. It was just that I couldn't give her the attention she deserved.'

'How long did that go on for?'

'Oh, about six months.'

'And other relationships?'

'I had a brief fling. But I decided that I didn't have time for a new relationship. I had my work.'

'OK,' said Kate. 'Now if we can move forward to the night of the trauma, could you start by telling me about your day out?'

Venn talked about how they had taken Olivia to a wildlife park during the day. Then Bruce had cooked and surprised the other two with the meal he created. The three of them had played board games and watched a DVD together.

'What time did Olivia go to bed?'

'About eleven.'

'And did you stay up with Fiona?'

'Yes. We talked a little longer.'

'Did anything else happen?'

'Yes. We got a little intimate.'

'A little intimate?'

'Yes, we kissed a bit. Cuddled. It was awkward because it was like she had one eye looking over my shoulder in case her daughter came in. But I relaxed her.'

'You relaxed her?'

'You know, she had . . .'

'She had an orgasm?'

'Yes.'

'How about you?'

'No. Fiona went to bed. She was a bit embarrassed, I think. It was like our roles were reversed. Like we were the teenagers and Olly was the mum upstairs.'

'So Fiona went to bed. What did you do?'

'I stayed up for a time. Couldn't settle. Watched some television till about midnight or later. Then went up.'

'Do you sleep well these days?'

'When I get off to sleep.'

'Have you been overtired?'

'I've been working long hours. That's what it's like in business these days. I often worry about work issues in bed.'

'And what do you remember about the incident with Olivia?'

'Nothing much. I must have got up about two, gone to Olly's room, pulled the covers back and had my evil way until Fiona pulled me off.' He held his head in his hands.

How Kate sometimes disliked the ambiguity of sexual innuendo. *Pulled me off.* But she saw no sign that Bruce Venn was deliberately being ambiguous.

'Can you describe the actual sex?' Kate asked.

'No, that's too embarrassing.'

'I asked you last time about the feel of her body.'

'I don't know. I want to forget about it and take my punishment.'

'So Fiona caught hold of you and pulled you away from her daughter?'

'Yes.'

'Had Olivia led you on in any way during the day?'

'No. We'd made eye contact a few times when we were out with the animals and playing games, and I think she liked me, but my date was with the mother. To be honest, I didn't want the girl around. I just wanted a tête-à-tête with Fiona. I think Fiona wanted to recruit me as a father figure because her daughter was going off the rails.'

'Off the rails?'

'Well, that's maybe stretching it. She'd had a boyfriend for six months and that had ended. She was seeing one or two other lads, including one of about nineteen.'

'What was Olivia's mood during the day?'

'She was a bit sulky and then she'd rally. She was good company for a teenager. I liked her. It could have all worked out between me and Fiona. I screwed it up big time. I must have had a brainstorm.'

SEVEN

Wayne made another drink for Buck Hanson. Then he sat at Hanson's kitchen table and thought about an action plan.

'OK, Buck,' he said. 'Here are some things we can do.'

'Huh,' Hanson said.

'We can phone every number in her address book.'

'Nah, she'll show up.'

'Well, maybe we could try to find out exactly when she was last seen. Talk to neighbours. Find out if anyone saw her leave.'

'Nah. I don't want the neighbours to know anything.'

'I could make up a story I could try on the neighbours – something about how she went off in a huff and you're worried about her and want to apologise.'

'That's not fuckin' funny.'

'It's not meant to be.'

Hanson stared at Wayne again.

'It sounds crap,' Hanson said.

'Yeah, you're right,' Wayne agreed. 'Does she have a computer we can look at?'

'Yeah, there's one upstairs.'

'Do you know her email password?'

'It's *her* computer. I don't know that stuff.'

'OK, I might have a look at it in a minute.' Wayne returned to his list. 'We could talk to her mobile phone company. See if they can trace the phone. Where were you when you rang her phone?'

'I was here.'

'So you didn't hear it ring in the house?'

'Nah.'

Hanson looked puzzled.

'Here's another idea,' Wayne said. 'We can contact the Missing Persons Network.'

'Nah, I told you, I don't want police.'

'They're not police.'

'They sound like police.'

'How about phoning all the hospitals?'

'Yeah, we could do that. That's a good one.'

'First, I'd like you to check if there's any evidence that she went away on a trip. Is there anything she would definitely take with her?'

'Fucked if I know.'

'Where does she keep a passport?'

'I'll go and look for it. Then we'll phone the hospitals.'

Hanson went upstairs. Wayne followed and Hanson regarded him suspiciously.

'Check whether suitcases are still there,' Wayne said. 'And whether any clothes have gone.'

'How the fuck would I know that?'

Wayne shrugged.

'Just have a look,' Wayne told him. 'See if everything looks normal.'

Hanson walked into the bedroom and did some foraging.

'Her passport's here,' he said. 'I dunno the rest.'

'OK, you phone the hospitals and I'll look at the computer.'

The phone rang. They watched it ring for a while.

'Probably her fuckin' mother,' Buck Hanson said.

'Only one way to find out.'

Hanson answered it eventually.

'Yeah,' he said. 'Yeah . . . Yeah . . . Who the fuck are you? . . . Don't fuck with me . . .' The pauses lasted ten to twenty seconds. 'Fuck . . .'

He ended the call and stared at the phone for a time. His eyes were popping and his neck veins were bulging.

'Who was it, Buck?' Wayne asked.

'Wrong fuckin' number,' he said.

'A wrong number doesn't make you that angry, Buck.'

He gazed at Wayne.

'Nah. They've got her. That was them.'

'Who?'

'Dunno. Some woman.'

'What did she say?'

'She said they had Rachel.'

'What else?'

'They told me to get cash by noon tomorrow or

something bad will happen to Rachel. She'll phone tomorrow and tell me what to do with it.'

'Holy mackerel,' said Wayne, dredging up a phrase he had once taught Bob Blazer.

Wayne sat down and weighed it up. A Premier League goalkeeper fake-kidnapped and returned safely after a collection for charity. The goalkeeper's wife really is kidnapped and a bigger ransom demanded. The two must be connected.

'Time to call the police, Buck,' Wayne said.

'Nah.'

'Better get the money first thing tomorrow.'

'There's no way I'm paying any money.'

'You've got it, haven't you, Buck?'

Hanson grunted.

'And she's worth is, isn't she?' Wayne added.

Hanson grunted again.

Here was one footballer who didn't part easily with money.

'You must tell the police,' Wayne said.

'I know what I should do,' Hanson said. 'I should talk to my agent. See what the score is. I'll handle it from here, Shakes.'

'OK, talk to your agent.'

'He'll know what to do. I should have got him straight away.'

'Do it your way. Let me know if you think I can help.'

Wayne hung around for a few more minutes, but felt redundant. He wanted out. He left Hanson's house, drove away and stopped the car a mile down the road. He used his mobile phone to call Tracey Holroyd's mobile, the only contact he had for her. A message service picked up his voice.

'Tracey, I need to speak to you urgently,' Wayne said.

At midday, after her return from Abingdon, Kate arrived unannounced at Caprice's barge. *Commuter's Fantasy* was moored in a prime spot close to the city centre, and Caprice was watering flowers on the roof.

'Hi, Caprice,' Kate called out, as she left her bicycle on the towpath.

'Well, Ophelia,' Caprice replied. 'Look who is honouring us with her presence.'

Ophelia?

Caprice was talking to one of her plants.

'Cup of tea?' Caprice asked. 'Would you care to share a pear?'

'Sure.'

Five minutes later they took their apple tea and half a pear on to the towpath. The weather was kind. They ate without talking. They watched the ducks and water for several minutes. Kate felt a painful glaze on the front of her face, and Caprice must have noticed.

'Oft have I heard that grief softens the mind,' Caprice said suddenly. 'And makes it fearful and degenerate.'

'My mind feels like mush,' Kate said. 'I can hardly put one foot in front of another. I'm supposed to be working a late shift today, on a ward I've never seen. I don't know if I can face it. And I'm teaching tomorrow. I've hardly done any preparation. I'm dreading it.'

'Is the man no comfort to you yet?'

'Wayne?'

'Of course.'

'We're finding our way. I can feel his eyes on me.'

'Wait until you feel his hands on you.'

'That won't happen. Why did you get involved with him, Caprice? Why did he get involved with you?'

'Wayne?' Caprice laughed. 'I am a dreamboat to him. An escape from his rugged world. And, for entrance to my entertainment, I do present you with a man of mine.'

'Is that more Shakespeare?'

'Thee talked about Shakespeare, so I quoteth Shakespeare.'

The two women laughed. Kate felt momentarily better. She'd needed some relief and Caprice's world was so far from her own.

'Besides,' said Caprice. 'I've always really liked his dog.'

'Rover?'

'Of course. Such a sweet artistic canine soul.'

'Wayne thinks you only like him because he's called Shakespeare,' Kate said.

'Does he now? But there is more to him than his name.'

'Are you still seeing him?'

'If I have to lie with him again, I shall happen to chance upon him. Thou are not ready for him yet. Thou needs to heal.'

Kate nodded.

'Goodness knows what sort of conversations you have with Wayne.' Kate said, looking at Caprice. 'Or maybe you don't talk much.'

They laughed together.

'Wayne understands more than he says,' Caprice said.

Kate nodded, without knowing why. She finished her tea and looked wistfully at her watch.

'Back to the coalface,' she said.

Later that night, around ten o'clock, Wayne Shakespeare exchanged a few words with Kate Park when she came in from her late shift. Then he said goodnight, told Rover he was still his best friend, and went up to his study. He finished off some bookkeeping and thought about what Juliet Bromage might be doing. He also wondered where Buck Hanson might have been on Saturday night.

Finally, Wayne phoned Tracey Holroyd's number again: 'It's still urgent – phone me whatever time you come in tonight.'

He went to bed with his mobile switched on and next to his pillow.

Wayne woke up wondering whether he should have asked Buck Hanson for a photograph of his wife. He checked his mobile and found no messages. He dozed fitfully and checked his phone fruitlessly the next time he woke. It was still dark and he could faintly hear someone creeping around the house.

Kate arrived at the kitchen table at 4.20 that Monday morning. The only thing she was nursing that night was a cup of camomile tea. She had come out of a short, restless sleep with thoughts of her morning's teaching. A few hours and she would be in front of a class.

She was relatively relaxed about not sleeping enough.

Sleep would come eventually, she thought, when the emotions and anxieties settled down. In the meantime she chose a heavy academic article in the hope that it would make her sleepy again. She stared at the wall for a few minutes, until she heard Wayne's footsteps on the stairs. She pulled her dressing-gown tight.

'I thought I heard you,' Wayne said. 'Are you all right?'

'Yes.'

'You've got tea?'

'Yes, thanks.'

'What are you reading?' Wayne looked at the cover of the journal. '*The Journal of Sexual Abstracts*.'

'Yes. Normally if I read books like this in public I put a cover on them.'

'A brown paper cover?'

'No. William Morris wrapping paper or something like that. Something to make the book seem more loving.'

'I think I understand. You'd like me to imagine that the books you read in the house have attractive covers so I can't see what you're reading.'

'Exactly.'

'I'm interested in what you're reading. I have a feeling that I've got a lot to learn from you.'

'I have the academic background, you have the experience?'

'I don't know about that.'

'Please stop looking at my legs,' Kate said.

'I was just noticing the scar on the outside of your right ankle. I was interested in its story.'

'Another time.'

'Are you size seven?'

'Yes.'

'Nice feet,' Wayne said.

'I'm sorry if I woke you up.'

'You didn't. I woke myself up with my thoughts. You're very light on your feet . . . but I'm strong on my hearing. Especially tonight. Would you like a hot chocolate?'

Kate looked at the tea she had hardly touched.

'Please,' she said.

Wayne boiled some milk while Kate unsuccessfully tried to read. She flicked the pages of the journal.

'Are you thinking about Juliet?' Kate asked.

'Yes. I was wondering where she spent Saturday night and who she was with.'

'Oh.'

'What were you thinking about?'

'I was thinking about teaching. I was thinking about my sister. I was thinking about rape. I went to see this man this morning. He's being charged with rape. At least I think it was this morning I saw him. It could have been three days ago. May I talk confidentially?'

'Of course.'

'It's bizarre. I'm working with a solicitor and he says it's an open-and-shut case. His client raped a fifteen-year-old girl and there was a witness. The police came and collected evidence and the man confessed.'

'The prosecutor could do it in his sleep.'

'So why should something bother me? It happened in the early hours of the morning.' Kate flicked the pages of the journal again. 'Oh, I do know why it bothers me. Of course, how silly.'

They were quiet for a moment.

'You're almost smiling,' Wayne said. 'Something's clicked.'

'Maybe. Now I have a theory that fits the facts. But I need more evidence.'

'Well done. Maybe now you could sleep.'

'Maybe I could sleep.'

Kate put the article in a folder, picked up her hot chocolate and walked to the stairs.

'Do I need to lock my door?' she said.

'No, you are very safe here,' Wayne said. 'If you and I were to ever make love, I would definitely want your consent. I would also want to see far more than a hint of a smile. I would love to see you smile lots and laugh heartily.'

Kate stopped and looked at him.

'Thanks for the drink,' she said, turning, walking up the stairs.

Wayne held up his cup as if to toast her. He walked back upstairs and stopped to pet Rover.

'It's too early for a walk,' he told the sculpture.

EIGHT

The sound of Wayne's mobile phone disturbed him from sleep. He reached for the phone, hoping it was Tracey Holroyd.

'Monday morning,' Wayne told the phone.

'It's Jim,' said Jim Bailey, who was Richard Bromage's key man and Juliet's godfather. 'Richard has a couple of little jobs we'd like you to help with. Come in as soon as you can.'

'Yeah, I'll put some clothes on.'

'You do that.'

Bailey disconnected.

The mobile phone rang again. It was still in Wayne's hand. Wayne stared at the phone like it was a wife's lover. Then he hit the green light.

'Still before breakfast,' he told the phone.

'Wayne?'

The Bromages were buzzing. This could only be Juliet

Bromage. Wayne could tell by the nervous tremble in his body and the way he fidgeted on the bed.

'Good morning,' he said sharply.

'I hear you're coming into the office, Wayne.'

'Yeah, as soon as . . .'

'See me before you see Jim.'

'Sure,' he said.

But she was gone. The brief unsatisfactory connection stirred all sorts of memories. He imagined her on a Florida beach, near naked, simultaneously planning a tour of the Everglades and a backdoor takeover. He did not find it too hard to imagine. It had happened.

Bodies are our essential lifeline, Wayne thought. Some bodies are cool, some are warm, and sometimes the fusion of two different ones creates the ideal temperature of a perfectly adjusted shower. Wayne had felt like that with Juliet Bromage. Winter or summer, their bodies seemed compatible. But all good things had to end. More or less.

Wayne pulled himself together and dressed for the boss's daughter.

The Bromage building was a three-minute jog from Wayne's house. Cars splashed and sprayed through the effects of a recent sharp shower while sunshine dazzled windscreens and reflected colourful scenes in the new puddles. Wayne shuffled towards the glass-fronted main entrance of the Bromage building, and went to talk with Mackie on the front desk.

Mackie nodded – his equivalent of 'Good Morning' –

and handed Wayne a note. It was a team line-up for their charity football match the coming week. Wayne was shown as part of a three-man midfield.

'No way,' Wayne said. 'I'm out of condition. The pitch will look like an aerodrome after ten minutes.'

Mackie laughed. He pointed at Wayne and said one word: 'Youngest.'

Mackie had played for Richard Bromage's club for fifteen years. His face bore the rugged testimony of broken noses and cut eyebrows, and his legs still carried scars from cuts and protruding bones and drill-holes. Wayne would occasionally ask Mackie to roll up a trouser-leg to see if he could make a middle-aged lady faint, or even a middle-aged man. Mackie was one of the many who didn't understand Wayne's decision to leave football.

'OK,' Wayne said, recognising Mackie's mood. 'It's only one game.'

Mackie nodded more approvingly. He was dressed in black trousers and a fashionable yellow shirt with a security emblem that looked like a designer label, until you got close. Wayne had designed these soft uniforms for the security workers inside the building. No peaked caps. No macho musclemen standing in doorways. None of that epaulette stuff. He liked security staff to stand out when needed and fade into the background the rest of the time. The important thing was that the Bromage employees and visitors could recognise them.

'I'd better go up,' Wayne said.

Wayne took the lift to the third floor. Then he

straightened his tie in front of a security camera, knowing that Mackie would see him. He buzzed through to the receptionist.

'Wayne Shakespeare,' he said. He went through the security system.

'Good morning, Mister Shakespeare,' said Mary Curtis. 'I'll tell Miss Juliet you're here.'

Wayne sat and read sport and crime in the newspapers. He wondered how close he and Buck Hanson had come to becoming a newspaper story.

A door opened soundlessly behind him. Wayne tossed the paper back into the pile.

'Wayne, can you come through,' said Juliet Bromage.

He certainly could.

Juliet Bromage's office was a high-class living space with two easy chairs and a sofa-bed as well as traditional office furniture. The artwork alone justified employing a security firm, and the ornaments symbolised countries rather than counties. Juliet waved Wayne to a comfortable chair and went back to her telephone.

'I can do lunch on Tuesday or we could meet here four o'clock on Thursday . . . Yes, Tuesday will be fine. One. I'll look forward to that.'

Juliet put the telephone down and input the arrangement on her phone. She looked up and switched on her smile.

'How are you, Wayne?' she asked

'Tickety-boo,' Wayne said.

'Good. I wanted to see you about tomorrow. I'm getting rid of someone. Remind me what we do.'

Wayne went over the procedure: how the manager approaches the employee; how the employee is told; whether counselling is available; how the employee collects personal property; and who escorts the victim off the premises.

'I'll tell Mackie,' Wayne said, at the end. 'I'll make sure I'm around, in case anything goes wrong – like it nearly did with Robin Hookes. Who's the lucky fellow?'

'Why do you assume it's a man? I'll tell you tomorrow morning.'

'Does he or she know this is coming?'

'Probably not.'

'I need to know if it's someone you're involved with. Had I known about your sleeping arrangements with your ex-husband I might have handled it differently.'

'That was unfortunate with Robin.'

'You're amazing, Juliet. You thought you could sack your man and expect him to continue sleeping with you.'

Wayne watched closely as Juliet's cheeks and neck turned red. He recognised the rouge from their love-making.

'We laid off Robin with a generous payment and gave him some freelance work,' Juliet said.

'I'll need to know what time the person comes in,' Wayne said.

Juliet made a quick phone call.

'Eight o'clock,' she told Wayne.

'OK,' Wayne said. 'I'll liaise with Mackie.'

'Phone me on my mobile if there's a problem,' Juliet said. 'And I have another job. You're really good at solving puzzles.'

'At your service.'

'Someone sent me an anonymous letter.'

'What type of letter?'

I don't really want to read one of her love letters, Wayne thought.

Juliet stood up and walked across the room to her briefcase. The effect was hypnotic. She was 5ft 7in but the shortest in her family. Her body seemed younger than her thirty-odd years and her legs moved quickly. The tight, tailored trousers told an accurate story of the shape of her thighs. She bent over, plucked a piece of paper from her briefcase and handed it to Wayne.

Wayne took the sheet with two fingernails at one top corner and laid it on the desk. There was one line of typing.

Juliet: you will die soon.

'Italics,' Wayne said.

'Yes.'

The telephone rang. It usually did.

'Yes,' Juliet said to the mouthpiece. 'Oh, yes . . . I can't talk now. I have someone with me. I'll phone you back. He's just leaving . . . Yes, yes. In Australia we want a cricketer and an Australian Rules player . . . Whoever has the best hands . . . I'll talk later.'

While Juliet dealt with her phone call, Wayne's eyes strayed towards seemingly neutral parts of the room. But everything he saw provoked thoughts of Juliet. Wayne wondered what Juliet really wanted from him now. He had fallen for her once and got hurt, but he had fought back and their relationship had become more intermittent and better balanced.

Juliet ended her telephone conversation and turned to Wayne.

'Did you send me the note, Wayne?' she asked.

He shook his head slowly from side to side. He was furious with her for even suggesting it, and he was also excited by her. He could sense she was luring him into something dangerous.

'No,' he said.

'I want to know who wrote it. I take the note seriously.'

'I'm not sure this is a job for me,' Wayne told her. 'I would have to ask you questions about who you are sleeping with, and who else you might have pissed off.'

'That's irrelevant.'

'I need to decide that.'

'Look, it wasn't easy bringing it up,' she told him. 'But it's your job to look into it. I'm telling you formally now. I don't know what this letter means. It sounds like a threat. There might be a stalker out there. Or some mad guy. I want you to find out who wrote it.'

Her voice had risen along the way.

'OK, OK,' Wayne said 'I'll look into it. But there's not much to go on.'

The telephone rang again. It seldom slept. Like the Bromage family. Wayne looked back at the note.

Juliet: you will die soon.

'Yes, it is,' said Juliet to the phone. 'Yes . . . I remember . . . I don't know . . . If you say so . . . Yes, I'll meet you for a drink . . . Tomorrow? . . . Tomorrow evening? . . . Yes, that will be fine. See you there.'

Juliet disconnected her phone call and turned to

Wayne. Her eyes were lively and excited.

'I have to ask some questions about the letter,' Wayne said, his voice calmer. Juliet nodded and he continued. 'Was it sent here or to your home?'

'Home.'

'Oh, my contract is for this building.'

'Look, Wayne, I'm telling you . . .'

'Just teasing. I'll look into it. When did it arrive?'

'Sunday, I think. I was in and out over the weekend.'

'Did it have an envelope?'

'Yes.'

'Do you still have the envelope?'

'I'd have to look.'

'Describe it to me.'

'It had the letter J on the front. That was all.'

'Handwritten?'

'Yes.'

'With a line across the top of the J or not?'

Juliet pondered.

'A line, I think. What difference does that make?'

'Look at the letters from your boyfriends. See who does the J like that.'

'I'll see.'

'I'll need a list of your boyfriends,' he said. 'To think through who might have sent that threat.'

Juliet nodded, her face flushed with anger.

A few names came to Wayne's mind. Robin Hookes, Buck Hanson . . . Wayne Shakespeare.

Robin Hookes had become some sort of consultant after being kicked out of the Bromage organisation. She had split up with him some time ago but perhaps still saw him. Hookes was well-spoken and well-educated. Wayne had strong opinions about Juliet's men. He disliked them from prejudice. Well, all except himself.

'I need a full list,' Wayne said. 'Go back further. Men will remember you for a long time. Write them all down. It will be a good exercise in affirmation.'

The words could have been flattering, but Wayne's voice had a bite.

'Look, I can't deal with this now,' Juliet said. 'We can talk about it later. You can come to my house one evening. In the meantime I want to feel safe. This has shaken me.'

'Shall I have someone watch over you?'

'Yes.'

'All the time?'

'Use your judgement.'

'OK,' Wayne said. 'Let me put it this way – who do you think it is?'

'I don't know.'

'Robin Hookes?'

'I don't know.'

Wayne didn't know much about Juliet's marriage. She'd met Robin Hookes at university and they'd joined the Bromage business together. She'd divorced Hookes because of his drinking and his associated business decline. But she'd continued to sleep with him occasionally. Then Juliet had discovered how physically attractive she was to other men.

'Can you talk to Robin?' Juliet asked. 'See if it's him.'

'OK, I'll visit him.'

Juliet gave Wayne an address for Robin Hookes. Then

she changed the subject.

'What do you know about Buck Hanson?' she asked.

'The goalkeeper?'

'Yes.'

'He's a difficult lad. Dedicated to his job. Uneven-tempered. He's having an affair with Juliet Bromage.'

Juliet tightened.

'Give me a written report on him,' she said.

'In what context?'

'We're talking to him about the condom campaign.'

'OK.'

'That's all, Wayne,' Juliet said.

'May I leave the threatening note here for the moment? I'll come back for it in ten minutes with a bag. I'll take to the private forensics guy we use.'

Juliet: you will die soon.

NINE

Kate Park had set sixteen students an exercise and the room was full of chatter. She'd asked them to rate different types of sexual activity in order of health risk. She watched as people in groups of four shuffled postcards with agreement or disagreement. She listened to the discussions.

The exercise also gave Kate time to think about Jeremy Spooner's case. She needed a conversation with Bruce Venn's ex-wife and she needed to visit the Law Library to check similar cases. She also needed to look through Teddy Merlin's files to test a theory.

When Kate had offered to take over Teddy's class, during the early stage of his illness, he told her that the university had only three problems – resources, resources and resources. Kate understood that. She had the same three problems in her own life. Tonight she would talk to Claire about making money through escort work, even though the thought made her angry. Well-educated, well-meaning people shouldn't be driven to this, she thought. What if her career suffered because a client recognized her? Maybe this was the sort of bizarre idea that bereaved people had.

Kate's eyes went from group to group. Soon she would interrupt and bring them all together. Then she would get feedback and sum up for ten minutes at the end. That was the part she was not looking forward to. These days, whenever she stood in front of a class, she felt as though she might cry.

'OK,' she said, eventually, her voice barely audible.

The students continued their discussions.

'OK,' Kate repeated, a little louder. She caught the eye of people in one discussion group and made contact with someone in a second group.

'OK, time to come together,' Kate said. 'Ready.'

The room became quiet.

She thought hard about what Teddy would do here. Then, when she had the gaze of the class, she called up a line that she had heard Teddy use as a starter. She breathed slowly and started talking in a calm and authoritative voice.

'Unaccustomed as I am to speaking in public,' she said, 'without a courgette and a condom . . .'

Wayne was back in the Bromages' third-floor waiting area, reading a catalogue he had lifted on his way out of Juliet's office. The catalogue was an example of Juliet's research into competitive products.

Chocolate condoms.

Tasty dental dams.
Lubricating jelly.
The femidom.
Contraceptive sponges.
Flavoured lubricants.

Mary Curtis watched Wayne like she was a first-day security guard.

'Has Juliet kept you informed about these condom developments?' Wayne asked Mary.

'She tells me what I need to know.'

'Do you think she will take to the condom business?'

'I need to get on with my work.'

The telephone rang to confirm Mary's words. Mary Curtis held the telephone with her left hand while her right hand covered her mouth. Wayne couldn't hear her from a yard away but it seemed like she was stopping someone from speaking to one of the Bromages. She did that all the time.

While Wayne watched, Jim Bailey came out of his office. Bailey trod the deep-pile carpet very gracefully, despite his solid build. His natural size could make others look small but he had also worked hard on perfecting a technique to go with it. He was in his late fifties, and had been with Richard Bromage for a very long time.

'Good morning, Wayne,' Bailey said.

'Morning, Jim.'

Wayne stood up and tossed the condom catalogue onto Mary Curtis's desk.

'Don't try them all at once,' Wayne whispered. He thought he saw Mary's left cheek twitch in search of an angry expression, but it might have been a trick of the light. Two seconds later her fingers were battering a computer keyboard and her usual tense look had returned.

Jim Bailey looked for a moment like he might make some comment. But he let it ride. Wayne followed him into his office and looked at the view. Good views of Oxford were declining by the minute, but this building had one. Half a dozen spires and a few dreaming cranes peeped over the city centre. He had to look quickly because Jim's chair took the best view. Wayne sat down on an older chair and felt smaller than Bailey.

'We have two little jobs for you, Wayne,' Jim said.

'You want me to take over as manager of the football club?'

Jim was stumped for a reply. For some reason he always took Wayne literally and it drove Wayne to new – and sometimes pathetic – attempts at humour.

'Richard has one little task for you,' Jim continued. 'He says it's very confidential and it needs great sensitivity. You must be very hush-hush.' Bailey's voice was even more serious than usual. He must have seen the puzzlement on Wayne's face because he held up his hands, palms towards Wayne. 'I know you're always hush-hush, Wayne, but you need to know that this one is special again. Obviously we're involving you because we can trust you.'

Wayne nodded and sat there expectantly.

'Richard knows you are here,' said Jim. 'He'll give us a call.'

While speaking, Bailey annotated correspondence on his desk. He was a man who could do six things at once.

'I can tell you about the other thing – before we go through,' Bailey said.

Wayne reached for his notebook.

'Keep an eye on Juliet if you can,' Bailey said. 'I'm worried she might go off the deep end.'

Their talk was interrupted by Mary Curtis buzzing through.

'Mister Richard has just freed himself up, Mister Bailey,' she said in a voice Wayne could hear.

'We're going through,' said Bailey.

'I'm interested in the issues that came up in your conversations,' Kate told her class, 'the issues that were part of the debate. When you do this exercise with teenagers the feedback will be more concerned with each particular sexual activity. What is the most risky? Why?'

'Can we use these cards for a group of teenagers?' one student asked.

'Of course. But you have to adopt the language to suit your group. Rather than anal sex you might have to use cock up the arse or dick in the bumhole or whatever. The variety in terminology is amazing. A year ago I attended a sex abuse court case and the young victim used the word breasts to mean vagina. When she was giving evidence she said that the man put his willie on her breasts, but she also said that he put his finger in her breasts and twisted it round. Next week I'll do a session on the language of sex and its ambiguity.'

Kate was suddenly aware that she was talking more self-consciously.

'Let's go round the groups,' she said. 'First group.

What issues came up in your discussion?'

'Well,' said a woman in her thirties, taking the initiative. 'We didn't think you could generalise. The same activity could be dangerous with one partner and risky with another. Take something like rimming. We put it at a higher risk than anal sex with a condom but it depends on all sorts of things.'

'Such as?'

'Well, we got a bit out of our depth then.'

Kate took a more directive stance.

'There are lots of germs in the anus,' she said. 'Hepatitis is one possibility. HIV is a possibility if the faeces contain blood and the person doing the licking or kissing has mouth sores or herpes.'

'Who's most at risk?' someone else asked. 'That's something we debated for all activities.'

'In the case of rimming, or analingus, it's the person doing the licking or kissing.'

The feedback session was under way, and Kate was engaged. She sensed a glimmer of normality.

Richard Bromage held up his palm to Jim Bailey.

'It's all right, Jim, I'll deal with this,' he said.

Bailey looked bewildered at being excluded. Wayne Shakespeare went through to Richard Bromage's office alone.

Richard Bromage pointed to a chair. He leaned back in his own chair and placed his hands behind his head.

'I want you to find a girl for me,' he said. 'Well, she would be a woman by now.'

As ever, Richard Bromage came straight to business.

No hellos and how-are-yous. Nothing about the great job Wayne had done for him last year.

Bromage's manner was always fierce and intense. He was medium-height, gaunt and wiry, the sort of man who would slip by in a crowd. But once inside his office you had to notice him. His skin was as tough as his temperament and the only fight Wayne expected him to lose was that against age. He was into his sixties and didn't look well. There again, he never had. This time, though, according to Jim Bailey, there was a bigger story behind the pallor.

'Her name was Claire. Surname something like Stanley or Stanway. She wouldn't recognise my real name.'

Bromage spoke in clipped sentences. He used the same tone when addressing shareholders. He was a man who knew everything of importance but probably had to ask Bailey for his own postcode. Yet this was a rare meeting when Bailey was not present.

'What do you know about her?' Wayne asked, 'Age? Where she was born? Name of her parents? Anything.'

'I met her six or seven years ago. She would be mid-twenties or late-twenties now. We met in Oxford and I think she came from this area. She was studying one of those vague subjects, like politics or sociology. She was at university somewhere in the Midlands.'

He paused.

'Leicester?' Wayne said. 'Nottingham? Loughborough? Birmingham?'

'No.'

Wayne was wondering if he could trace Claire Stan-whatsit through an alumni network. These days university fundraisers scour the world for likely targets.

'Aston?'

'No.'

'Keele?'

'That's it. Keele.'

'Good,' Wayne said.

'Let me repeat the basic facts,' Wayne said quickly. 'To make sure I've got them correct.' He knew the old man had appreciated him not taking notes but he wanted to be sure of his details. Wayne went over it again and Richard Bromage nodded when he had finished.

'I may need more of the story,' Wayne said.

'Get by if you can,' said Bromage. 'If you can't, get back to me.'

Wayne had been dismissed.

Downstairs, Wayne waited for Mackie to come free.

'Can you do two jobs for me?' Wayne asked.

He prepared Mackie on the drill for the next day's sacking, and explained about Juliet's strange threat.

'She needs to feel secure,' Wayne said. 'Put someone on it for a few hours each evening. You'll get a feel for whether there's a problem. Let me know if you want me to take a shift.'

Mackie nodded. Mackie was so quiet that Wayne sometimes thought he must have been raised on a London Underground train.

'I'll be fit for your charity match,' Wayne said, as he started for the door. 'As long as the referee'll let me use a golf-cart.'

Mackie put his thumb up to Wayne.

'And could you collect a note from Juliet's office,' Wayne continued, 'put it into a bag and take it to our private forensic guy David Boyle?'

Mackie nodded.

Wayne sprinted home, thinking *I'll show Mackie*. It was probably what Mackie wanted him to think.

'We need you to watch the money and see who collects it,' Buck Hanson's agent told Wayne on the telephone. 'When Buck gets the phone call, my assistant and I will follow him and we'll keep watching until the money is picked up. We'll need some relief cover, in case it's a long job. That's where you come in. Can you manage a couple of hours later today?'

'Have you done this sort of thing before?' Wayne asked.

'I don't have time to discuss it.'

'I don't fancy driving to Glasgow,' Wayne said.

'They won't send him there, will they?'

'We don't know yet, do we?'

'I'll phone you when I know where he's going.'

They disconnected.

Wayne had done many things as a security consultant but watching ransom money would be a first.

Wayne was home when Hanson's agent phoned at one o'clock. Buck Hanson had been told to put the money in his Mercedes and drive towards Stratford-upon-Avon. Hanson had set off dutifully, while his agent phoned Wayne to communicate the plan.

'I'll leave in twenty minutes,' Wayne said. He was shaking his head. 'Let me know when they phone him again.'

Wayne made arrangements to borrow his friend's car. As he ended the call, Kate arrived back from her class. She was breathless from her cycle ride.

'Would you like a trip?' Wayne asked. 'I'm driving somewhere.'

'Where?' Kate queried.

'I haven't a clue.'

'A mystery tour?'

'Somewhere around Stratford-upon-Avon. Come on, it'll do you good to get out of Oxford.'

'Yes, I'll come. I'll just change quickly.'

TEN

On the journey, Wayne explained to Kate how he had been contacted by Tracey Holroyd to set up the fake kidnapping of Buck Hanson. He also told her how Rachel Hanson had disappeared and a ransom had been demanded.

'This sounds dangerous,' Kate said.

'It doesn't feel dangerous at the moment but it could get that way. I'll drop you off in Stratford-upon-Avon and pick you up later – you could do the Shakespeare tour.'

'I seem to be on one already.'

'Very sharp. I think that's the first time I've heard you tell a joke.'

'I'm sorry I'm so serious. My sense of humour has been stolen by a thief called grief.'

'Your sense of humour will return,' Wayne said.

'How do you know I ever had one?'

'That's very funny.'

Wayne laughed. Kate smiled briefly.

'It might need a pick-axe to find my sense of humour,' she added.

'I'll go to Headington Homewares in the morning.'

'Do they sell humour?'

'Pick-axes. And everything else.'

'I'll take one of everything else.'

'It does you good to get out of Oxford.'

'Apparently.'

'My partner died seven weeks ago. It might explain how I can be too serious at times. I miss all the things he added to my life. He had that confident optimism that so many Americans have. I think it counterbalanced my earnestness.' She hesitated and then added, 'So much of bereavement is about change.'

Wayne's mobile phone rang. He pulled off the road and answered on the sixth ring.

'Twenty miles south of Stratford-upon-Avon,' he said, when he saw it was Buck Hanson's agent.

'Christ, I thought you weren't going to answer,' the agent said.

'What news?' Wayne asked.

'Buck Hanson's dropped the money off.'

Wayne leaned across Kate and took an Ordnance Survey map from the glove-compartment.

'Where?' he asked.

'South of a place called Ilmington,' the agent said.

Wayne found it on the map. They discussed the details of where the money was being left – hanging on a tree at a quiet road junction.

'Money grows on trees,' Wayne said.

'It's in a bag,' said Hanson's agent.

'Describe the bag.'

'A red bag.'

'Make? Style? Size?'

'I don't know. Buck put the money in the bag. I'm just watching the area.'

'Where are you?'

'Up a hill with my assistant. One of us will stay here and the other will stay by the car.'

'I'll be in the area in twenty minutes.'

'I'll be in the village pub but my assistant will be here.'

'What does your assistant look like?'

He gave Wayne a poor description.

'I'll make contact with him within an hour,' Wayne said. He cut the connection.

'There's probably two guys in suits sitting in a field, not knowing what to look for,' he said. 'Where can I drop you that will be entertaining for you?'

'I'll come with you.'

Wayne looked at Kate and nodded.

Fifteen minutes later Wayne Shakespeare parked the car on a grass verge near a village called Nebsworth. Kate and he planned a walk of a mile along a country path towards the tree that held the money.

'Ready?' asked Wayne.

'It will be nice to get some fresh air. It's wonderful to be somewhere other than Oxford.'

'We need to be in role,' Wayne told her. 'Man and woman on a romantic afternoon walk. May I hold your hand?'

Kate looked at him suspiciously.

'OK,' she said. 'But that's about all I can handle.'

Wayne put his hand in hers. They walked in silence for half a mile until they had to break their grip because two horses came up behind. Women in helmets and jodhpurs, with rucksacks on their back. Wayne and Kate exchanged hellos with the riders and were thanked for stepping out of the way. The horses broke into a trot.

'Is that a string?' Wayne asked Kate.

'I think a string is more than two horses, and they are usually racehorses. Sometimes women.'

'Women?'

'Yes. Like the string of women you've left trailing in your wake . . .'

'Ah ha, more humour?'

'No, I was serious.' Kate said. Then she looked at him and smiled.

They walked in silence until they passed an elderly couple walking from the other direction. Wayne studied them closely.

'They seemed harmless enough,' he said aloud.

When they got to the drop point, they saw a red bag in a tree. Wayne wondered how much a branch should sag if a bag held hundreds of notes. Not as much as he thought. He could sense they were being watched, and it took him less than ten seconds to spot a pair of binoculars glinting in the sun.

'Let's double back and take the footpath to the right,'

Wayne said to Kate.

They left the bridleway for a designated path. Wayne saw a young man in smart casual clothes about fifty yards off the track. Wayne left Kate on the path and crept up slowly. He watched the man for a few minutes before deciding this man was the agent's assistant.

'Nice day,' Wayne said, sitting alongside him. Wayne held out a hand. 'Wayne Shakespeare,' he said.

'Oh, yeah. We're expecting you. You're my relief.'

'If needed. Anything happening?'

'No.'

'All quiet?'

'Yes.'

'Anybody gone past?'

'A few cars.'

'Did you note their numbers?'

'I wasn't asked to do that.'

'What about the elderly couple?'

'Oh, yeah. They walked past.'

'And the two horses? They passed us on the bridleway which runs across the road. Two horses, two riders. One had a red bag on her back.'

'Oh, yeah, I saw them through the trees. Galloping. Till they got near the road.'

Oh dear, Wayne thought.

'Is the bag still there?' he asked.

The look-out used his binoculars.

'Still there,' he said.

'Is it the same bag?'

'I suppose.'

'Is the money still there?' Wayne asked.

'I can't see the money from here.'

'I'll go down and have a look.'

'They might see you.'

'I wouldn't worry about that.'

Wayne walked down with Kate, and they looked at the bag. It was empty.

'One of the riders switched bags,' Wayne said to Kate. 'Might as well take the bag.'

Wayne studied his map and then phoned Buck Hanson's agent.

'You can go home now,' Wayne told him. 'Someone switched bags and went off with the money on horseback. My guess is that they galloped to the end of the bridle path and then had a horsebox waiting. You could check the local riding schools. Have you got people stationed at the main roads?'

'No, there's just me and my assistant.'

'In that case, the money's gone and you have to wait for them to make the next move.'

'Christ. How can I tell Buck?'

'Want me to?'

'Yeah.'

Wayne ended the call in disgust.

'Would you recognise the riders if we saw them again?' he asked Kate.

'It would be difficult. I might recognise their cheekbones.'

'I might remember their bums and thighs.'

'Of course.'

'Would you recognise the horses?' Wayne asked.

'Probably not.'

They walked in silence.

'Your friend who died,' Wayne said. 'Was he an academic?'

'Yes. He bequeathed me the book to edit. He set it all up for me.'

'And you miss him enormously?'

'Enormously.'

'If you want to talk, I can listen.'

'I may talk at some time. At the moment I am enjoying the countryside. I just want to breathe real air.'

When they reached the car, Wayne phoned Buck Hanson.

'Sorry, Buck. A rider came along the bridle path and picked up the money without the agent's assistant seeing her. That was one thing your agent didn't think of.'

One of many, Wayne thought.

'Fuck,' said Buck Hanson.

'At least you gave them what they wanted, Buck. She should still be safe.'

Buck Hanson was silent.

'Are you still there, Buck?'

'Yeah.'

'Tell me the bag had real lawful British money in it.'

More silence. Buck Hanson was not telling Wayne anything.

Wayne disconnected and phoned the agent.

'Tell me that Buck left all the required money in that red bag,' he said.

'As far as I know.'

'You sure?'

'Not absolutely.'

Wayne ended the call.

Wayne dropped Kate in Wolvercote, as she wanted to walk along the canal and do some thinking. Then he took advantage of having the car. Ten miles north of Oxford there was a 1980s housing estate which was ideal for football personnel. The houses were large, the neighbours protective and a motorway was nearby. People in football management, like snooker players, travelled long distances, and some located themselves where they could keep the same house throughout their careers.

Bob Blazer came to the door with a wine bottle and corkscrew in his hands.

'Just in time,' he said, waving the bottle.

Wayne noted the tainted wine glass on the lounge coffee table. Blazer poured a big helping for himself and one for Wayne, who took the drink reluctantly. Drinking at five o'clock in the afternoon was not Wayne's forte.

'Sorry to hear about the job,' Wayne said.

'That's the fuckin' game,' Blazer replied.

'Flippin' game. Something better will come out of it.'

'Yeah, it always does.'

Wayne sat awkwardly and looked around the room. A thin layer of dust covered most of the surfaces. Wayne wiped a finger across a table.

'Yeah, life's not been great since the wife left me,' Blazer said. 'Over a year ago. I've been staying in hotels. I haven't been here much the past month.'

'A bad time for you.'

'Yeah. Wife leaves me, daughter hates me and then I get sacked.' He looked across at an empty bird cage.

'Fuckin' budgie gets cancer of the beak and drops dead off his perch, just when I've taught the fuckin' bird some proper fuckin' swear words.'

'You taught the bird to swear?'

'Nah, it learned anyway.'

They both laughed.

'What should I tell the press, Wayne?' Blazer asked.

'What do you want to tell them?'

'That the bastard directors didn't know their arseholes from a goal-net.'

'How about telling them that objectively the health of the club increased exponentially from the time you and the manager took over but now the subjective opinions of the directors seems to imply otherwise?'

'Write that down.'

Wayne wrote that down.

'What was that shoeshine word you once taught me?'

'Insouciant?' Wayne asked.

'That's it.'

'You used that a lot at one time.'

'Yeah. That's because we had a fuckin' insouciant team. No-one could give a fuck. Isn't that what insouciant means?'

'Sort of.'

They settled in to a football conversation. Blazer told Wayne a couple of stories about the executives at the club and Wayne told him a couple from his late grandfather's archive. Before long they were having a good time and Blazer was drinking more wine.

'Are you living on your own?' Wayne asked.

'Yeah. You think I should get a new budgie?'

'Find someone to live here. It always works for me.'

'A woman?'

'Maybe. A friend. Anybody. It stops me wallowing.'

'I'll get through it, Wayne. Makes it easier in some ways not having the wife around.'

Blazer's phone rang. He answered it.

'Yeah,' said Blazer. 'Yeah.' He waved frantically and pointed at a piece of paper in front of Wayne. He took the paper when Wayne handed it over. 'Yeah. Well, objectively the health of the club increased exponentially from the time we took over but now the subjective opinions of the directors seems to imply otherwise . . . Yeah, I thought we were on the right track. We were playing well enough but not winning enough points . . . No, no, they won't go down. It doesn't feel like a relegation dressing-room, and the players were far from insouciant . . . insouciant . . . I don't know how to spell it, you're the fuckin' journalist . . . OK.'

Blazer disconnected and sat down.

'Vituperative bastard,' he said.

'Vituperative?' Wayne asked. 'I can't remember teaching you that one.'

'Got it from Martin O'Neill. Do you think I could have a career in the media?'

'Nah. You're a bit too easy to wind up. You might let a swearword slip out.'

'Stuff that.'

Blazer slumped in his seat and became subdued. It seemed out of character to Wayne, but Wayne had generally seen Blazer at a football ground where he reigned as Boss or Gaffer, and his word was law.

Wayne stayed for another half-hour and then bid Blazer goodbye.

'Thanks for calling by, Wayne,' said Blazer. 'That means a lot.'

Approaching Oxford, Wayne swung the borrowed car off the Woodstock Road towards the address he had been given for Robin Hookes. He parked the car and knocked loudly at the door to the secluded flat. He wanted to confront Hookes about the note that had frightened Juliet.

Juliet: you will die soon.

No reply.

Wayne knocked loudly again.

'He's probably down the pub, mate,' a neighbour shouted from his garden.

'Which one?'

'Any of them or all of them. Try the one by the tennis courts.'

'He's a big drinker, is he?'

'He's big and he drinks.'

'Does he give you any trouble?'

'No. He knows when he's had enough. He just falls over.'

The neighbour laughed and Wayne joined in.

'Thanks for your help,' Wayne said.

Wayne parked the car at the pub. He had met Hookes on a few occasions, including the time Hookes had been forced out of the Bromage empire. There was a scene that day – Wayne was called to escort Hookes from Juliet's office – but the scene was more to do with Juliet and

Hookes than Hookes losing his job. The episode was eventful enough for Wayne to recognise Robin Hookes in the pub lounge, even though the months had not been kind to the man. Hookes looked a little older, greyer and heavier.

Wayne appraised Hookes's body. Less of a chest, more of a tummy, muscles underused and undeveloped. Wayne wondered what it had all meant to Juliet.

'Ah, the chief superintendent,' Hookes said, when he saw Wayne. He held up a half-full pint of beer. It was obviously not his first of the day. 'Get yourself a drink. Let us bury the Bromages. Get me a drink too.' Hookes swallowed most of the remaining beer in his glass.

'Yeah, best drink 'em quickly, Robin,' Wayne said. 'In case you get one knocked over.'

'What a wit.'

'I'm not staying,' Wayne said. 'I'll just say something and then leave.'

'Take a pew.'

'I'm trying to find out who sent Juliet Bromage a threatening note,' Wayne started.

'How dramatic,' he said.

'Do you know anything about that?' Wayne asked.

'Not at all,' he said. Wayne was tempted to believe him.

'Have you seen her lately?' Wayne asked.

'We would meet occasionally for lunch. We would meet occasionally for, er, other matters.'

'Were you still . . .'

'Yes, I was still *involved* with Juliet,' Hookes said.

Wayne was thrown off course. He took a minute to

focus.

'So what went wrong between you two?' Wayne asked. He had only heard Juliet's side of the story.

'I'm probably prejudiced about what happened,' he said. 'She was seeing me when I was working for Bromage and then when I left she was seeing someone else.'

His answer made Wayne feel uncomfortable.

'It got rather irksome,' he said. 'I think Juliet felt we should stop seeing each other. But then I would see her again. Very complex. Rather awkward.'

Wayne knew all about that.

'Yeah, well,' Wayne said.

'I wish I'd known Juliet as a mistress rather than as a girlfriend and wife,' Hookes said. 'I bet she makes an ideal mistress.'

Hookes looked at Wayne. 'She's not the sort of woman a man would leave a wife for,' he said, 'but she copes with things. She gets on with life. She has high standards too. She has style and she needs someone of high status. She's someone who mixes with important people. A drink?'

Wayne declined and watched Hookes walk to the bar to order another pint. He waited for him to return.

'Were you angry at Juliet?' Wayne asked.

'At times,' he said. 'Weren't you?'

'Weren't we all? I didn't want to kill her. Well, maybe some days. Did you want to kill her?'

'Did she want to kill me?' Hookes asked. He stared at the table like a man who sees depression in a beer glass and drinks it.

'Anyway, if it is you sending threatening notes, I want

you to lay off Juliet,' Wayne said. 'Stop frightening her.'

Hookes laughed. 'Who's frightening who?' he asked.

'I think you're frightening her. If you carry on frightening her, someone might frighten you.'

'It's frightening enough trying to get past the dragon on the desk.'

'Mary Curtis?'

'The same. Does she tell anybody anything?'

'Don't know. Not my business.'

'Don't you security people check out everybody?'

'Mary learned discretion when she'd worked at the football club. She brought that with her to the Bromages.'

'I can't seem to contact Juliet through her.'

'Yeah,' Wayne said.

Hookes looked directly at Wayne.

'I'm trying to decide whether you're a cad or a bounder,' Hookes said.

Wayne laughed. 'A cad or a bounder?'

He imagined Bob Blazer on the training ground.

Wattsy, you're a bounder.

Moggsy, stop being a cad.

'Yes,' Hookes said. 'A cad sleeps with your woman while you're on the battleground. A bounder sleeps with your woman and then fights alongside you.' He paused. 'I'm getting another drink.'

'I'm off,' Wayne said. 'I have work to do. Just remember, don't frighten Juliet.'

Robin Hookes grew morose. The mood in the pub grew dark and heavy.

Wayne left. As he drove back to return the car, he wondered if Robin Hookes would remember their conversation in the morning. He hoped not. Wayne wasn't proud of it.

ELEVEN

The woman with black hair was the second visitor for Robin Hookes inside two hours. She used the door knocker to good effect, but the house seemed deserted. She peeked through the window and saw a large room made out of two smaller rooms and a kitchen. Hookes's work station was at one end of the room, a chair and a couch in the middle, and a cooking area at the back.

She tried again. Knocked even harder.

'He's popular tonight,' said a man with his dog as he walked past. 'If you want him, try the boozer by the tennis court.'

'Thanks,' the woman said. She liked the idea of picking up Robin Hookes in a pub. 'How will I recognise him?'

'Early forties. He has a well-enunciated voice with a sprinkling of the south-east. He'll probably be on his own in the pub.'

The black-haired woman turned and walked towards the pub. She was planning another perfect murder. No court in the world could convict her.

'Are you seriously thinking about entering the oldest profession?' Claire asked.

'I'm not sure that prostitution is the oldest profession,' Kate said. 'I thought shamanism was older.'

They were sitting in Claire's chic two-bedroom flat. The hint of money was a good advertisement for the escort business.

'You dodged my question,' Claire said.

'I know. I'm sorry. I don't know where I am in my life. I am considering options.'

'Of course.'

'Do you own this place?' Kate asked.

'I rent it cheaply from a client.' Claire looked at Kate. 'I was sorry to hear about Teddy Merlin. He was very helpful to me. Otherwise I wouldn't be seeing you.'

'I appreciate it.'

'We talked about the hepatitis B vaccine. I went and had it done. He thought it should be given to all babies. The positives seemed to outweigh the negatives for someone in my line of work.'

'Some people think hepatitis B is a bigger world problem than HIV and AIDS.'

'Yeah, that's what he said.'

'Teddy talked to me a little about your dissertation,' Kate said.

'Yes. I did a few modules to get on to my MSc course. I needed to get back to studying. It had been a while since my degree. Teddy was my supervisor for an independent study. He also helped me with a refuge idea.'

'Your independent study was about what attracts people to prostitution?'

'Something like that. Punters and workers. I think it's different for the different types of work. You can't compare streetworkers with what I do.'

'You work through an agency?'

'I do. I also have three organisations who call on me directly for a confidential service. Most of my colleagues need the money because they don't have any other way of getting themselves out of poverty.'

'Could that be any woman these days?'

'Yes, it could. But it's more likely to be those without qualifications and with nothing else to look forward to. Or immigrants. Most people have some hope about another way of life even if it rarely pays off.'

'And students?'

'Yes, students. I certainly don't want a huge debt hanging over me for years. It's difficult to start paying that back. How many graduates commit suicide later because of unpayable debts?'

'How many?'

'I don't know. But I keep reading stories.'

'I understand,' Kate said.

'A lot of prostitutes have had a difficult home life and a background of abuse,' Claire continued. 'Drugs and alcohol play a part in the street life.'

'I don't really fit that profile.'

'Yet you're interested. Maybe you want to learn more for your other work.'

'As a sexologist?'

'Yes.'

'I always want to learn more as a sexologist. I'm also wondering if I can sneak the escort life past myself for a few months while I'm still numb and have no capacity to feel anything for men.'

'You might get used to the money.'

'I might.'

'You might not feel so numb. You might have really bad feelings.'

'True.'

'Let me tell you something that Teddy told me.'

'Go on.'

'A study in the United States showed that two-thirds of prostitutes suffer from post-traumatic stress disorder. That's a bigger proportion than Vietnam veterans.'

Kate nodded aimlessly.

'Was the prostitutes' post-traumatic stress caused by events before prostitution or events during prostitution?' Kate asked.

'Good question,' Claire said. 'Try sleeping casually with someone. See if you can walk away without feeling anything for them.'

'For free?'

Claire smiled.

'You're learning,' she said.

The pub was subdued – no more than eight people inside – and the black-haired beauty picked out Hookes immediately. He had to be the man sitting in the dark corner; he looked as though he'd stopped at an unsigned crossroads with the wrong map on his lap.

She bought herself a soft drink – she'd given up alcohol for health reasons – and went over to him.

'You look like you need cheering up,' she said.

Robin Hookes took his time to reply.

'Have we been introduced?'

'I met you briefly at a party. You were with Juliet.'

'Ah, Juliet. My ex-wife.'

'Sorry, is that painful?'

'She was a risk waiting for an accident to happen.'

'She takes big risks, doesn't she?' the woman said.

'She has an adventuresome spirit. She lives a full life that is full of intrigue.'

The woman raised her eyebrows.

'She was manic rather a lot,' Hookes continued. 'All that energy. Yet she sometimes fell flat. She wasn't the happiest when she was on her own. She needed someone to be there.'

'Were you married for a long time?'

'Too long and yet not long enough.'

'So what went wrong between you?' the woman asked.

'She was seeing me when I was working for Bromage and then when I left she was seeing someone else. She got rid of me slowly. She hasn't got rid of me yet. She can't fully let go of me.'

'Do you still sleep with her?

Hookes smiled.

'Occasionally,' Hookes continued. 'It is very awkward and rather irksome. We got divorced. But then I would see her again. Her friends thought I was good for her –

she seemed grounded.' He was away in his own mind now. 'She has too many other men.'

'Who else?'

'Buck Hanson the footballer, Wayne the security man.'

'Wayne?'

'Wayne Shakespeare. He escorted me out of the building when Juliet laid me off.'

'That must have been awful for you.'

'She thinks that because she doesn't talk about her amorous adventures, nobody knows. The secret with Juliet was not to expect reciprocation. Expect only as much as she could give.'

'You expected more?'

'That was probably my mistake. I expected to be treated like I treated her. She couldn't do that. Something must have happened in her childhood. Her mother had been in and out of hospital when Juliet was young. That was probably when she needed her mother. And then there's her pater.'

'Her father?'

Hookes nodded.

'A one-off,' Hookes said. 'He works hard. Hardly sleeps. Lean and mean. Treats you well if you help his profits. Step out of line and he treats you bad.'

'I see.'

The black-haired woman could feel the darkness in the bar. But her mission fitted well with darkness.

'I'm getting another drink,' Hookes said.

'No, I think you've had enough. Let's get you home. Come on, you can lean on me.'

The pick-up became more literal. As the black-haired woman steered Hookes out of the pub she could smell his beery perfume; Wadworth Number Six.

'My mother died a month ago,' Hookes said, as she walked him home.

'I'm sorry to . . .'

'Oh, she'd been ill for a while, but it's always strange, isn't it. It never happens in the way that you anticipate. I got there too late. She was dead.'

Kate looked closely at Claire. She noticed cold eyes, toughening skin and a black wig. Was this the prototype for a future life, even at the top end?

'Where's the streetwalking business in Oxford?' Kate asked.

'All sorts of places. Off the Cowley Road. In the car parks behind the pubs and bingo hall. Wherever there's a trail of used condoms.'

'Nice.'

They went silent for a while.

'I don't see it as too different from a lot of jobs,' Claire said. 'Labourers and sportsmen sell their bodies. Politicians sell their souls.'

'I read a study about the positive and negative factors about acting in porn films,' Kate said. 'Women went into that life for fame, money, glamour, freedom, independence, being naughty, having sex and all the rest. But they need the opportunity, which usually comes through the suggestion of a friend.'

'That sounds like an American study.'

'It was,' Kate said.

'I get the impression that European porn actresses are a bit more desperate. I think that's the case with streetwalkers. It's probably family abuse that drives them away from home and then coercion from a pimp that drives them to the game. Then they need the money to support drugs or alcohol.' Claire paused. 'I can see how you would handle some parts of the profession well.'

'Such as?'

'You know all the disease risks. You'd think it through and only decide to do it if it was the right thing to do.'

'What might I not handle?'

'Physical danger. I'm very good at that. My father was a wrestler. He taught me the holds. I've done martial arts. I make sure I keep my hands and feet free when I'm with a client. I never wear necklaces or scarves. I don't wear tight skirts and high heels in case I need to run away. I check the clients for weapons as subtly as I can. I try to get them to shower before sex.'

'That's a good rule for everyone.'

'Some people think that because they are paying they have a right to be rough and dirty. It's not true.'

'What about staying on the right side of the law?'

'I've had no problems.'

'As I understand it you only get charged on the third arrest.'

'Two cautions and then an arrest. If you're found guilty and fined then it is back to the streets to pay off the fine. But that's the workers on the street. The police spend more time on them. I always double-check directions and hotel room numbers, that sort of thing. I don't want to be knocking on the wrong door and annoying people. The police seem to react to complaints more than anything.'

'I need to think about all this,' Kate said.

'I can talk to my agency whenever you're ready.'

'I need some more time. I'm not even sure I'll be good at it.'

'They'll love your eyes. Then it's up to you, how well you pleasure them, how you counsel them. Returners are better clients than newcomers.'

'I'm not sure I could work the local scene.'

'Go down to London. I have contacts there.'

The two women went quiet again.

'I can separate my inner self from my work,' Claire said. 'But I found it hard when I was doing that independent study module about escort work.'

'What are you saying?'

'Well, if you've taken on some of Teddy's work, like that teaching, then you'll be getting it from all sides. Sex work will be your life.'

'Are you saying it would be too confusing for me?'

'I have three identities. Claire is my real name. Claire identifies a personal past which is largely beyond my control. These past few years I've called myself Tracey in preparation for my legitimate future. And Cat is my working name. Call me when you've decided and I'll call my agency. I have another engagement now.'

'Thanks for fitting me in so late in the day.'

'We are ladies of the night.'

Kate said goodbye. She unhitched her bicycle from a lamp-post and cycled a mile across North Oxford. On the journey, she began to think that prostitution was a wild and stupid idea for her.

As she entered Wayne Shakespeare's street, she saw an old man hesitate on the path to the house. Kate stopped and watched. She even wondered if Claire had sent her a client to test her reaction. He looked the type – a wizened businessman in his sixties.

Kate stopped and watched from several houses away. The old man walked up to Wayne's door and rang the bell. It was shortly before midnight.

Wayne Shakespeare was lying in bed when the doorbell rang. Probably someone looking for the party three doors down, he thought. He tugged on a dressing-gown and stole a glance out of an upstairs window.

Wayne answered the door. Standing on his step was Richard Bromage, out of breath from the hike and looking paler than usual. Wayne made a mental note to upgrade the hall light from 40 watts.

'Good evening,' Wayne said.

'Just a quick word,' Bromage said.

Bromage was a step lower than Wayne, ferret-like, looking as though he would dash into the house. Wayne stood there, frozen to the doorstep, while three doors away John Lennon asked him to *imagine arrrll the pee-hee-pull*. Wayne was inactive because he was baffled. Richard Bromage was a man who sent for people. He was not the visiting type. When Wayne registered Bromage's fierce expression, he invited him inside.

'Sorry,' Wayne said. 'I'm a poor host. Come this way.'

Richard Bromage grunted something and entered.

Wayne showed Bromage through to the lounge and saw him frown at the cushions on the floor.

'Come downstairs,' Wayne said.

They sat at the kitchen table. Bromage's mood was still subdued. Wayne assumed it was the surroundings. He hoped Bromage wouldn't look in the fridge.

'Coffee? Tea? Whisky?' Wayne said. He heard Kate come in.

'No, just a quick visit,' Richard Bromage said. He seemed to want Wayne to take the initiative, so Wayne started talking.

'I've got on to the little task you set me this morning,' he said. 'I've started to search for the girl.'

Wayne had phoned Janine, his people searcher, and told her about Claire Stan-whatsit.

'Yeah, I wanted to say something,' Richard Bromage said.

'Go ahead.'

'I want *you* to handle it, Wayne. I don't want you to farm it out.'

'The . . . er?'

'Talking to the girl.'

'Miss Stanley. Or Stanway. Or . . . '

'Yes.'

'I'll do it discreetly.'

'It may be difficult to find her. She may not have been honest with her name. I wasn't with mine.'

'What did you call yourself?'

'Rick, I think. No, Alec.'

'OK.'

'There's one more thing.'

'Go ahead.'

'I want to see the girl again.'

'I could arrange a meeting when I find her.'

'No, it's more than that.' He paused and looked around the house furtively. He was building up to something interesting. 'You see, I think of that weekend a lot. I'm an old man now and I would give a lot of money to repeat a weekend like that. She was a young girl. I want to be with a young girl again.'

'She'll be older now, Mister Richard.'

Richard Bromage's expression was scathing.

'Men remember women by the age they were when they met them,' he told Wayne. 'Some young girls grow up. Some stay young girls. I want to see which she is. But I'll always think of her as a young girl. It's worth a lot of money to me. It's worth a lot of money to her. If you find her, Wayne, offer her ten thousand for a night, or whatever it takes. Start lower and work up.'

'I'll see what I can do.'

'I want something from her,' he told Wayne. 'And I'll pay for what I want.'

He spoke through clenched teeth when a different man might have cried. Bromage had something to settle, and yet his generosity was completely out of character.

'OK,' Wayne said.

'She had the body of a child,' Bromage told Wayne. 'She made love like a gymnast. She used the bed like it was a gymnast's mat. She was uninhibited and experienced, but she was still a child at heart. Red hair. You don't forget a girl like that.'

'No.' Wayne thought about his words. 'Did you meet

any of her friends?'

He shook his head.

'How did you meet?'

'It was through the football. She was at a hotel where the team were staying, and I picked her up.' Bromage was gazing at the loose plaster on the side wall and for a moment Wayne could have been a psychoanalyst. 'I loved her in the bed and I loved her in the bathroom and I loved her on the bedroom floor. Saturday night and all day Sunday. Then I left early on Monday morning and I've never seen her since. I still remember the exact . . .' Then Richard Bromage twitched as if he had suddenly remembered that he was talking to the staff. He looked at Wayne again and his whole personality changed. Wayne nodded uneasily; he knew that confessions changed relationships, especially confessions from a powerful man.

'Right,' Bromage said, and suddenly he was Wayne's master again.

Bromage stood up. He was on his way out when he turned and asked Wayne a question: 'Mackie says there's a charity game's coming up.'

'Yeah.'

'Sunday. Is that right?'

'Yes, Sunday at three o'clock.' Wayne gave him all the details.

Bromage turned and went off into the night. A man whose past was catching up with his future. And it was Wayne's job to help it.

Wayne walked into the lounge and stared at the

sculpture.

'You're a good dog, Rover,' Wayne said. 'You don't chew the mail, you never wee on the carpet, and you don't bite my boss.'

He turned round, sensing Kate in the room.

'Has your visitor gone?' Kate asked.

'Yes. Richard Bromage. Strange things are happening.'

Kate nodded.

TWELVE

In bed, Wayne couldn't settle. He thought he heard Juliet Bromage breathing next to him, he could sense Kate Park in the lounge, flushed from her cycle ride, and he wondered about Tracey Holroyd. In the morning he would have to find Tracey.

He thought more about Richard Bromage. He was grateful to him for advice when starting his security business. Just get in there and do it, Bromage had said, the best predictor of success is a previous business failure. If you worry about VAT and National Insurance you'll never start anything. But now Bromage looked like an unhealthy man.

What Wayne heard most of all was the imaginary voice of Bob Blazer telling him he was abject and inconsequential. Wayne turned his head through ninety degrees and tried to muffle the voices. Something disturbed him. His knee was stiff and his heart ached, or was it the other way round? Life often replays the same stories to an experienced man, but not always. Certainly not this time.

In bed, Kate Park couldn't settle. Her life was too chaotic. She had little to hold on to. She could remember the stabilising effect of Teddy Merlin's smell in her bed. She could imagine the tone of his voice when he was imparting wisdom to her. She could visualise him talking to Claire about prostitution or hepatitis B. Thinking of which, she had some work to do for Jeremy Spooner. She would do that tomorrow. Then report to him as soon as possible. It might bring in some money.

Maybe I should talk more to Wayne, Kate wondered. Ask him to treat me as he would treat a grieving widow. Tell him that I may disappear into my room for hours but I'm all right . . . well, not really all right.

Wayne would want to help. He would probably want to solve it through sex. Well, she could be firm about not wanting sex. She needed laughs and hugs more than sex. Maybe Wayne could provide that without strings. Or maybe not.

In the unfamiliar double bed, at five in the morning, the black-haired woman wasn't making much progress. She was listening to Robin Hookes talk about his dead mother.

'Maybe I'll get a therapist,' said Robin Hookes. 'I always intended to sort it out before she died.'

The woman thought about intentions. We judge

ourselves by our intentions and judge others by their actions. That was her view.

'Never mind, Robin,' she said.

He looked at her.

'I've forgotten your name,' Hookes said.

'Em,' she said.

'Em for Emma?'

'If you like.'

No, she thought, not Em for Emma. M for mankiller.

She had helped Hookes home, helped him into bed, but he had fallen asleep without taking much interest in her. During the night he had got up to visit the toilet. Now he seemed more lively. Once he'd got over the shock of seeing her in his bed.

'What work do you do?' she asked.

'I do research for management. But no one wants research these days. They make decisions without any research. Five minutes of imbecilic scribble on the back of an envelope. Someone will employ me to do research, but the decision has been taken before I report. And it's usually an erroneous decision. It always comes down to someone coming up with a sensible solution and someone else not listening to it.'

'What did you do for Richard Bromage?'

'Feasibility studies. New products. New companies. A few other things. But I've not done much for Bromage in the past year. It didn't end very well. My contract came to an end. Oh, they put some freelance contracts my way and the Bromages gave me a bit of money, but it has not been the best of times. The Bromage Building is a facade.

All the real work goes on outside the building. They rely on freelancers to do everything.'

The woman thought that Hookes' voice was losing some of its depression. All it had taken was an hour's talk about his mother, some anger at his ex-wife and a tirade against his ex-employer. All healthy stuff. She felt that she was nurturing him. She had almost forgotten how angry she was. Now she was stroking him and getting a reaction.

'You shouldn't drink so much,' she told him. 'It will spoil your beautiful body. You might get cirrhosis of the liver.'

'I don't want to get cirrhosis of the liver,' he said. 'But I wouldn't want to miss it by much.'

He laughed and she laughed with him. You're not having my cirrhosis, she thought. Not yet anyway.

'You're funny,' she said, before crawling down the bed, spreading her hair across his chest and taking him in her mouth.

I'll get him good and hard, she thought, and then I'll do the deed.

It took a while. When she was sure he was ready, she straddled him and took him inside her. Lowered her torso. Grazed his chest with her breasts, grabbed his skin, his love handles, felt his hands over her back. He was more cuddly than she had first thought.

She took it slowly, worried about her energy levels, but she started to feel him grow more and more excited. He hugged her close so she breathed in his ear and quickened her rhythm, now eager to finish the job.

'That's a lot of cum,' she told him afterwards, as she wiped herself with tissues. 'Have you been saving it all up for me?'

'I hope you don't get pregnant with it,' Hookes said.

'No, that won't happen. I'm still bleeding a little.'

'And as long as you're not HIV positive.'

'No, I am not HIV positive and I haven't got AIDS,' she said, truthfully. She kissed his chest and held him close. 'You should go and find that Juliet while you're performing so well. Try to get her pregnant.'

'Do you think so?'

'I know so.'

The things you do for a new friend, she thought.

That Tuesday morning, Wayne phoned an administrator he knew at Tracey Holroyd's university. Wayne asked some questions. He heard fingers tap a keyboard.

'She's not a full-time student here,' the man told Wayne.

'She must be – she's on the Rag Committee.'

'Hang on.' More keyboard tapping. 'There's a part-timer called Claire Ann Tracey Holroyd doing an MSc in Psychology.'

'Possible.'

'Try the Student Union office if she was on the Rag Committee.'

'At this time?' It was ten past nine.

'I'd wait an hour,' he said.

'Have you got an address for Claire Ann Tracey Holroyd?'

'Term-time or vacation-time?'

'Both.'

He read them out. 'Anything else?' he asked.

Wayne imagined the screen in front of him. Holroyd's eight-digit enrolment number and her percentage marks for her courses. The name of her personal tutor.

'What courses is she doing?'

He gave Wayne the courses and the class times.

'Anything else?'

'No,' Wayne said. 'You've been a great help.'

He hung up, thinking it was ironic. In Wayne's report to the university he would suggest a review of the policy for access to students' addresses. Students should be protected. He had come across too many cases of staff harassing students at home.

He heard Kate come up to his den and knock on the door.

'Come in,' Wayne said.

'I'm out for the day,' she said. 'Visiting libraries in the morning, working a late shift and then meeting a solicitor in a pub.'

'Watch you don't get solicited.'

'Have a good day,' said Kate.

'Don't tell me what to do,' Wayne replied, softly, when she had gone, laughing to himself.

Wayne spent a couple of hours trying to write his report on university security, but he occasionally had an idea about Tracey Holroyd, so he made a few phone calls.

Wayne tried the Student Union office and they said they could pass on a message. When he pressed for her phone number, Wayne was given the mobile number he already had. He phoned another member of the Rag Committee and she gave him the same mobile phone number. Eventually he ran a mile to Tracey's last year's address and got an answer to his persistent door knocking. The new occupants gave him a forwarding address.

The forwarding address for Tracey Holroyd was off the Cowley Road, in an area of East Oxford where space was so scarce that cars were parked on pavements and four or five people lived in two-bedroom houses. Someone had once told Wayne that this was the most crowded sector in Britain.

Wayne rang the doorbell and asked to see Miss Holroyd.

'No,' said the youth who answered the door. 'She isn't here.'

'But she lives here?'

'She comes and goes. Collects post.'

'How often?'

'Most days.'

'Any particular time?'

'In the next hour or two. Do you want to leave a message?'

He stared at Wayne for a moment, as if he needed to rub sleep from his eyes.

'No, thanks.,' said Wayne. 'She still has a key, I presume.'

'I guess.'

A row of shops across the road gave Wayne a good view of the house. He went in one where he knew the owner and started chatting.

'The whole road's changing,' the shop-owner said. 'The Russians are here. There's blokes getting done for carrying scimitars.'

'Are the Pakistanis still controlling the bouncers? Didn't they used to go and smash up a pub and then come back and offer security?'

'I don't know. I haven't heard that. Where did you get that from?'

'You told me last year.'

The shop owner laughed.

Wayne stared through the window for some time. It was like watching a drama programme. A dirty street cleaner hugged a woman who was wearing a business suit. A big bear of a man walked past with a bullhorn through his nose. A man went into a telephone box, rattled the coin tray and stepped out empty-handed.

'The areas going to the dogs, Wayne,' the shopkeeper said. 'Condoms and syringes in your front garden. Dog dirt and dried vomit on the pavements. There's more rubbish on the paths after the binmen have been than there is before.'

'They call it the Bermuda Triangle.'

'Have you seen this advert on my board?'

'Which one?' asked Wayne. He walked over to look.

'At the bottom . . . next one . . that's it.'

'This one looking for love actors and love actresses, girls and guys between twenty and twenty-eight?'

'That's it.'

'Why would I see that? I'm too old?'

'We didn't have those opportunities in our day, Wayne,' the shopkeeper said.

'No,' Wayne agreed, laughing.

Wayne was just thinking he had wasted half an hour when he saw Tracey Holroyd walk past the shop. She was wearing the same faded jeans as before (or a very similar pair) and a frosty frown. A sweatshirt hung loosely over her athletic frame. She was in and out of the shared house before Wayne had said goodbye to the shop owner. When he came out, Tracey Holroyd was fifty yards down the road, assuming a commanding presence while flagging down a taxi. The driver stopped for her.

Wayne looked around for another taxi. Then an apparition appeared in front of him – a dreamlike woman in her early thirties. Wayne caught a flash of jeans, dark hair and a healthy outdoor complexion that had ejected the strains of life. This was Caprice, the woman who had steered Kate his way. As Caprice leant her bicycle against a pillar, she saw Wayne looking at her. She was smiling, but that was nothing special. The smile was omnipresent.

'Good day, kind sir,' she said. 'My knight needs a haircut.'

Her response was good news for Wayne. Sometimes he didn't suit Caprice's mood. Sometimes she smiled straight past him.

'Your knight needs to borrow your trusty steed?' Wayne said. 'I need to follow someone in a taxi.'

'Take my trusty steed, you brave and reckless knight. He will serve thee well.'

'Here's five pounds for a taxi fare home,' Wayne said, which was ridiculous because no taxi driver could drive along the canal to Caprice's boat.

'What is money when I am the King's servant?' She reached in her multi-coloured shoulder-bag, held up a bicycle key and spoke loudly: 'May God be with you on your crusade, my gallant knight, and if you shall return with this key I can promise you that my defence will be minimal.'

'I will keep the key between my armour and my loin cloth,' Wayne said. 'I shall call on you for a haircut when I have conquered the enemy.'

'I shall await your return. Fare thee well,' she cried as Wayne lifted his leg over the bicycle and started the wheel turning.

The conversation with Caprice was just one more cameo on Cowley Road. But the bicycle quickly brought Wayne back to the present, because it was typical Caprice. The frame was beautifully painted, but the mechanism was loud and the brakes were bad. By the time Wayne had travelled a hundred yards, his shoes needed new heels. He caught a distant sight of Tracey Holroyd's taxi, which was stuck in traffic.

The taxi crawled around town and eventually accelerated along Banbury Road. It was disappearing out of view when Wayne noticed it make a left turn. By the time he'd turned the corner, Tracey Holroyd had paid the driver and was walking up a path to a block of flats.

This was one of the better areas of the city, but it was usually the world of the Bromages rather than the recently graduated. He watched Tracey Holroyd let herself in with a key. Then he found a secluded spot and observed.

Wayne watched and waited for two hours. Just as he got bored, he came across a small sticker on a wall.

Does the question give you the illusion of choice? Yes. No. Don't know.

He thought about that one for a while.

At ten minutes before nine a car arrived outside the apartment block. Wayne recognised the car. The driver stayed inside, but Wayne spotted a woman of Tracey Holroyd's height and gait as she left the building and elegantly took her place in the back of the vehicle. Had he not been expecting her, Wayne might not have recognised her. The rubber band had been discarded and her hair was black and flowing. She wore a long black evening dress, flat black shoes and carried a violin case.

Do concert violinists leave home about nine o'clock at night? Well, maybe they do. Or maybe she played in a late-night jazz band.

As the car sped away Wayne cursed his helplessness. This was where he needed a car the most. But he tried to make up by doing some thinking.

Why had Tracey Holroyd been collected?

The answer came to Wayne after a couple of minutes.

Where was he taking her?

Ah.

Next came the legwork. Wayne cycled to the first hotel, walked to the second and then hailed a taxi to take him to the third, fourth and fifth. Finally, he spotted the car that had collected Tracey Holroyd. Wayne paid off the taxi and walked across to where a man was slumped in the driver's seat. There was no sign of Tracey.

THIRTEEN

The Black Horse in Broad Street was smoky and crowded, but Jeremy Spooner had saved Kate a seat. She had changed from her nursing uniform, after her late shift, into an Oxfam dress shirt and her best jeans, but she still felt tired and scruffy. What she really wanted was a good night's sleep.

'Let me get you a drink,' Jeremy said. 'What would you like?'

'Horlicks,' Kate said.

Jeremy's laugh was a little forced.

'That's funny,' he said. 'You're very funny.'

He seemed to mean it, but Kate had meant Horlicks too.

'Gin and tonic,' she said now.

For some reason Jeremy Spooner had been keen to meet her in the pub at ten o'clock tonight. Either something in the case was urgent or he wanted to meet her away from the office. Kate suspected the latter. It was also odd because Kate had little to report, even after her morning in the Law Library.

When Spooner returned with the drinks, he wriggled the stool closer so that their knees were touching.

'So how are you getting on?' he asked. 'What did you think of my client?'

'He's very fatalistic about going to prison. The assault seems completely out of character. At heart he seems a decent bloke, hardworking, sensitive at times.'

'Yes, that's what I found. That's partly why I needed you.'

'I have some theories. I need to do some more research. I spoke to him on Sunday and I'm still trying to process all that he told me.'

'Bill me for your telephone time.'

'I went to see him.'

'What! Alone?'

'Yes. I went to his house because . . .'

'Kate, you shouldn't have done that. The man's a self-confessed rapist. It's not safe for you to do things like that.'

'I thought it was.'

'Ummm,' said Spooner. 'I wish I hadn't got him bail now. The thought of you in his house alone with him . . .'

'I actually felt quite safe with him,' Kate said. 'That's what makes it a really interesting case.'

Wayne was twenty yards away from the car in the hotel car park when he was noticed. The man in the car was as vigilant as Wayne had expected him to be. He reached across and opened the passenger door for Wayne to get in.

'A bit of moonlighting?' Wayne asked, sliding into the passenger-seat.

'Helps,' he said.

'Is the Cat good to work for?'

The man nodded.

'Did you help with the Buck Hanson stunt?' Wayne asked.

'Car. Poker.'

'And you suggested me to fix it up?'

The man nodded.

'Good choice.'

The man smiled.

'You were with him all that Friday night?'

The man nodded.

'All weekend?'

The man shook his head.

'He wanted an extra night with the Cat?' Wayne asked.

The man looked puzzled.

'Or Juliet?' Wayne asked.

'Friday night, Saturday morning,' the man said.

More silence. They sat and watched a young lad scouting the cars for the easiest steal. They sniggered at the boy's furtiveness.

'Shall we see how fast he can run?' Wayne asked.

A nod from the driver's seat.

Their car-lights went on and the engine kicked.

Wayne opened the passenger door lightly and yelled

'Hey.' The boy went off like a hare in trainers.

'A bit of pace,' Wayne said. 'Wonder what he's like with a ball?'

They returned to silence and darkness.

'I wished I'd known you were doing this,' Wayne said, after a while. 'I've spent the week looking for her. I could have written a book called *Tracing Tracey*.' He looked across. 'But I guess you wouldn't have given me her address anyway.'

'Nah.'

'So what's the story here?' Wayne asked. 'You bring her, wait for a phone call when she's inside the room to make sure she's safe. Then wait for a call when she's finished.'

The driver nodded.

'Hope you've arranged coded messages in case she thinks she's in trouble.'

Another nod.

'Probably pays more than I pay you.'

'Same,' he said.

'But the company is much more attractive,' Wayne said, his voice sounding demoralised.

The man in the driver's seat laughed.

Wayne always enjoyed hearing Mackie laugh.

Jeremy Spooner sat closer to Kate. It was loud in the pub and they were talking about confidential matters.

'I've familiarised myself with some of the precedents in these rape trials,' Kate said. 'I spent the morning going through one of Teddy's cuttings file and looking up some stuff in the Law Library. Teddy kept a lot of legal cuttings. He didn't write about it in his book because it dated so quickly.'

'There's not much of a market for second-hand law books.'

'I'd like to talk to your client's ex-wife in order to test one of my theories.'

'While you're doing that, try to pick up some character references we could use to ask for a reduced sentence.'

'I may want to talk to one or two other ex-girlfriends of his.'

'Do what you need to do, but the case isn't made of money.'

'The case interests me. Especially if it becomes a landmark case.'

'How do you mean?'

'I don't know yet. I need more information. And the data might prove me wrong.'

'Talk to me about what you find out. And let me know where you're going so I can come with you if need be. Don't walk into any threatening situations. Don't visit Bruce Venn on your own again.'

Kate looked at Spooner to assess his understanding. All she saw in his face, though, was evidence of lust. Kate felt safer with Bruce Venn than she did now with Jeremy Spooner. She looked down at her notes.

'Bruce and Fiona had been canoodling on the settee before they went to bed on the night of the assault,' Kate told Spooner.

'That's interesting,' he said. 'But they slept in separate beds.'

Kate was reassured to know that he was listening to her. She thought about his last comment for a while.

'Are you all right, Kate?'

'Yes. According to Bruce Venn, Fiona felt inhibited by the presence of her daughter in the house.'

'That's not a very threatening position to put over.'

'How do you mean?' Kate asked.

'Well, it's not going to make the mother and daughter withdraw from the case. It makes our client look more of a villain. We'd have to find something more sordid than that to give the mother and daughter second thoughts, especially when our man is claiming he is guilty. Is there any chance he walked in the wrong bedroom and thought he was with Fiona?'

'He hasn't said anything to indicate that. There had been a discussion about Olivia having the room next door.'

Kate was aware that she was almost yelling to make herself heard. The pub was crowded now, and she had been talking and teaching too much this week.

'You're very seductive when you talk about your work,' Spooner said.

Oh, well, Kate thought, here it comes.

'It is only work,' Kate said. She smiled her best smile.

Spooner smiled back and rubbed her thigh with his knee.

Well, Kate thought, I've done something to keep him interested. Maybe he'd pay for sex as well as for sexpertise.

'Did Teddy talk to you about cases where men or women had infected their sex partners with HIV through unprotected sex?' Spooner asked.

'Yes, we had long discussions.'

'Will there be more of that kind of case?'

'Yes.'

'Let me ask you about one that went to trial,' he said. He named the case.

'That was a very complicated case,' Kate said.

'Leave the law to me.'

'And they had to go through it twice. The two women involved must have suffered real heartache.'

'Yes, there was a retrial. The appeal judges ruled that grievous bodily harm could be inflicted through having sex. The original judge dismissed the issue of consent and the appeal judges ruled against him.'

'The issue of consent being . . .'

'. . . whether the complainants did or did not have the requisite knowledge, whether they were consenting to the risk of infection. The trial judge ruled that whether or not the complainants knew of the HIV, their consent, if any, was irrelevant and provided no defence. That was a mistake.'

'If a woman is in love with a man she trusts him,' Kate said.

'There is the issue of whether or not she asks the right questions.'

'Such as "have you been tested recently?" and "do you have HIV?"'

'"Yes" to the first and "No" to the second,' said Spooner, with the smug smile of a barrister who has swung the case.

Kate went quiet and thought about the case.

'One of the women in the case met a man in a night

club and went out with him for three months. The man claimed he was unmarried, a Gulf War veteran and a lawyer. In fact he was married with three children and living on benefits. He didn't like using condoms, so the woman allowed him unprotected sex because she trusted him. He hadn't mentioned HIV. She left her marital home and then got ill. He disappeared when she got ill but she traced him. The man got himself tested and said he was HIV positive. Then the woman located the man's previous girlfriend and she was HIV positive too. Apparently this guy had known for eight years that he was HIV positive. They did a DNA sequencing of her blood and found that the virus came from him. The woman felt sad that a big love of her life didn't work out, but at least he couldn't infect anybody while in prison.'

'Have you thought about specialising in that sort of case?'

'I prefer to stick to the therapeutic side rather than the forensic side of sexology. But I do need to earn some money.'

'Let's talk more about it.'

'Yes.'

'Good,' said Spooner.

'I must go,' Kate said suddenly.

'Another drink?'

'No, thanks.'

She kissed him on the cheek and hurried to her bicycle. She felt a little wobbly on the way home.

Wayne had one more visit to make – to Caprice's canal boat *Commuter's Fantasy*.

Welcome to Dreamworld.

Caprice had changed to black. Black trousers hugged her thighs. A black T-shirt blended neatly with long black hair which curled around her shoulders. The hair had two white streaks. Her face was in very good shape for thirty-odd years. She had spared it from make-up, and her pheromones were uncomplicated. Wayne looked her up and down, and saw her bare feet, each toe-nail painted a different colour. The butterfly tattoo at the top of her left thigh was colourful too. Wayne couldn't see it, he just knew.

'Is it too late for a haircut?' he asked her.

'It is never too early for tomorrow's news,' she replied, smiling as she improvised. Their arms brushed lightly as he stepped on to the boat.

'Are you short of news from the front?' Wayne asked.

'Are you tall for a former football player?' she said.

'It's the length of my hair that makes me tall.'

'And does the beard detract from your strength?'

'Take off the beard. These days men do not wear hair anywhere.'

'It should not take long, sir,' Caprice said. 'I shall eschew our profession's customary viewpoint on vacations in favour of pragmatism and expediency. Tomorrow you can take me belly-dancing in the Antarctic without being recognised.'

'You can't belly-dance in the Antarctic,' Wayne said.

She moved behind him and whispered huskily in his ear: 'I can make anything possible.'

Caprice spread newspapers on the floor and pulled across a chair.

'Sit,' she ordered.

As he took off his jacket and sat down, a pair of scissors magically appeared in her left hand. She picked up a plant-sprayer with the other hand and wet his hair. Then she leaned over his shoulder and undid the buttons of his shirt slowly. Her face came within two inches of his.

She pushed him forward lightly and pulled off his shirt. He noticed how long and thin her fingers were.

The boat had no mirrors, but he could tell she was peeling off her T-shirt by the smell of her skin.

'The first thing one larns at Haa-dressing Univarsity is to work at the proper height,' Caprice said, her voice unusually plummy but not totally out of character. 'One's nipples should be always in line with the section one is cutting.' Then her voice softened to its normal soothing pitch. 'And your black hair would show up so on this black shirt of mine,' she said.

'Have you sent the mirrors to bed early?' Wayne asked. His mind was beginning to bend.

'The mirrors sleep together. They look into each other's eyes.'

Scissors started to work on the back of his hair. The boat rocked slightly as she moved from side to side. The effect was sensuous. In her mystical way she reassured Wayne that she knew how to cut hair. It didn't stop the tension rising. When she clambered over the furniture, to get to the front, she teased him with her breasts.

'Could Sir stay still, please. I would not want an accident with these scissors.'

Caprice's aura was peaceful and comfortable. A pile

of black hair grew on the floor. Inch-long hairs remained on Wayne's head. The air felt good. Or something did. He didn't care what he looked like.

'Stay still now, please.' she ordered. 'I have only your eyebrows to do.'

She clipped once, twice, three times. Then she offered him a very slow wink and a quarter of a smile. The range was short.

She went to the kitchen and returned with a bowl of water, scented soap and a razor. She lathered his face.

Wayne spoke while he had the chance: 'If three men with machine-guns come in, tell them they have the wrong film.'

'Perhaps,' she said, still smiling. He felt her concentration as she held his head in her right hand and worked the razor slowly up and down his skin. She cut him very slightly and licked off a small dab of blood. Her tongue was warm and wet.

'Finished,' she said, eventually.

'Thank you, Caprice,' he said.

'Now we shall pass you over to our manicurist,' she told him.

'Why would I need a manicure?' he asked.

'I would like your nails short and your fingers clean,' she said. Then she leaned over and whispered in his ear. 'So you can touch me where I would like to be touched.'

The words *touch* and *touched* came out like sighs. She sounded like a woman on the edge of an erotic breakthrough.

'No nail varnish for me,' Wayne said.

When she had finished working on his hands, she

kissed his fingertips lightly, one by one, until he was almost devoid of straight thoughts. Then they merged their topless bodies, and kissed and stroked and nuzzled, and found a space on the floor where the only threat to health was a pair of left-handed hairdressing scissors. After they had shifted positions several times, Wayne undid a button at the front of Caprice's jeans and tweaked at the zip catch.

Then Caprice stopped him.

'Remember the boat rule,' she said. 'No hairs in the bed.'

Caprice took his hand and led him along the boat. She completed the undressing – first Wayne, then herself. He studied the butterfly tattoo at the top of her left thigh and bent low to kiss it lightly.

The boat's shower room was hardly big enough for two. They wedged tightly together under the water and were jointly responsible for their mutual cleanliness. They soaped each other, rinsed themselves and rubbed bodies. They dried each other and arranged the towels where they would dry.

'Come,' said Caprice. She took his hand and led him along the boat to the bed. He lay down on the bed while Caprice lit four candles and then joined him.

'Tell me about your favourite fantasy,' Wayne said.

'It changes on different occasions, following a system which is unknown to me.'

'That's helpful.'

'Max Morise,' she said. 'A French surrealist.'

Ah, Wayne thought, maybe I'll understand Caprice one day.

'Come, Caprice,' Wayne said. 'Let me make the canal move for you.'

The boat rocked a little as their bodies closed on each other.

FOURTEEN

Kate woke up with a start at four-fifteen in the morning. The house felt very empty and her loss felt acute. Her bed was barren without Teddy.

She picked up Teddy's address-book and found a friendly note against one of the entries: *A sympathetic voice for the middle of the night, she knows about grief and AIDS.*

Kate crept downstairs with the address book and found the phone furthest from Wayne's bedroom. She punched in a number for a woman in California, where the time difference made it mid-evening. The call was answered on the third ring and lasted forty minutes. During that time they talked about grief, sexology, relaxation techniques and how anal cancer was three times more common in women than men.

Kate ended the call. She stroked Teddy's address book and then kissed the cover. It was as though he was still taking care of her. The woman in California had the soothing voice of a surrogate mother. Unlike her own mother, who Kate had not heard from since she had sent a change-of-address postcard. All her mother could talk about these days was plants and gardens. Her mother had too much unresolved grief herself.

Kate sobbed loudly without warning. Then she thought about the woman in California and returned to bed.

Wayne and Caprice slept soundly until the ducks began eating plant growth from the side of the boat. They cuddled and snuggled, showered again, aroused each other and calmed each other, ate breakfast, and then it was time for Wayne to go.

'Thank you for the haircut and the manicure,' he told her.

'And?' Caprice said, smiling.

'And for being you, and for your love, and for your beauty and wit.'

'And?'

'And for breakfast and for the loan of your bicycle.'

'And?' she asked, still smiling.

'And for the shave and the showers.'

'And?'

This time Wayne looked at Caprice's red chin and thought for a while.

'Ah,' he said. 'And for telling Kate Park about my spare room.'

Caprice smiled more widely and nodded her head slowly. She hugged him and put her mouth to his ear.

'You are both students of sex,' Caprice whispered. 'You are her Don Juan and she is your Virginia Johnson, you are a Casanova and she is a Kinsey. You will meet somewhere in the middle.'

'Is that a promise?' he asked. He had no idea what Caprice was saying, but it sounded exciting.

'Her eyes are the daylight at the end of your tunnel.'

'Leading to where?'

'To a library run by the old souls of wise women.'

He hugged Caprice and kissed her cheeks. She bit his ear lightly and helped him off the boat. When Wayne looked back from the towpath, Caprice was waving from the deck of *Commuter's Fantasy*, her arm fully extended.

Wayne arrived home at eight o'clock that morning. When he went downstairs to the kitchen he found Kate reading a book at the table. She didn't look up at first. When she did raise her head, she stared through Wayne to the wall beyond.

'Ah, it's my new image,' Wayne said. 'You didn't recognise me with shorter hair and clean-shaven?'

'Oh, it's easy to recognise you – you're wearing the same clothes as yesterday.'

'Ah, clever.'

'You stayed out last night,' she said. There was no edge to Kate's voice. It was gentle and supportive.

'Yes, I did.'

They found silence. Kate looked at him some more.

'What is it?' Wayne asked.

'What is what?'

'You're looking at me as if you're expecting me to say more.'

'You don't have to say more.'

Another silence.

'I saw Caprice,' Wayne said, 'I borrowed her bicycle during the day. Then I took it back. She cut my hair.'

'I figured somebody did.'

'We had a surreal night.'

'That sounds like Caprice.'

'Do you understand her?' Wayne asked.

'A little. Caprice needs to see the world through Shakespeare and surrealism. That gives her two strong frameworks to deal with all that life offers. She fascinates me because I am always liable to get stuck in realism.'

'Why surrealism?'

'Surrealism can be an effort to subvert society. It's also incredibly playful. It unlocks our creativity.'

'Sexual creativity?'

'All sorts. Surrealist sex can seem too casual for my liking. It's not what I aspire to but I can see how it can work for some. You're probably better placed to judge Caprice as a sexual muse.'

'Caprice thinks that you and I are destined for each other. She said you and I will find a common ground somewhere between Don Juan and Virginia Johnson, somewhere between Casanova and Kinsey.'

'She said that? She remembered Virginia Johnson?'

'Who's Virginia Johnson?'

'Of Masters and Johnson. They researched human sexual response and created a stir in the mid-sixties.'

'Caprice said we were both students of sex.'

'Caprice and you?' Kate asked.

'No, you and I.'

'You and I?'

'Yes.'

'Oh.'

That led to a peaceful silence.

'I have to get ready for work,' Kate said. 'This has been an interesting conversation.'

She smiled, picked up the book in her right hand, waved lightly with her left and walked out of the room.

Wayne sat for a few minutes. His night with Caprice had been erotic, elliptic and elusive. He realised that Kate could generate real intimacy. He had to be straight with her.

He debated whether to change his clothes but decided to smell Caprice for a little longer. His mobile phone jolted him into the present.

'A wonderful morning,' he told the caller.

'It's about to get even better,' came the reply.

'Whenever you phone, Janine, my day gets better.'

Wayne had briefed Janine to search for Richard Bromage's girl of the past.

'I've got one here that looks possible,' Janine said. 'It's been a task.'

'I expected that. Wing me your bill.'

'I'll tell you what I've done. Then you can decide whether it's worth it.'

'OK.'

'I've got a Claire A. Stanworth in Oxfordshire. Her parents are still at the same address. Or they were a year ago. I can give you their names and their address.'

'Go on. This sounds good.'

Wayne made a note of the Stanworths' details, including telephone number. Strangely, it matched a parental address he had for Claire Ann Holroyd.

'I sent off for Claire's birth certificate – Claire Ann Tracey Stanworth – and I checked my disks.'

'Any luck?'

'Yeah. She got married young. To an uncommon name – Pocklington.'

'And?'

'I can't find a Claire Ann Tracey Pocklington.'

'Oh.'

'I got stuck.'

Wayne thought awhile.

'What was her mother's maiden name?' he asked.

'Er, Holroyd.'

'Now why doesn't that surprise me?'

'I give up. Why doesn't that surprise you?'

'Try Claire Ann Tracey Holroyd in Oxfordshire.'

'Trying . . .'

Wayne could hear the sound of fingers on keyboard. A minute later Janine read off last year's address for Tracey Holroyd. Wayne had that one already too.

Claire Ann Tracey.

The Cat.

'A great job,' Wayne said. 'Pump up the bill.'

'My aim is to please.'

'Janine, we can't go on not meeting like this.'

'Janine and Wayne had never met,' Janine said. 'They were like two hummingbirds who had also never met.'

'Mr and Mrs Hummingbird,' Wayne said.

'Hummmm, hummmm,' hummed Janine and she disconnected.

Wayne smiled to himself at the playfulness. Then he considered the logic of his discovery. Claire Stanworth, who had had an affair with Richard Bromage when she was young, was the same person as Tracey Holroyd who was on the Rag Committee. And Tracey Holroyd, an escort known as Cat, had lured Buck Hanson away from his wife Rachel while Rachel was being kidnapped.

Wayne was trying to make sense of the complexities when his mobile phone rang.

'A truly wonderful morning,' Wayne said.

'No, it's not.'

'Who's that?'

'Wayne?'

'Yeah.'

'It's Buck Hanson's agent.'

His voice was dull. He was very subdued.

'You'd best get here straightaway,' the agent said.

'Is it really necessary?'

'Yes. It's not good news.'

'What isn't?'

'His wife's dead.'

'Rachel?'

'Yes.'

'I'll be there in about two hours.'

Wayne disconnected and set about borrowing the car.

'How often did you have sex?' Kate Park asked Holly Venn.

'About twice a week, I would guess,' the other woman replied. 'It varied, obviously. Towards the end of our time together we made love more rather than less.'

The two women were sitting on a bench in a cemetery near the centre of Oxford. The setting wasn't ideal for intimate conversation but Bruce Venn's wife – nearly his ex-wife – didn't seem inhibited. She had eaten sandwiches and was now talking freely about her marriage. She seemed matter-of-fact about that period of her life. But it had taken Kate twenty-five minutes to get to this point.

Kate had spent some time explaining about Bruce Venn's plight. Holly Venn seemed unfazed by her husband's potential loss of income from a prison sentence. Kate guessed that she was a woman of independent means. Or the impact hadn't fully registered yet.

'Now that you've told me about that incident, it makes me wonder about his treatment of me,' said Holly Venn.

'In what way?'

'Well, sometimes he would make sexual demands on me when I wasn't expecting it. Although I actually enjoyed it. I'd be asleep and he would wake me up in the middle of the night and we'd have passionate sex without any conversation or communication between us. Sometimes he'd last half an hour. It was quite cool. Quite anonymous. Then we'd both go back to sleep immediately.'

'Was he more passionate during the night?'

'Yes. I think those quiet times in the dark are often wonderfully freeing. You've got some rest and the body's more relaxed.'

'What are you calling the middle of the night – around four or five in the morning?'

'Yes. Or earlier.'

Yes, Kate knew about those hours. But they were now producing anxious thoughts for her rather than sexual freedom.

'I sometimes wonder if we woke the neighbours,' Holly Venn said. 'He'd be panting away and I'd be having an orgasm and trying to muffle my sounds. We'd end up breathless. Thinking back, it was really cool. It's a shame we're not still doing that.'

'What went wrong for you?'

'He was never there. He was in his business. Totally married to his business. I gave him an ultimatum and he chose to build up his business rather than build up our relationship. The trouble about ultimatums is that they commit you. I couldn't go back. I certainly wouldn't want to go back after what you've told me about these recent events. That's a nasty story.'

'Did the story surprise you?'

Holly Venn thought a while.

'Yes and no,' she said.

'He struck me as quite a sensitive person,' Kate offered.

'Yes, he was. He noticed things. He could be attentive. He lost all that towards the end. I think he was quite troubled underneath.'

'Was he different when you met him second time around?'

'A little edgier. But he had drive. That attracted me more the second time around. He seemed like he'd make a good father. I was in a different place when we got married. I was more serious about my life. Now, after what you've told me, I'm pleased we didn't have children together. The last year he seemed edgier, but he wasn't the type to talk about the underlying stuff. He was striving, always chasing, always stressed, always tired. He was building up a business and getting more ambitious about his running. Doing half-marathons, that sort of thing.'

'May I ask you a little more about those sex sessions during the night?' Kate said.

'Sure.'

'How often did they happen?'

'Only twice. I just remember them vividly.'

'Did they continue up to the end?'

'No, I moved out into another bedroom. Well, actually . . .'

'Yes?'

'A couple of times he came into my room during the night. That was amazing. That was like stranger sex, like having it off with someone whose name you didn't know, not that I've ever done that. It was funny, I suppose.'

'Funny? In what way?'

'I don't know. Probably funny in both ways. I suppose some men are more passionate in the middle of the night. The guy I'm seeing at the moment, I think I'd quite like it if he woke me up and ravished me.'

Kate smiled.

'Just one more thing,' Kate said.

'Sure.'

'You said that you moved into another bedroom at the

end. Which bedroom did you move into?'

'The one at the end of the corridor.'

'Not the one with the single bed?'

'No. The double bedroom past that one, past the bathroom. Where did the assault take place? No, don't tell me. I don't think I want to know.'

Kate didn't tell her.

'Thank you, Holly,' she said. 'I really appreciate you talking to me like this. I'll keep you informed.'

'Thanks. I don't want to speak to him at this point.'

When Wayne arrived at Buck Hanson's house, the door was answered by his agent. Wayne always thought an agent's job was about finding plumbers, arranging close-season holidays and negotiating employment contracts. Dealing with sudden death looked a step too far. The agent couldn't seem to find the word *hello*. Instead he flicked his head towards the lounge and Wayne followed him through.

Buck Hanson was slumped on the couch. He looked leaden and downcast.

'I'm sorry, Buck,' Wayne said, as he sat on a chair. 'I'm really sorry.'

Buck slowly ran his safe hands from his forehead to his chin.

'I'll make you a drink and you can tell me about it,' Wayne said. 'If you want to.'

Wayne walked through to the kitchen and felt the emptiness. He made a coffee for Buck and two teas, took them through to the lounge, and the three of them sat in silent mourning for a few minutes.

'We heard nothing more till this morning,' the agent said. 'Nothing since the delivery of the money.'

'And then?'

'A letter and some pictures,' said Buck Hanson, coming out of his stupor. 'I could have fuckin' paid them all they wanted but they weren't gonna have me over a barrel. They'd have kept coming back.'

'What's done is done,' the agent said.

'Them?' Wayne asked.

'Whoever the bastards are,' said Buck Hanson. He had suddenly swung into anger. 'I'll get them one day. I'll kill them.' He stood up and paced around. 'There's not enough hand-chopping-off in this country.'

'So what happened?' Wayne asked.

Buck sat down again.

'I got another note. *Your wife's dead.* And photographs of her laid out in a coffin. She was like a skeleton. A box of bones.'

There was a delay while he composed himself. Then the anger returned to his face. Wayne waited until he was sure the anger wouldn't be turned his way.

'Can I see the letter and the photographs?' Wayne asked.

'No,' He sounded guilty. 'I tore them up.'

'What did you do with the bits?'

'Dunno.'

'Do you remember anything about the letter? Postmark? Handwritten or typed?'

Hanson shook his head.

'Can you describe the photographs? Can we find them again?'

'Tore them up and binned them.' Hanson shook his head again. He drank some more tea and spoke: 'When a photograph of your dead fuckin' wife arrives in the post you don't look to see whether the fuckin' thing's overexposed or not,' he said. He picked up his coffee cup and hurled it across the room. It missed Wayne by a yard and smashed into the wall. Wayne watched a brown mark dribble towards the floor. The agent sighed and walked towards the kitchen.

'There was a lot of blood and she looked very pale and very thin,' Hanson continued. 'I just said, "The bastards've killed her."'

The agent returned with a cloth and started dabbing at the wall. He looked relieved that he had found something he could manage. Wayne drank his tea before it became part of the decorations.

'You was probably right,' Buck Hanson told Wayne. 'I shouldn't have messed with the pay-off. I thought we'd get them at the pay-off place.'

They thought about that for a while.

'What would you like me to do now?' Wayne asked. 'Have you informed the police and her family?'

The agent shook his head.

'No one needs to know,' Buck said. 'I can sign Rachel's name on birthday cards and Christmas cards to all the relatives.'

Wayne's jawbone set off towards his chest. He took a few moments to recover.

'You need to tell everybody,' Wayne said.

'I don't know whether I can do that.'

'Her family need to know. They have a right to know.

They have a right to a proper investigation. Did you report her missing to the police, like I said?'

His body language showed that he hadn't.

'You must tell the police about this,' Wayne insisted.

'Fuck off, Shakes,' Buck Hanson said.

Wayne looked at the agent.

'Buck's decision,' the agent said.

'What can I tell them?' Buck said. 'I mean, there's no fuckin' body and I've destroyed the photographs. They'd think I was out of my mind.' He got up and stomped around. 'I'd be better off going after them myself. I just need a bit of time. Do you know any good private detectives, Shakes?'

'Maybe,' Wayne said. 'But most would feel a responsibility to report a crime to the police.'

'I'll get one of the others,' Buck Hanson said.

'Look, Buck, it'll all come out eventually and you'll be the prime suspect for not telling anyone.'

You probably are anyway, Wayne thought.

'Nah,' Hanson said. 'I want to find these bastards.'

'Let me know if you think I could help.'

'Yeah, sure. You've been a great fuckin' help.'

Buck Hanson didn't mean it.

'Call me when you're ready to talk,' Wayne said. 'Let me know when you've informed the police.'

Wayne stood up and walked to the front door. The agent came with him.

'Find that letter and the bits of the photographs,' Wayne told the agent. 'Look everywhere until you find them. Look in the dustbin, waste-paper bins, behind radiators, under cushions, in the compost-heap, amongst newspapers, everywhere. When you find them, stitch the pieces together and send a copy to me. Here's my email address. You must find that stuff – unless he flushed it down the toilet. If you don't find it, he might be in big trouble. There'll be nothing to back up his story. They'll try to pin it on him even if they can't find a body.'

The agent nodded a lot. He may or may not have been listening.

'Buck's worried about all the publicity,' the agent said. 'He's worried some other stuff about his life might be discovered.'

Wayne nodded. He left them to their grief, confusion and worries.

Wayne got into his borrowed car and started it up. As he drove out of Hanson's close, a car passed him going the other way. The driver was a woman with black hair. Wayne thought she was worth a second glance . . . so he gave her one.

FIFTEEN

When Wayne returned to his house, late that afternoon, Kate was lying on her back on the lounge floor with the sculpture of Rover just behind her. Three paperback books supported her head, her knees were bent at ninety degrees and her feet were eighteen inches apart. She was wearing blue jeans and a blue T-shirt which proclaimed *The University of Perversity*. She opened her eyes to check Wayne over and then closed them again.

'Nice T-shirt,' Wayne said.

'Caprice gave it to me.'

'Of course.'

Wayne watched Kate for a minute and then found three paperbacks of his own. He lay down next to her, two feet away, in a copycat posture.

They stayed like that for a few peaceful minutes. Then Kate wriggled a little.

'I hope I'm not disturbing you,' Wayne said.

'No. It's me who's disturbing me.'

'In what way?'

'I'm still trying to heal. I'm still adjusting to being on my own, and I'm still learning to be a sexologist on my own.'

'Tell me more about him,' Wayne said. He was almost whispering.

'Teddy?'

'Yes. How did you meet?'

'I went to a talk he gave about HIV research. I stayed and asked him some questions. He invited me to dinner. We asked each other more questions; we gave each other answers. He said he was looking for a research nurse to work on a project. I put myself forward and . . .'

Her voice faltered. Wayne reached for her hand and squeezed it gently.

'We even had our own language,' Kate said.

'You made up your own words?'

'Not so much that. More like using real words as codes. We used flowers. If there was trouble brewing, we'd say, "There is a problem with the clematis." Ridiculous really.'

'But it had meaning for you.'

'Yes,'

'You weren't married to him?'

'No.'

'So he left you the book?'

'Yes. He knew his ex-wife would fight for everything else.'

'So why aren't you working as a sex consultant and earning loads of money?'

'I'm not ready yet, and I can't face more change. When I've sorted out a few things I'll look for a full-time job.'

'May I ask you something about your work?' Wayne said.

'Sure.'

'I'm trying to understand the woman who organised the rag stunt. I think she works for an escort agency. Is that something students do?'

Kate looked across.

'Some of them. Students are body-rich and money-poor.'

'This student went to a hotel wearing a black wig and dressed up as a concert violinist. A security man stayed in a car in the car park as back-up.'

'Body work takes all sorts of forms.'

'Tell me more.'

'Let me have another two minutes lying like this, and then I'll get a few books out.'

'Don't go to any trouble.'

'No. I want to do it.'

They went back to silence for a while and then Kate got up to go to her room. She returned with a book called *Sex and Sexuality* by Theodore Merlin.

'This is the book I have to update,' Kate said. She sat on a cushion.

'That's a very big book.'

Kate breathed deeply and nodded her head.

'OK,' she said, eventually. 'Let me talk to you about the student escort. What do you know about her?'

'She is mid-twenties with a degree from another university, and she's doing courses in psychology. She's astute and business-minded, and she works for the Rag Committee. She must use a gym, because she looks very muscular.'

'This sounds like a familiar story. It sounds like someone I know. Can she look after herself?'

'Definitely.'

Wayne climbed on to a cushion.

Kate looked dreamily at the wall.

'OK,' she said, finally.

'Would the university know she worked for an escort agency?' Wayne asked.

'I don't think the university cares. As long as students pay fees and pass exams. I think the university accepts that students have to work part-time to get through their course.'

'OK,' Wayne said. 'I'm trying to put myself inside Tracey's head.'

'Your escort friend is called Tracey?'

'Yes. Perhaps I shouldn't have told you that.'

'No. But I'm glad you did.'

'OK,' said Wayne.

'Some people think it's a glamorous profession but you can end up feeling abused,' Kate said. 'She would have no illusions about what she was doing.'

'Only the clients have illusions.'

'She probably wouldn't get emotionally involved with clients,' Kate said. 'She may have regular clients or she may meet several strangers every day. She may have stuck with it because she has easy clients or some sort of specialism that brings in more money. She may or may not have orgasms while working. She may or may not take a selection of props with her to a client.'

'Such as?'

'Vibrators. Whips. Bottle-opener.'

'What would she do with the bottle-opener?' asked Wayne.

'Open a bottle of wine or champagne.'

'I never thought of that.' Wayne laughed.

'When escorts are with clients their bodies are present, but their minds could be anywhere. In their heads they could be shopping or preparing an essay. Business and pleasure mix for some, but not for others. Tracey would also have a particular attitude to her work. She may consider herself grubby or she may feel virtuous. Or she may feel something in between.'

'Virtuous?'

'Escorts can become virtuous by removing their own selfish needs. They may eventually discover that there is not much difference between having sex with someone seemingly attractive and someone seemingly ugly. Freed from the demands of their own needs, they can cater to the needs of others.'

'You know your stuff, don't you?' Wayne said.

'I've been thinking about it a lot lately.'

'Thinking about earning some money?'

Kate stared hard at him. She opened her mouth as if to speak and then closed it again.

'Look,' Wayne said. 'You don't need money to live here. Let's call it free rent. Just pay me bills and a share of council tax.'

'No, I must pay my way.'

'There are many routes to altruism,' Wayne mumbled. 'You have yours.' He pointed to Kate's copy of *Sex and Sexuality*. 'Let me have mine.'

Kate hid her face.

Wayne watched her for a few seconds.

'You'll never be out of work,' Wayne told her, as he stood up. 'As long as you live, people will make love.'

'Let us hope so,' Kate said.

Wayne waited until the room felt peaceful and then left her alone.

Kate returned to her prone position on the floor and considered Wayne's questions. The discussion about Tracey resonated with what she knew about Claire – escort services, psychology courses, physically intimidating and also known as Tracey.

She hadn't thought about Wayne much until now. He suddenly seemed a complex man with troubles running deep, too good-looking for his own good and too confident for a woman's good. A real heartbreaker.

She clambered up from the floor and set off upstairs towards Wayne's study.

'Wayne?' she asked.

'Come in.'

'The student you were asking about, the professional escort, was she involved in the kidnapping of the goalkeeper for Rag Week?'

'Yes.'

'Did the goalkeeper's wife come back?'

'No.'

'Has something happened?'

'Not that I can discuss.'

'Let me know if I can help. I may know her.'

'Buck Hanson's wife?'

'No. The escort.'

'You mix in interesting circles.'

Kate nodded automatically and went to her room to think.

The Mankiller sensed that Buck Hanson might be the easiest victim of them all. That night she followed his car around town, from one secluded high-class drinking-place to another. She parked outside the third one, saw Hanson enter, then waited fifteen minutes before going in.

Hanson was sitting on a high stool talking to another man. She set out for the ladies' room and paraded towards Hanson, wiggling her hips, tensing her stomach muscles and arching her back. She caught his eye when she was three yards from him. She gave a flick of her jet-black hair and sent a quick, darting glance his way.

On her return she watched him surreptitiously for nearly five minutes. When he was alone she walked over and stood alongside him.

'You look as though you need cheering up,' she said. She twisted her hair through her fingers.

Hanson shifted his head slowly and looked at her face. Then he moved his eyes up and down, and peered down her short black dress. She hoped that he had guessed that she wore nothing restrictive underneath the dress. She thought Buck Hanson was a man who knew the cost of everything and the value of nothing. Maybe his wife had taught him the market value of jewels.

'Oh, dear,' she said, placing her hand lightly on his upper arm. 'Has your girlfriend walked out on you or something?'

'My wife,' Hanson said. 'My wife has fucked off.'

'I'm sorry,' she told him. 'You poor thing. But every cloud has a silver lining. You have to look at the positive side.'

'What's the fuckin' positive side when your wife walks out?' Hanson asked.

She smiled at him. She was on a spree now. She thought this one needed a direct approach. No subtleties. She took a deep breath and moved close to him.

'Well,' she whispered. 'If your house is empty, you can take me home and fuck the arse off me.'

Hanson was still for ten seconds, looking at her. Then he picked up his drink, drained it, and turned to the woman.

'Come on then,' he said.

'What do you know about Claire, also called The Cat?' Wayne asked Mackie.

Mackie pointed to the pack of cards. Wayne cut them obediently. Mackie dealt.

'I don't ask questions,' Mackie said.

'That's what I like about you, Mackie,' Wayne said. 'You're a good listener, but you don't ask questions. That's great until I need to know stuff.'

Mackie shrugged.

'How did you meet her?' Wayne asked.

'Club.'

'A corporate client?'

Mackie nodded.

'Three directors,' Mackie said.

'Including Mister Richard?'

Mackie looked shocked. He shook his head. Except maybe once, Wayne wondered.

'Can you tell me who her clients are?' Wayne asked.

'I only do one night a week.'

'Who does Saturday night?'

'Ask her.'

'OK.' Then Wayne looked at the cribbage board. 'How did I get so far behind?'

'Outclassed,' Mackie said.

Inside Buck Hanson's bedroom, the black-haired woman peeled off her little black dress, shook out her hair and stood naked before him. He tore off the rest of his clothes. He had barely tossed them aside before she was down on her knees, taking his erection in her mouth. Her lips went down and up twice and then she disengaged and stood up. She had practised her lie.

'Come on then,' she told Hanson, her right hand holding his penis. 'I want to feel you come in my arse. That's what I really like. I want your spunk in my bum.'

She lay face down on the bed and waited for him. She wasn't a total stranger to anal sex but she hadn't enjoyed her previous experience. This time she had prepared well. She had applied lubricant and was prepared to relax. Not too much lubricant though. A little rectal tear might help her cause, help her to kill him.

Then Hanson frightened her with his savage goalkeeping hands, and the way he battered her buttocks with his body. He banged her around the bed, losing his place once, plunging desperately to regain it. Even so, it was over fairly quickly and Hanson collapsed in a heap on the bed. She moved gingerly away from him. In her opinion bums should be exercised only on toilet seats.

They had nothing to say to each other afterwards. She felt very sore.

'OK, you've got what you wanted,' Hanson said, eventually. 'Now fuck off, and leave me alone.'

Yes, I've got what I wanted, she mused. I've done what I needed to do for sisterhood. Your words can wound me, but not as much as I can wound you.

'Thank you,' she said aloud. 'Lots of wonderful things are waiting to happen to you now that your marriage is over.'

And one of them is death, she thought, picking up her dress from the floor, walking uneasily out of the bedroom, looking for where she had left her shoes. She knew it would take her a while to recover from this one. Then Wayne Shakespeare was next.

SIXTEEN

The next morning, a Thursday, Wayne took a taxi across Oxford to the university where Tracey Holroyd was a student. After five minutes of dodging students Wayne found a man of the security trade. He handed the man a card.

Wayne Shakespeare – Security Consultant

'Have we been taken over?' the security man asked. He was a bent man in his fifties.

Wayne laughed.

'No, don't worry,' Wayne said. 'I'm mainly office blocks and football grounds.' In fact, he was also doing some consultancy for the university.

'How can I help?'

'I'm looking for a class.'

'You need Admissions.'

'No, I'm trying to meet someone out of a class.'

'Which department?'

'Psychology.'

'I think that's up the road. Out the door. Turn left. Turn right . . .'

'Whoa,' Wayne said. 'Is there a phone number I could try before I run the London Marathon? Just in case the class is next door.'

Wayne pointed at a lecture theatre.

The security man thumbed the internal telephone book. He read Wayne a number and passed over a telephone.

Wayne spoke to a helpful secretary. Tracey Holroyd's class was in seminar room twelve. The class would be over about three o'clock. Wayne had twenty-five minutes.

He returned the phone to the porter.

'Where's seminar-room twelve?' he asked.

'Just next door.'

They smiled at each other.

'What's it like working here then?' Wayne asked.

'Not bad. A bit military. Checking library cards. Car parking. Computer rooms are the big thing now. Twenty-four hours. They need surveillance. I don't understand it – they say they're short of money but they get more and more computers.'

'Beats issuing identity cards and checking CCTV,' Wayne said. 'And you get to go to lectures free, eh?'

The security man grunted a reply.

'Where do you work then?' he asked Wayne.

'Here in Oxford. I look after a business empire. Our access control is a bit easier than here – one building and not so many visitors.'

A handsome couple walked by, a male and a female, each with a hand in the far back pocket of the other's jeans. Their bodies bumped together on every step and every three paces they stopped and turned to each other and kissed deeply.

'I thought they were supposed to be studying,' the security man said, acidly.

'They're studying each other,' Wayne said.

'Studying each other,' he repeated, shaking his head. 'Look at her showing her stomach. They can't seem to make tops long enough or trousers high enough these days.'

'Thanks for your help,' Wayne said. He left the security man to his navel-gazing.

Wayne spent ten minutes in the library, studying the security system, and then stationed himself outside seminar room twelve. Just before three o'clock a score of students decanted from inside and Tracey Holroyd was among them. She was carrying an armful of knowledge.

Tracey didn't notice Wayne. He followed her to the coffee bar and sat down opposite her as she thumbed through a rag week magazine.

'I'm an envoy,' Wayne said, speaking quietly.

'You again?' Tracey said.

'I'm an envoy for someone who once spent a sensational weekend making love with you. About six or seven years ago.'

Her steely, intelligent eyes smacked Wayne's from a yard away. The effect would have been stunning, except that the rest of her face had discarded sexuality in favour of business.

'Go on,' Tracey said. She put down the magazine.

'It was one of the best times of his life,' Wayne added.

Her grey eyes continued to stare at him. He could see more than intelligence in them. He could see puzzlement and dispassion.

'He called himself Alec. Do you know who I mean?' he asked.

'I meet a lot of men.'

'I know.' He looked at her and tried to call up some compassion. 'This one would like to meet you again.'

'I work through an agency.'

'He wants to spend time with you. He wants to spend another night with you.' Wayne put Richard Bromage's proposition to her, but he didn't mention his real name. He saw her stiffen when he mentioned the money. 'It will set you up for the year, just for spending a weekend with him.'

Wayne let the woman think.

'Are you serious about the money?' she asked.

'Perfectly serious.'

'Is he – Alec – serious about it?'

'Yes.'

'And what would the tax man think of that?'

'We'd put it through as consultancy, I suppose. There are people around Rich . . . Alec who can organise that sort of thing.'

'Richard? Is he called Richard?'

'No, he's rich Alec.'

'As opposed to Smart Alec, huh?'

'That's *me*.'

She shook her head and tried not to laugh. It didn't seem hard for her.

'Tell me again,' she said. 'Tell me about the money.'

'The man who calls himself Alec wishes to spend a weekend with you, and he is willing to pay several thousand for that privilege. We can set it up in a way that makes you feel as safe as possible. But we don't have to put it through the agency.'

'I need time to think about this,' she said. 'There must be a catch. Why does he want to do this?'

'He must have been thinking about you for years.'

'Why now? Why has he waited until now?' Then she looked at Wayne with a psychologist's curiosity. 'You're an odd man.'

'Aren't we all odd? My numbers are on the card. I'll phone you if I don't hear from you. And please return my calls next time.'

'Thanks for organising Buck Hanson,' she said.

'No trouble. He's a good lad is Mackie.' She looked at him. 'Oh, don't worry, he didn't say anything to me. I found him outside a hotel waiting for you. I just observed.'

'Were you the one who called at the Cowley Road house the other day?'

'Yeah. You really should have answered your phone.'

'I thought we'd finished our business.'

'We had. But there was a development.'

He looked at her, but didn't see a reaction.

'Hanson sent you?' she asked.

'No.'

'Someone from Bromage's football club?'

She caught him unawares with her mention of the Bromage name.

'That's why football clubs hire me,' Tracey said. 'I give a confidential service.'

Wayne wasn't sure what to say. He picked up a copy of the rag magazine that Tracey Holroyd had put down and opened it near the centre.

What's the difference between a condom and a coffin? They both take stiffs, but you come in one and go in the other.

'Where do you get these jokes?' he asked.

'It's dealt with centrally now. We go in with a bunch of other colleges and sell each other's rag mags. We get the jokes from a supplier in London.'

Wayne closed the magazine and turned to Tracey Holroyd.

'Buck Hanson reacted very well to the news that you would be there at his kidnapping,' he said.

'Looking for something more, is he?'

'I don't know what happens between you and Buck Hanson. That's not my business.'

'Asking on your own behalf?'

Wayne was puzzled. 'No, it's about his wife,' he said.

Now Tracey looked baffled.

'What does she want?' Tracey asked.

Wayne didn't know what to say. Tracey knows nothing about Rachel's death, he thought, nothing about the Hanson family since she had last seen Buck Hanson.

'I have to leave,' she said. She removed the rubber band from her hair and began styling.

Wayne stayed silent. He was fairly sure that Tracey

Holroyd did not know what had developed since she had last seen Buck Hanson.

'You're good at raising funds, aren't you?' he said.

'If you think of the question you really want to ask, try writing it down before you come to see me. My time is important to me.'

She jumped to her feet like an eight-year-old and flexed her muscles. Richard Bromage had wanted to know how much of the child remained. Her physique had developed far beyond childhood, her mind acted as if she were a hundred, and inside the bottomless pit of her grey eyes Wayne could almost see the earth forming.

Mackie was on the desk at the Bromage Building. He was a glutton for work. He signed Wayne in without saying a word and handed over a note.

Wayne read the note in the security office. Mackie had listed details of his hours watching Juliet's house. It was probably Mackie's way of asking if it was essential. Well, Wayne would enquire. He was meeting Juliet in thirty minutes.

Wayne picked up the phone and tried the number for his private forensic man.

'I expected to get your voicemail,' Wayne said when he heard David Boyle's voice.

'Wayne Shakespeare. I'd ask for your autograph if I thought you could write.'

'I always sign mine *Wayne you know Shakespeare.*'

David Boyle laughed.

'Nothing on the note or envelope, Wayne,' said Boyle. 'Just the set of prints that you expected.'

Juliet Bromage, Wayne thought.

'I thought it was probably a lost cause,' he said.

'Have you told the police?'

'Not yet,' Wayne said. 'Thanks, David. Send me a bill.'

'Shall I send it to Wayne You Know Shakespeare?'

'Do that, you know,' Wayne said.

'This threat is worrying me,' Juliet said, ten minutes later, in her third-floor office. 'Have you dealt with it?'

'I'm working on it,' Wayne said. 'I went to see Robin Hookes. I think I frightened him a little. I have a forensic report on the note. Nothing much we can use.'

'I hope you are taking this threat seriously.'

'I've had someone watching over you, but not all the time. Have you heard something else?'

'Two more notes.'

'Two more? Can I see them, please?'

Juliet handed them over.

Juliet: death is on its way.

Juliet: you will definitely die soon.

'When did they arrive?'

'Both today.'

'Two at the same time?'

'One came by mail. The other one had no stamp on. It must have been pushed through the main door.'

'OK, that's useful. I might be able to look at CCTV footage. Did Mary open them?'

'Yes. She saved the envelopes.'

'OK. I'll think about this.'

'I think I'm being followed,' Juliet said.

'Probably my guys.'

'It doesn't feel like it.'

'You've always got men tracking you, Juliet. We're like drones to the honeypot.'

'This feels menacing. I'd like you to watch over me tonight.'

'I'll make sure Mackie's there.'

'No. I want it to be you.'

'Me?'

'Yes. I want you in my house tonight.'

'If I come to see you, will you tell me all you know?'

'Yes,' she said, without a moment's thought. Wayne didn't know whether she meant it.

Juliet was as tense as he'd ever seen her. Wayne thought of Tracey Holroyd. The similarities were very strong now that stress was enveloping Juliet. Two slim, attractive women with stunning eyes and quick body movements. How similar had they looked when the teenager Claire Stanworth had met Richard Bromage several years ago?

'I'll bag the notes and envelopes and send them off to my forensic guy,' Wayne said.

'I need you there tonight,' Juliet repeated. 'I need a night of feeling safe.'

'I'll be there,' Wayne said.

'That's all, Wayne. We'll talk tonight.'

Wayne left. He was already in a heightened state of anticipation. He sensed that the foreplay would last all day, and it was all in his mind.

Wayne sought out Mackie.

'Could you do me a favour?' he asked his colleague.

Mackie nodded.

'Could you look through last night's CCTV tape for the main door, see if anyone pushed a letter through the door?'

Mackie nodded.

'Let me see the footage if you find anything,' Wayne said.

Mackie nodded.

'Thanks,' Wayne said.

The phone call from Tracey Holroyd reached Wayne's mobile phone while he was still in the Bromage Building.

'Answering the phone,' Wayne said.

'Wayne Shakespeare?'

'As far as I'm aware.'

'It's Tracey. I'm a bit better prepared for you now,' she said. 'You took me by surprise earlier.'

'I'm sorry I had to spring it on you like that. Have you thought any more about my suggestion?'

'Your suggestion or his suggestion?'

'His suggestion. A night away with him.'

'I've thought about it. I'd like to keep talking about it.'

'How do you mean?'

'How much do you know about it all?'

'Only a little. But I can find out more. I have a direct route to Alec.'

'Rich Alec.'

'Yes, rich Alec.'

'I need to talk about it,' Tracey said.

'I'm not sure what I can tell you.'

'Well, let me put it this way – if we don't carry on talking then I just say no to the whole idea. Then we are all frustrated. Me, you and Alec.'

'OK, let's talk. Where and when?'

'At my home. Can you come tomorrow afternoon?'

'Afternoon?' Wayne queried. 'Yes.'

'Make it two o'clock tomorrow. I must get some work done in the morning.'

'That'll be fine. Where's home?'

She told him the address. North Oxford. Wayne knew it already of course. He was standing outside the place when Mackie came to pick her up.

Wayne went home and phoned Richard Bromage from his landline.

'I'll be meeting your girl from the past tomorrow,' he said.

'Good,' Bromage said.

'Is there anything else I need to know?'

'No. Do your best. You'll know how to handle it.'

'OK. It's just that she seemed to imply that there was more to the story.'

Richard Bromage thought for a while.

'Not that I know of,' he said, eventually.

Wayne said goodbye and fantasised about Richard Bromage's daughter.

Kate walked through the kitchen wearing a long black skirt, a white blouse and a jacket.

'You look very smart,' Wayne told Kate. 'You must have a hot date this evening.'

'I've been invited out to dinner.'

'I'll stay out of the way for when you bring him back.'

'It's work. I won't be bringing him back.'

'I'll be out tonight,' Wayne said.

'So you're the one with the hot date?'

'It's work. I have to see Juliet Bromage. Someone is sending her notes to say that her life is in danger.'

'Notes?'

'Three notes over the last few days. Someone sneaked one past Mary Curtis.'

'Mary Curtis?'

'Juliet's secretary. Juliet's ex-husband calls her the dragon on the desk. Juliet seems frightened.'

'It sounds like Juliet needs you,' Kate asked. 'Have a good evening.'

'You too.'

Kate collected her bag, walked up the stairs and left the house.

Jeremy Spooner greeted Kate with a big smile. He kissed her cheeks and stroked her upper arms. He had a bright-eyed look which suggested he was excited about something.

'Let me get you a drink,' he said, summoning the waitress. 'Something alcoholic. It's too early for Horlicks.'

He laughed.

They were in Pizza Express in the centre of Oxford. Kate had walked into the city rather than cycle wearing a skirt, and she had enjoyed the stroll.

'So how've you been?' Jeremy Spooner asked.

'OK,' she said. 'I've spoken with Bruce Venn's ex-wife and thought some more about my theory.'

'Are you ready to tell me about it?'

'Well, I'm waiting for a book to arrive from the United States. I'll know more when I've read that.' Kate had felt rushed into this meeting by Jeremy Spooner. 'We've still got some time, haven't we? The book should arrive in the next two or three days.'

'Yes, of course.'

'Is there any way I could get to talk to the mother and her daughter?' Kate asked. 'Fiona Coates and Olivia.'

'Why would you want to do that?'

'I would like to find out more of the detail.'

'Let me think about that. I'd rather go to them with something I can use against them.'

'The defence I'm building up might need expert witnesses and I don't know of any in England.'

'The Americans would charge the earth.'

'There may be one or two in Scandinavia. I'll look harder in England.'

'Please do. Now tell me more about yourself.'

Wayne walked round the corner of Juliet's street and saw Mackie's car cruising towards him. Mackie stopped and Wayne crossed over to talk.

'Were you just doing a once-over?' Wayne asked him.

Mackie nodded.

'To see if anyone was watching her house?' Wayne checked.

Mackie nodded again.

'And no one was?'

Mackie shook his head.

'I can take over for the evening,' Wayne told him. 'I'm going to call in to see her.'

Mackie smiled, winked at Wayne and drove away.

Not a word from Mackie.

'I would like you to take on more rape cases,' Jeremy Spooner said. They had finished eating and were lingering over coffee.

Kate winced.

'I'm not sure I could handle too many rape cases,' she said. 'It brings up stuff for me.' 'Have you been a victim?'

'Someone in my family was.'

Spooner let it drop, as Kate wanted him to.

'How about AIDS cases?' he asked. 'I take it AIDS is still a problem, and we'll get more cases of that type.'

He wasn't actually rubbing his hands, but the implication was there. He kept smiling at Kate.

'AIDs will always be a problem,' Kate told him. 'We just move into different phases. We did well in this country to keep our epidemic under control in the early nineties but now we face different problems, different escalations.'

'Such as?' Spooner asked.

'We are keeping HIV-positive patients alive longer, which is wonderful, but that means they have to learn how to adapt their behaviour while they are around for longer. We're learning that circumcision is one way of reducing the risk of HIV infection.'

'So they don't pass it on?'

'I tend not to use that expression,' said Kate.

'Why not?'

'Some kids think it means passing it on like you pass the parcel – you get it and then you get rid of it on someone else. There's a lot of confusion over language.'

'Like the Bentley case?'

'What was that?'

'A policeman told a boy to drop the gun. The accomplice shouted, "Let him have it." The boy shot the policeman. What did the accomplice mean by "Let him have it"? Was it "hand over the gun" or "shoot the policeman"?'

'Words and their meanings,' Kate said. 'That's how it always is with sex and love. We each bring our own frameworks and meanings.'

'I hope it doesn't make you negative about sex.'

'Not at all. Far from it. People should enjoy sex, but they should also take calculated risks and communicate as well as possible.'

'That's what I was hoping you'd say.'

He leaned across the table. Kate sat up straighter.

'Maybe I should be clear in my language,' Jeremy Spooner said. 'I would love to go to bed with you. I would like to take care of you and myself by using condoms. It doesn't have to be tonight. My desire for you will last.'

Kate was speechless for a few minutes.

'Do you have a place of your own?' Jeremy Spooner asked.

'I have a room in a house. My landlord is a security consultant called Wayne Shakespeare.'

'The former footballer?'

'So I believe. Do you know him?'

'I know of him. He was a good player.'

'Oh.'

Kate didn't know what to say next. She watched while

Spooner paid the bill. The solicitor took her arm and led her out of the restaurant.

'Thank you for the meal,' Kate said. They were standing in the High Street.

'Let me take you home,' Spooner said.

'Thank you. I'd rather walk.'

'Let me walk you home.'

'I'd like to be alone, thanks. I'd like to think about a few things.'

He kissed her on the cheek and pulled her towards his chest and thighs for contact that felt somewhere between a hug and frottage.

'I would be very generous,' Spooner said. 'More work.'

'I'll think about it.'

'Are you seeing someone?'

'No. But I'm hoping to go abroad.'

'To sell Teddy's property in Princeton, New Jersey?'

'Yes.'

'Don't forget that you can claim expenses from Teddy's estate. We can be very generous about those expenses.'

'Thank you for a nice evening.'

They were walking together.

'That's where I'd like to take you for our first night together,' Spooner told Kate, pointing at the Randolph.

'I'll think about it,' she repeated. She broke from him and walked quickly away.

On the way home she zigzagged around the streets just in case Spooner had followed her. Wayne Shakespeare's house felt very empty when she arrived.

Wayne stood at Juliet's gate and watched the front of her large North Oxford building. He felt the kind of nervous excitement that came immediately before a football game or talking to a large audience. There was something about the evening that promised a performance.

He walked up the path slowly and rang the bell.

Juliet let him in. She wore a red shirt and tight trousers the grey of a stormy sky. She smelt wonderful and it all felt familiar.

'I'm so glad to see you, Wayne,' she said. She kissed him on the left cheek. 'I prefer you without the beard.'

'Is everything all right?'

'I feel safe now that you are here.'

Wayne inhaled deeply. Juliet did the same.

They stood in the corridor like two people who could explode.

What happened next was a frenzied, concentrated sex scene like something in a movie. Wayne's evening with Caprice had been relaxed and drawn out, while the candles burned lower and the clock's minute hand ticked through thousands of degrees, but this was the opposite. It was one of those clothes-tossing scenes where the co-stars find the first available location and intercourse is all over in ninety seconds, so fast that a movie audience would be unsure whether body doubles were used.

Juliet's eyes were all the foreplay Wayne needed. Without leaving the hallway he and Juliet found a sprinter's route to nudity. Then, with her back against the wall, his hands under her bum, they settled into an athletic rhythm of barely-controlled body collisions, until their legs shook and their cries bounced back off the ceiling. It was sudden and visceral, but Wayne had one moment of clarity. He fished a condom out of his back pocket and used his mouth to tear it open without damaging the condom itself. Afterwards, when Juliet went to the bathroom to urinate, as recommended for cystitis-sufferers, Wayne stood awkwardly in the hall. He occupied himself by dealing with the condom.

SEVENTEEN

Kate awoke at five o'clock that Friday morning. In her dream Teddy was helping her to write a talk on the complexities of language in sexual settings. Kate got out of bed and put on her dressing gown. She sat on her bed, picked up pen and pad, and started making notes for Monday's class.

A ten-year-old takes the witness stand in court. The prosecutor asks her a question and she breaks down and cries. How should her crying be interpreted? Is she crying because she has been through a traumatic event? Is it because she doesn't know what to say? Or has she been frightened by the judge's wig?

Teddy always relied on William Empson's book *Seven Types of Ambiguity*, because he enjoyed telling people about how Empson had been expelled from his Cambridge college for having contraceptives in his rooms.

Now Kate tried to remember some of Teddy's examples of ambiguity. There was the story of the sex educator who told a class of twelve-year-olds that the man slides his penis inside the woman's vagina, and one boy asked, seriously, 'How does he get his hand out again?' And a comment from another child: 'If they don't get pregnant do they have to do that again?'

Kate thought through a case study. A man and woman are naked and petting heavily. She says, 'I wish you could get inside me.' Does that imply she wants his penis inside her vagina? Or that she wishes she could let him but she can't? Or that she wishes him to get to know her better, like getting inside her mind, before they go all the way?

In the same set of circumstances – a naked heterosexual couple – the female says, 'I want more of you.' Does that mean more of the same, more than just sex, or does she want to raise the level of sexual activity, say, from heavy petting to full intercourse?

She needed to find the exercises that Teddy used in this class. The students had responded so well to Teddy's funny stories. She couldn't do any class as well as him. She missed him so much.

Kate got back into bed still wearing her dressing gown. Today was a day off. It should be a good day to get on with other work – updating Teddy' book, preparing classes, some reading and writing, talk to Wayne, talk to Caprice – but all she could think of was hiding under the covers and feeling the warmth of her dressing gown and the bed linen.

When Wayne returned to his home at midday, after a morning at the Bromage Building, Kate was sitting at the kitchen table, still in her dressing gown. A copy of *The Sex Researchers* by Edward Brecher lay open on the table. Wayne pointed towards the book.

'I was looking for something I'd read a few years ago,' Kate said. 'I can't find it.'

'Are you OK? You don't look great.'

'I didn't sleep well,' Kate said.

'I didn't either.'

'You probably had better reason than me.' Kate said, smiling. 'Do you need to talk about something?'

'Me?' said Wayne. 'I'm a man.'

'Why don't you sit down and tell me what's happening in the outside world, where everybody is spending hours having sex.'

'It only takes some people a minute,' Wayne said.

'That may be your idea of sex,' Kate said, smiling.

'We men enjoy the post-coital closeness so much that we like to get to it as soon as possible.'

Wayne sat at the table.

'I want to move on from Juliet but I can't seem to,' he said.

'It takes time, doesn't it?'

'I went there expecting that we would talk. She said she would tell me more about the threats she'd received.'

'Uh-huh?'

'As soon as I stepped inside the front door, it all went back a few weeks.'

'She brought out your animal side?'

'Yeah, I froze like a rabbit in the headlights.'

'I bet you didn't.'

Wayne shrugged again, and then smiled.

'OK. What happened with Juliet?' Kate asked.

'Well, the sex was fine.'

'And afterwards?'

'The sex afterwards was fine too. In fact it was probably better than it used to be.'

Kate nodded.

'Sometimes I wonder if we try to lift a sexual relationship to greater heights when a relationship is under threat,' Kate said. 'I'm not saying that's happening with you and Juliet, but it's happened with me in the past. Sometimes it gets creative, like it's a device to win the battle. As if they are saying, "We must preserve this" or "You must preserve this."'

'Yeah, we must preserve this like we preserve pickled eggs.'

'Wayne,' Kate said. 'When you asked about why women don't use condoms, were you thinking about Juliet?'

He nodded automatically.

'I wonder if Mister Richard will use condoms with Tracey Holroyd,' Wayne said.

'Tracey Holroyd?'

'I wonder if it runs in the family.'

'I don't follow.'

'He asked me to track down this heartthrob he'd been with years ago. When Tracey was a teenager called Claire.'

'Oh.'

'He's having a night with her tonight.'

'Hmm. Part of his past must have tapped his shoulder now,' Kate said.

'What's that mean?'

'I don't know. Especially in the case you describe.'

'I fixed up an appointment for you with Juliet. I sneaked you into her diary for three o'clock this afternoon for five minutes.'

'Why?'

'I think there may be some work for you as a condom consultant.'

'It would have been nice had you asked me first.'

'Sorry. I just saw an opportunity while I was with Juliet. Five minutes at three. That's the way Juliet works.'

'Are you sure it's not to see what I think of Juliet?' Kate asked.

'That too. I have one question: Should I take these threatening notes seriously?'

'What did they say?'

Wayne told her.

Juliet: you will die soon.

Juliet: death is on its way.

Juliet: you will definitely die soon.

Wayne stopped because he was absent-mindedly opening his mail. Buck Hanson's agent had sent copies of pieced-together photographs.

A woman bloody and dead on a bed.

The coffin being loaded on to a white van with covered number plates.

The white van setting off.

The woman in her coffin surrounded by grass, ground and a pile of soil.

Wayne put the copies in his wallet, not knowing what he would do with them, or whether it was his job to do anything.

'Come in,' said Tracey Holroyd, opening the door to her North Oxford flat. Her reddish hair was held by a yellow rubber-band but she wore a white blouse, a long black skirt and some jewellery. Wayne felt like he had misread his invitation.

As he walked through the spacious flat Wayne assessed the fitted carpets, tasteful wallpaper and select furniture. It could have come from the Bank of Dad, but Wayne had a feeling it hadn't.

A black cat rubbed against Wayne's legs.

'That's Wolvercat,' Tracey said. 'He followed us home from Wolvercote and we never got rid of him.'

'We?'

'I used to live with someone. Now I don't. Coffee?'

'Yes, please.'

Wayne took time to bond with the cat.

Tracey Holroyd brought Wayne a coffee. They sat at the table.

'Thanks for coming,' she said. 'I wanted to talk more. I wanted to find out more.' Her grey eyes took up a position of challenge. 'Tell me more about him.'

'He's a wealthy businessman. He's in his sixties. He works hard. He earns a lot of money.'

'Oh, really. I didn't know he was wealthy. I thought maybe he was a poor boy who wanted to spend his enormous life-savings on a weekend with me.'

Her voice was harsh and her gaze threatening.

'Look at it from my point of view,' Tracey said. 'All I know about him is the price he puts on me. The price is very high. The price is that high that I'm suspicious. People get killed for that amount.'

'You can trust me. Mackie and I go a long way back.'

'I know. I take you seriously, but this is not how I normally do business.'

'You have safety concerns?'

'Of course. I don't want to end up in a snuff movie.'

Wayne nodded.

'Why do you think he asked you to contact me?' Tracey asked.

'I don't know. I can only guess.'

'Guess.'

'He's been totally and utterly in love with you for a few years but doesn't have the language to express it. Or he just wants a weekend of casual sex.'

'Is he dying?' she asked.

That shook Wayne a little.

'It's possible,' he said.

Wayne realised he needed to make Richard Bromage more real to Tracey. He had to make the seduction personal. He wasn't sure how to do it.

'I feel as though I'm in a Mafia movie,' she said. 'There must be a catch to the weekend.'

'Not that I know about – but I might not know everything.'

'Are you family?'

Wayne thought about the question. There had been a

short time when he had thought he might marry Juliet and become family.

'No,' he said.

'You hesitated.'

'Your question threw me a little because I had an affair with his youngest daughter.'

Tracey waited for Wayne to go on. She wasn't a woman he could fool. He leaned forward in his chair and looked at her more closely. Her grey eyes were still keen and sharp.

'OK, let me tell you what I think,' Wayne said. 'But most of this is guesswork. I'm guessing that Alec has thought of you often over the years. He's not a man who displays his vulnerabilities. Not a man who talks to people about his emotions. It doesn't sound as though he revealed much of his inner self when you first met him. That's how his daughter is – you learn about her life through other people rather than her. But he probably wants to talk to you. I bet that weekend with you has preyed on his mind. He wants to reprise it. He needs some peace of mind.'

Wayne stopped to study her reaction. Her eyes were still attentive, but they'd darkened.

'I assume your contract with clients includes confidentiality?' Wayne asked.

'Yes. That comes with the fee.'

'OK. Let me put it this way – he's obviously thinking about his mortality and wants to do the most important things *now*.'

'Go on,' she said. 'You're doing better.'

'He is a man of resources. He knows he can help you

financially.'

'I would do it for far less money,' she said. 'It's what I do all the time. It's the amount that shocks me. He should have been able to find out the proper rates.'

'Yes,' Wayne said quickly. 'But what if you were married and settled now? What if you'd left the escort business? He needed to pitch a sum that could tempt a woman, whatever her financial standing, whatever her marital or relationship status, whatever her circumstances.' He waited a moment. 'Would he have known that you worked for an escort agency then? Would he have known at the time?'

'Depends who he is. Sometimes someone would call the agency on behalf of an organisation. Then they'd send a car for a few of us. Everything had been arranged and taken care of.'

'What sort of organisation?'

'A business conference. A football club.'

'Was that how you met Buck Hanson?'

'Through the agency. Sometimes Buck came to me directly.'

Wayne thought a while.

'I'd like to work with you to make it safe for you,' he said. 'I'll ask more questions of the man I represent.'

'The one you called Alec.'

'Yes.'

'What's your best guess about his motives?'

'I'd guess that the weekend he spent with you was probably one of the most eventful and exciting of his life.'

'His football team won,' she said.

'Don't mock yourself,' Wayne said. His voice was sharp. 'Maybe his relationship with you had an intensity he's always remembered. Let's look at it as it was then. He was an ageing man going through a crisis and his sex life was zero. Then he met a beautiful and nubile university student of nineteen or twenty.'

'Eighteen,' she said.

'Ah, so you remember it. A beautiful young girl full of life, energy and intelligence. Her face is open to him. Her eyes are wide and grey, and the years drop away from him. He suddenly has a day's freedom in a life where all his time is usually accounted for. I don't know what happened between you two but I guess you transported him from his repressed world to an era that was uninhibited and pure and raw. Look at yourself. You're still attractive and young. He wants to rediscover that for another weekend. What's so strange about that? If I had his money, I'd spend it on a weekend with you.'

Wayne's words just came out. Wayne didn't know why he had said it. He looked at her and was relieved to see that cynicism remained in her eyes.

'That's very nice,' she said. 'All that's missing is some poetry.'

'Part of his past must have tapped his shoulder now,' Wayne said.

'Seduction doesn't work through an envoy.'

The air was fraught with something Wayne didn't understand.

Tracey stood up and started pacing the room.

'I'll get some more coffee,' she said. 'Then *I* want to talk.'

Wayne used the time to visit the bathroom. It was neat and orderly and feminine. On the way back he looked at her bookshelves. Tracey's books were about healing her life, complementary medicine, sex, women and psychology. The books on cults interested Wayne.

Tracey and Wayne resumed their positions at the table.

'I had a termination sometime around then,' said Tracey. 'I had an accidental pregnancy.'

'So you did get pregnant by him?'

'Unlikely,' she said.

'No way to tell?'

'No way to tell.'

'You've had no children since?'

'No.'

'But a weekend with him would bring back all your loss?'

She shrugged. 'I'm not worried about that,' she said.

Wayne searched for something to say.

'Something good is going to come out of this for you,' he said. 'Some part of your life will shift. I think you need to meet it halfway. I know you're suspicious, I know you have a hundred and one things to worry about, but here's a chance to shift something. If you're worried about anything or if you need help to deal with other stuff, just say. My boss is a resourceful man and we can find help for you.'

'One word with the Godfather,' she said.

'Something like that.'

'You're a strange bloke for a footballer. You're not like Buck Hanson.'

'Good.'

'How did you become a footballer?'

'A number of clubs watched me closely because my grandfather had been a professional footballer.'

'My father was a professional wrestler,' Tracey said.

'So your grappling skills are hereditary?'

Tracey laughed. It surprised Wayne. He didn't believe Tracey Holroyd would ever laugh.

'I've never made that connection before,' she said.

Wayne looked at her.

'I bet you're good at what you do,' Wayne said.

'I am.'

'Have you been an actress?'

'An actress?'

'Alec remembers you as a blonde. I've seen you with black hair.'

'I'm good with wigs. Psychodrama is an interest of mine.'

'He also knows you as Claire.'

Tracey nodded.

'When I was new to the life I foolishly went by my real name. I was naive.'

'Then you chose your third name – Tracey.'

'Yes.'

'Or the first letter of each name – Cat.'

She nodded.

Wayne took out the photographs of Rachel Hanson's death scene.

'I saw your books on cults,' he said. 'Do you recognise this setting?'

Wayne gave her the pictures. She looked at each one for a long time.

'I see nothing symbolic in them.'

She loosened her hair and shook it.

'I have to finish getting ready,' she said.

She ushered him towards the door.

'With your name you should be a writer,' she told him.

'I'm working on a play about my life,' Wayne said. 'It's called *A Comedy of Errors* by W Shakespeare.'

Tracey Holroyd's eyes twinkled momentarily, but they still held too many grey clouds.

EIGHTEEN

Kate sat in the third-floor reception area waiting for Juliet Bromage. For several minutes she watched as the woman on the desk, Mary Curtis, handled telephone calls with an effective blocking technique. Kate and Mary occasionally exchanged glances.

'You can go through now,' Mary said, eventually.

Kate walked through. Her first thought was that Juliet Bromage looked too small for her office. Juliet was sitting down, talking on the phone.

'I have to go now. I have an appointment.'

She hung up quickly, turned to Kate and waved to a seat.

'What can you do for me?' Juliet asked. 'You have five minutes as a favour to Wayne.'

By the time Kate replied, she was aware that ten seconds of her five minutes had already disappeared.

'I'm a gatekeeper for the community of sexology researchers,' Kate said. 'I have an archive of research materials which I can lay my hands on quickly. All matters of importance to condoms – condoms and risk, condoms and health, condoms and the law.'

'We're market-driven here, not research-driven.'

Kate hesitated for another few seconds, feeling the pressure of talking to the five-minute manager.

'Condoms and publicity,' Kate continued. 'Condoms and marketing campaigns. I can set up specific market research and I'll be going to the United States shortly. I can do market-driven research while I'm there.'

'Do you have a card?'

'I'll leave my details with your secretary.'

'OK. That's your pitch?'

'I'm not an expert on the business side, but I know something about condom research. I know about condoms sold with the St George Cross flag and the slogan "Lie Back and Think of England", and I know about National Condom Week. I can tell you about the woman who sued a condom manufacturer for the cost of raising her daughter because a condom was defective. I know about breakage rates, slippage rates, unintended pregnancy for different types of use, sensitivity . . .'

Juliet looked up and Kate saw her eyes for the first time.

'OK, that's your five,' Juliet said. 'Leave your details with Mary.'

As Kate stood up, she studied Juliet Bromage for a few more moments. Men probably saw her as an exciting mixture of intellect and independence. She came over as dynamic, exciting and a free spirit. Men saw her as how they wanted to be themselves. But Kate wasn't so sure about Juliet's stability. Kate thought Juliet was a frightened woman. Best take the threats seriously, Wayne, if only to calm her down.

Wayne entered Mackie's office, and Mackie held up a finger. Wayne waited as Mackie loaded a CCTV tape. When Wayne watched the screen he saw a dark-haired figure walk up to the main door of the Bromage building and push an envelope through the letter-box.

'Wednesday night at two-oh-two, androgyny came in view,' Wayne said. 'Posting an envelope through the door with gloved hands.'

'Female,' Mackie said.

'She's up late and she knows what to do. She is always side-on to the camera. Huddled up in baggy clothes. She could be male.'

'Female,' Mackie repeated.

'Indeterminate age,' Wayne said. 'We could get her height by one of us standing in that position when she comes into shot. Seeing where the top of our heads come to.'

'Five six.'

'You've done it already?'

'Sent a secretary.'

'Well done. Baggy Trousers may be the messenger. But we should try to identify her. Can you see anything individual?'

'No.'

'Is that an earring?'

'No.'

'No,' Wayne agreed. 'Let me watch her walk. Let me learn her gait.'

They played the tape twice more.

'Anything?' Mackie asked.

'Well, she doesn't walk like you, Mackie. No evidence of broken legs.'

Mackie laughed.

'She moves like a lightweight. Doesn't look well-built enough to threaten anybody. Just a messenger. But she knows what she's doing. At no point in the sequence does she face the camera. Her caution is threatening. We should take this seriously.'

Mackie nodded.

'Thanks, Mackie,' Wayne said. 'You're man of the match.'

Kate left the office feeling glad that she had come, even though she had no desire to work for Juliet Bromage. She had learned who Wayne was dealing with – a clever girl, a pretty girl, a rich girl, a girl who asked 'Where's the next spotlight?'

On the way out Kate left all her details with Mary Curtis on the desk.

'What is it that you do?' Mary asked.

'I study sexology.'

'What's that?'

'It means I study sexuality and sexual behaviour from all disciplines – the medical side, the psychology, the sociology, the geography, all the subjects.'

Mary looked at Kate plaintively as she held the paper with Kate's details.

'I also listen to people's problems,' Kate said. 'Please give me a call if you need to.'

The two women looked at each other longer than they should have done. Then Kate left.

Later, Wayne and Kate shared hot chocolate and conversation over Wayne's kitchen-table. It was nine-thirty in the evening and Wayne had just returned from football training. Kate was wearing jogging pants and a T-shirt with the slogan *Love and Passion – Condoms Back in Fashion*. Wayne stared at the lettering and Kate covered her front.

'I only dare wear this around the house or in bed,' she said.

'Do you know anything about cults?' Wayne asked.

'Are you thinking of leaving home?' Kate asked.

Wayne laughed. This woman could be fun, he thought. He took out the photographs of Rachel Hanson's funeral. 'Have a look at these,' he said.

'Ugh,' Kate said. 'It looks like a dead body in a cardboard coffin.'

'This is Rachel Hanson.'

Kate looked up sharply at Wayne.

'The footballer's wife?' she asked.

'The same.'

Kate held a hand to her chest.

'I thought that mission felt dangerous,' she said.

Kate studied the pictures some more.

'She looks as though she starved to death,' Kate said. 'Was she anorexic?'

'I don't know. What do you think of the scene?'

'Well, if it is a cardboard coffin, the police could probably trace the firm that made it.'

'If the police were involved.'

'Assuming that.'

'This afternoon I showed the pictures to a woman who knows about cults, and she said there was nothing symbolic in it.'

Kate continued to stare at the photographs.

'I can sense why she said that,' she said. 'But I know nothing about cults, except the sexual mores of certain ones.'

'That sounds interesting.'

'Not really. All cults have their own sexual systems. Some are known specifically for it.'

'Such as?'

'Oneida was one. That was in the mid-1800s. Everyone in the community was essentially married to each other, and the men practised *karezza*.'

'*Karezza*?'

'Or *coitus reservatus*. It's the art of prolonged intercourse where the man does not ejaculate but the woman can orgasm as much as she wants.'

'Do you have a reading list on that one?' Wayne asked.

Kate ignored him and put the photographs on the table.

'I think the letters to Juliet are to be taken seriously. May I see them?'

'I'll get them in a moment. What were you thinking about when you saw the photographs?'

'Loss and death.'

'I've been dealing with death since I was a child,' Wayne said. 'Ever since my grandparents came in my room and told me my parents were dead.'

'I didn't know that.'

'That explains everything, doesn't it?'

'I'm sorry,' Kate said. 'I didn't mean to . . .'

'A car crash. They were coming home from a night out. I was awake anyway. I could sense the babysitter was agitated. I heard her reaction to the phone call. Half an hour later my grandparents arrived. I knew what they were going to say.' Wayne thought for a while. 'Looking back, it must have been really hard for my grandparents. They had just lost their daughter and they had to tell me the news.'

'What a tragedy.'

'It's hard when you're not with loved ones when they die.'

'It's hard when you are with them too.'

'Was that your recent experience?'

'Yes,' said Kate. 'The image stays with you for life.'

'Yes.'

Wayne took Kate's hand as a few tears came slowly to her face. Wayne flicked a tissue-box towards Kate with his free hand.

'It's hard, but at least I know where I stand,' said Kate. 'I know my relationship with him is over. You don't know about Juliet, do you?'

'How do you mean?'

'You don't know whether it's over or not. Rationally you want it to be over. But when you see her you always want to replay it one more time.'

'I suppose.'

'You could decide that it is over.'

Kate let go of Wayne's hand and blew her nose.

'I would still see her at work,' Wayne said. 'She would still lure me in.'

'So you think she is controlling the relationship?'

'I think she controlled the other night. She wanted me to come round because her life was in danger, and yet she didn't seem frightened.'

'Perhaps that was because you were there,' Kate said.

'Maybe.'

'She looked scared when I saw her today.'

Kate picked up the photographs again.

'Do you think they've offered Rachel up as some sort of sacrifice?' Wayne asked.

'I don't know,' Kate said. 'What did the notes to Juliet say? The threatening notes.'

'Sorry. Let me get them.'

He was back in twenty seconds.

Juliet: you will die soon.

Juliet: death is on its way.

Juliet: you will definitely die soon.

'They used colons?' Kate asked.

'Yeah, pretty well educated, eh?'

'Who else reads Juliet's mail?'

'Mary Curtis, the administrator and office-manager.'

'You need a clear way to end the relationship with Juliet.'

'What do you suggest?'

'Make a note of the negative things and keep the list

with you. Write down how you always feel the morning after a night with Juliet. Are you seeing her tonight?'

'No. She's away for the weekend. Back Sunday lunchtime.'

Kate stared at the wall.

'It takes years to get to know a sexual partner and find out what he brings to the bedclothes,' said Kate. 'If I was thinking of sleeping with someone I would want to know more about him first. I wouldn't want it to be some opportunistic encounter for genital gymnastics.'

Wayne laughed.

'Genital gymnastics?' he said.

Kate blushed.

'You heard,' she said.

'I see sex as athletic and exciting and fun,' he said. 'But I also see it as a way of creating intimacy. I know it can be damaging, and I know it always affects a relationship. I know it always changes things.'

'Well, at least we agree about that,' Kate said.

Wayne looked up but Kate had gone to her room, leaving him to wonder what it all meant. He thought it over for a while.

'Well, Rover,' he said, even though the dog was upstairs. 'It's time I didn't take you out for your walk.'

NINETEEN

'Shaving,' Wayne told the telephone.

It was eight o'clock the next morning. Saturday. Wayne had a relatively uncluttered day with no home match to supervise.

'It's Jim Bailey, Wayne. I have a task for you.'

'Go ahead.'

Wayne put down the razor and went for a pen.

'We need a check on the background of a senior executive we're looking to hire.'

Bailey gave Wayne the details.

'I'll see what I can find,' Wayne said.

Curricula vitae were riddled with lies and omissions. He had discovered exaggerated salaries, fabricated qualifications and invented experience.

He finished shaving and made breakfast.

His phone rang again. He caught it on the second

ring, pleased at his speed off the mark. Not too stiff from the football training the previous night.

'Yeah?'

'Is that Wayne Shakespeare?'

'Yeah.'

'It's Tracey Holroyd.'

'How are you?'

'I'm fine. I'm phoning to say that I agree to do it.'

'Yes!' More snappy now. 'I'm sorry, my mind was elsewhere. I'm really pleased that you are agreeing to this.'

'I've thought about it,' she said, 'I've realised that I can't make it totally safe. But you must convey to him that he mustn't have expectations.'

Richard Bromage probably believed that his money bought him a lot of expectations. It usually did.

'Do you have a particular night in mind?' Wayne asked, aware that too many questions might change her decision.

'No, the sooner the better. I can be free most nights. Tonight if need be. I can cancel any appointments that interfere.'

'What about your college work?' he asked.

'I'll have to busk it,' she said, almost carefree.

'Let me know if we can help in any way.'

'I'd like some sort of contract,' she said. She was all business now. 'The name of a hotel. The times. The money. Some questions I would like answered.'

'All in the contract?'

'Yes.'

She gave Wayne more details of what she wanted.

'OK, I'll speak to Alec right now.'

'Oh, and one more thing.'

'Yes?'

'Put the contract in his real name.'

'I'll see what I can do.'

'You don't have to cover for him any longer – I know who he is. I've known since the start.'

Wayne thought about it. Yes, she could have worked it out from the information he gave her. He would have had no problem doing so.

'OK. What's the fifth letter of his surname?' he asked.

'The fifth letter?'

'Yeah.'

'A for apple. A for alpha. A for Alec. Come on, I know you work for the man.'

'OK. Where will you be for the rest of the day?'

'I'll be at home.'

'I'll get the contract to you as soon as I can.'

'Thanks.'

Wayne finished eating toast and preened himself for a trip to the Bromage Building. First he logged on to his home computer, typed up a short contract and printed off two copies.

At the Bromage Building Wayne tried to impress Mackie by walking jauntily on his toes. Then he took the stairs to the third floor.

'Ah, Mary,' he said, when he arrived. 'Fancy seeing you here. Any chance I can see Mister Richard? It's important.'

Mary buzzed through and spoke softly.

'He'll see you in half an hour,' she told Wayne. 'Will you wait here, in case it's sooner?'

'I will.'

Wayne waited. He used his phone to make more two quick calls about the executive Jim Bailey had been looking to hire. Then Richard Bromage opened his door and gave Wayne a wave. Wayne walked in, shut the door and came to the point.

'The woman called Claire . . .' Wayne said. Bromage looked up from his correspondence, so Wayne ran the sentence on: '. . . has agreed to spend a night with you. She would prefer sooner rather than later. From six at night to noon the next day. I had a hard time convincing her, so I suggest we seal it today. She might change her mind if you postpone it too long.' Wayne plucked two pieces of paper from his inside jacket pocket and handed them to Bromage. 'She wanted a contract. I drew up some details and typed them myself. No one else has seen them. I left out the date. She wants you to sign it, in your real name, date it, and then I can deliver it today. It says where and when, and it has some weird precautionary demands. Her idiosyncrasies. I think it's just because she doesn't know you that well.'

Richard Bromage had already read the contract with his customary speed. He looked up. His expression was part outrage, part embarrassment. Wayne was certainly seeing different sides of Richard Bromage. He must have read the two clauses prohibiting particular types of sex, the one on contraception and the one on listening to her story for an hour with no interruption.

'Why my real name?' he asked.

Wayne had to be careful here.

'It may be better to offer your real name rather than have her quiz you about it over the weekend. And I think she would be able to work it out anyway. She is very bright. And safety is her major concern. She'll feel safer if she knows that you can be traced if anything untoward happens.'

Richard Bromage looked at his diary.

'I can cancel an engagement for tonight,' he said. 'I'd rather meet her tonight. Saves me a sleepless night in anticipation.' He smiled. 'Well, you know what I mean.'

He wrote in the dates, signed the contract and handed it to Wayne, keeping the copy.

'Set it up,' he told Wayne. 'I'll deal with the payment. We'll put it through as consultancy.'

'I'll make her feel safe.'

'Do what you need to do,' Bromage said. 'We all need our health, Wayne. That's number one.'

Wayne knew then that Richard Bromage was dying sooner rather than later. Wayne envisaged chaos in the empire and corporate loggerheads.

Wayne simply nodded. He got up and walked to the door.

Bromage called him back.

'Keep this quiet,' he said. 'You know a few things about me, but I know a few things about you.' And then he smiled the youngest-looking smile Wayne had ever seen on his face. 'Well done,' he said.

Wayne returned his smile.

Have a nice night, he thought. But he kept his mouth

shut.

'Hey, Wayne,' Bromage called, in a tone of voice that Wayne had never heard before. 'When's that charity football game?'

'Tomorrow,' Wayne said.

Richard Bromage dismissed him with a wave and a smile.

Downstairs, Wayne took another photocopy of the signed contract and put the original in an envelope.

He put Tracey Holroyd's Oxford address on a label and stuck it on the front. He was about to phone for a courier but he remembered what the text book said: *sensitive documents should be carried by trusted staff.* Wayne tracked Mackie down and handed him the envelope with the contract. Mackie nodded and set off immediately with the strangest piece of erotica Wayne had ever seen.

TWENTY

'I need to earn some money,' Kate told Deborah as they walked along the river the following day. 'So I'm thinking about high-class prostitution.'

Deborah stopped walking. Turned and looked at Kate. Shook her head.

'I think you're too sensitive and too vulnerable,' Deborah said, 'especially at this time.'

They were on the River Thames towpath on the north side of Oxford. Deborah had asked that they do the walk. It was what Deb missed most about leaving Oxford. She had left the city for a relationship which hadn't worked out, but she had built up a client base as a sex therapist.

'I may be numb enough to do it,' Kate added.

'But you're not dumb enough to do it.'

'I've always envied you and your practical knowledge about sex.'

Deborah laughed.

'Yeah, practical knowledge,' Deborah said. 'That was just my way into it, Kate. Some of us are experiential learners and others are academics. I'm in the experiential camp. It also means we have different ways of working. I have to be more emotional, more intuitive, because I don't have the strong grounding that Teddy and others gave you. You're a book person. You're rational and analytical. I am not so good at that side. I would love to have your research background. It means you are calmer than me, more thoughtful, more considered. Please don't put that part of yourself at risk in an attempt to gain more experience.'

'I miss the physical contact too.'

'I know. But that's different. Being an escort helped my career in some ways, but it's made my personal life more difficult.'

'Watch out for the bike,' Kate said.

The two women separated as they saw a young male rowing coach cycling fast and one-handed towards them on the towpath. The youth held a megaphone to his mouth, yelling instructions. A women's eight zipped along in the water at a similar pace to the bike.

'Keep going, keep going,' the youth shouted. 'I want to see you working your bollocks off.'

One or two of the girls in the boat started smiling.

'Metaphorically speaking,' the coach added.

The crew went to pieces and dissolved into laughter. So did Kate and Deborah.

'Classic,' Kate said.

'That's what I miss about Oxford,' said Deborah, as

they walked on. 'The uncouth and the couth. You stick to the couth, Kate. Now tell me about this interesting case.'

That Sunday a team of ex-professional footballers, including Wayne, Mackie and Bob Blazer, won their charity game seven-three. Afterwards, the ex-professionals' dressing-room was lively. Everyone talked at once.

'We've made some money for charity. Over a thousand spectators.'

'Does that include our two strikers?'

'Hey, Wayne, you're still good in the air,' said Bob Blazer. 'Take the air away and you're not much good.'

'Shut up, Mackie,' someone said, because Mackie hadn't said a word. Mackie laughed.

'I'm first in the shower,' Wayne told his team-mates. 'I'll be needed at the press conference as man of the match.'

Someone tossed a boot at him. Wayne caught it and lobbed it back.

'Quiet everybody,' Blazer yelled. 'I've got a team talk to give.'

Everyone hushed, especially Mackie.

'Listen to me,' Bob Blazer said, although they were all listening already. 'Listen, lads. LISTEN. I don't want to dwell on all the things you did wrong so I won't. Instead I want to tell you something important. Try to remember it for the next ten minutes.'

'Listen, everybody,' someone shouted.

'Listen to your gaffer.'

'There's a buffet in the pub across the road,' said Blazer.

Bob Blazer dodged a hailstorm of useless objects.

'I love it when you talk tactics, Bob.'

'He doesn't even tell you the name of the pub,' said Crossy. 'What kind of a manager doesn't tell you the name of the pub?'

'I think it's called the Red Lion,' Blazer shouted.

'Aren't they all?' someone said.

They were laughing even harder when they saw the pub was called the Golden Lion.

'What kind of manager gets the name of the pub wrong?' someone said.

'The ex-wife's story interests me,' said Deborah, after Kate had summarized her theory of what had happened between Bruce Venn and Fiona Coates' daughter.

'Me too,' said Kate. They were sitting on a tree stump.

'He went to her room during the night and screwed her?'

'Yes.'

'Holly Venn told you that?'

'Yes.'

'Not Bruce?'

'No. She told me.'

'It would be nice to talk to the fifteen-year-old.'

'I don't think there's any chance of that,' Kate said.

'I could pose as someone who is researching assault victims.'

'I think not.'

'You're so ethical.'

'My downfall.'

'I hope the young girl is having therapy,' Deborah added.

'I hope so too. Sometimes I worry that the mother's reactions might have been more traumatising than the actual event.'

'And the arrival of police.'

'That too.'

'Did you say that the mother pulled him off?'

'I think that was in her statement,' Kate said.

Deborah laughed.

'Pulled him off the young girl?' Deborah asked again.

'Yes. Phoned the police. Told her not to wash.'

'Very strategic.'

'Maybe she had been through it herself,' Kate suggested.

'Maybe. But it's not a good post-coital precedent. No cuddling.'

'No "that was great, darling".'

'No revelations about the past.'

'No "Did you come?"'

'No "How was it for you?"'

'Could you speak to the ex-wife, please?' Kate said. 'Maybe talk to her on the phone? Test my theory for me. There's money in the kitty.'

'That's where your reading is so good. I couldn't have come up with a theory like you, but I'd be really interested to test it.'

'Thanks, Deb.'

'But there's something else,' Deborah said.

'What's that?'

'The young girl. If Bruce Venn had staying power, like his ex-wife suggested, especially in the middle of the night, then did he last as long with the fifteen-year-old? Did he last half an hour with her?'

'Or maybe he was so excited at her young body that he came quickly?'

'That would disprove your theory.'

'Good point,' said Kate.

'If he did last half an hour, why didn't she shout for help?'

'Another good point. Maybe she was enjoying it.'

'And if he did last half an hour, your theory would hold up.'

'It might mean that he wasn't distinguishing between the two,' Kate said, getting excited.

'There's something more important.'

'What's that?'

'The solicitor, what's his name?'

'Jeremy Spooner.'

'Well, Jeremy Spooner will have a good reason to ask the question in court: how long was he inside you became he came?'

'I would have to be sure first. I would hate to put the young girl through the ordeal if it was only going to cause damage.'

'It wouldn't come to that.'

'You think the mother would withdraw the case?' Kate asked.

'Or the police would decide that it was too difficult to prosecute. Let me talk to his ex-wife first.'

'Holly Venn?'

'Yes.'

'OK. Are you happy to do it by phone?'

'It's how I do a lot of my work now. Thirty per cent of my clients are outside my area. Having the magazine column helps. When I get to fifty per cent I'll be able to move anywhere in the country.'

'I can hardly see you living in a backwater.'

'Oh, no. I still want some experiential learning about sex. In fact I wouldn't mind Bruce Venn's number.

'Get away with you, Deb.'

They laughed.

Kate spoke to Holly Venn by phone and explained what she would like to do. 'It's just that I need a second opinion on something and Deborah is very experienced,' she added.

'It sounds interesting,' said Holly Venn.

'You can talk privately and confidentially to her. But you can ask her questions if you wish. Anything you like. We are trying to understand Bruce rather than you.'

'Right. I'll look forward to hearing from her.'

'Thanks, Holly. Can I just ask one question before you go?'

'Of course.'

'You said that you moved into the big bedroom at the end of the corridor.'

'Yes.'

'Not the small bedroom next to Bruce's room?'

'No. Not that one.'

'He didn't come to you when you were in the bedroom at the end of the corridor?'

'No, but . . . '

'But.'

'I was in the small one for a short time. One or two nights. When I first moved out of the master bedroom. That was when we had that great sex in the night. It was great but it confused me. That was why I went further away, to the other end of the corridor.'

'Thank you.'

It was late on Sunday night and Wayne was lying alone in Juliet's bed, naked and sleepy. Immediately after sex Juliet had risen silently and disappeared to the bathroom as part of her routine to fight her cystitis.

Wayne was suddenly restless. He wondered what he was doing in Juliet's bed.

Juliet returned and lay against him. He detached himself slowly but Juliet followed. He sensed that she was restless too. Maybe she was unsettled by jet lag or threatening notes.

'Do you want some water?' Juliet asked.

'No thanks,' Wayne replied, but he did really.

Juliet got out of bed again and Wayne admired the rear of her body in the moonlight before she slipped into her robe and flicked back her hair. They were on the top floor of her house, too high to need curtains, but she had to go down two floors to the kitchen.

While she was away, Wayne decided to leave. He didn't know why. Was it because Juliet's cat would disturb him at six o'clock, pawing his shoulder and humming in his ear? Or was it the imbalance of their sleep patterns? He couldn't explain it. He just knew he wanted to be alone.

Juliet returned with two glasses of water.

'I brought you one anyway,' she said.

They sipped water, both awake now, not touching.

'I want to talk to you about Buck Hanson,' she said. Stroking him. Her voice was excited.

'What about?'

'I want a man with safe hands for my condoms.'

That was the nearest Juliet had ever come to making a joke.

'Why talk to me about Buck Hanson?'

'I hear you have influence with him.'

'I would guess that you have far more influence with him than me.'

'I was told that you could persuade him into anything.'

Wayne couldn't imagine Mackie saying anything to Juliet about Buck Hanson. He couldn't imagine Mackie saying anything to anyone about anything. It must have come from Buck Hanson himself. Who else?

'Who do you think sent you the threatening letters?' Wayne asked.

'Don't quiz me, Wayne.'

'But it's all right for you to quiz me, Juliet?'

Wayne's comment was greeted by silence.

'Was it definitely Robin Hookes who sent you the threat?' Wayne asked.

Silence.

'Buck Hanson?'

Silence.

'Me?'

Silence.

'Somebody else?'

Silence.

More silence followed. The undercurrent was anger. Wayne thought of how he enjoyed sharing silences with Kate Park. This silence felt very different.

'What do you want with Buck Hanson?' Wayne asked.

'That's none of your business,' she said.

Wayne was back to being the paid help. The distance between them increased.

'I see.' Wayne raised himself on to his elbow. 'So Buck Hanson is just a good commercial proposition to you? Just another good idea. Like buying football clubs. Or promoting a condom business.'

The bedroom was a boardroom now.

'Well, you could take a helicopter view of the condom business,' Wayne said, 'then organise a few meetings, pre-meetings, breakfast meetings and toilet-visit-in-the-night meetings.'

Juliet had pushed buttons that connected Wayne to his perversity. Or maybe he had pushed hers first. He should have backed off then, but he fancied a tirade.

'You could host international corporate pre-warm-up meetings in executive condom lounges before football matches,' Wayne continued.

While Juliet reddened and fumed, Wayne prepared the next stage of his ridiculous monologue. He couldn't remember later what else he had said. He couldn't recall the stick she had given him in return. Later he recalled only the mood. They had locked into something hostile with no middle ground and, eventually, their only way out was to return to the frenzied physicality of sex. They didn't make love, they wrestled it. They squeezed the affection out of each other and hammered it through the mattress. They threw in a spot of trampolining and synchronised swimming, and after their climaxes they had very little energy for anger. It was a victory for sport, and very nearly a defeat for the condom business.

And then the phone call came. Juliet reached for the bedside telephone. Her breasts were streamlined in the moonlight.

'Oh I see,' she said. 'Tomorrow . . . yes . . . well, if you have to . . . give me your number . . . wait for ten minutes . . .'

By then Wayne was wearing his clothes.

He regretted it all later. Had he stayed the night, everything would have been different. Education took so many forms and one lesson was never to argue in bed – the place is too sacred.

On his way out, Wayne passed the cat in the hallway and the cat spoke to him in catspeak.

Row . . . row . . . row . . . row . . . row . . .

Or so Wayne heard as he slammed the front door.

TWENTY-ONE

The next day started as a sunny morning, but there were people in anoraks and overcoats who had not predicted the upswing in temperature. Wayne saw a girl on a bicycle peel off her jacket as she cycled along. She stuffed the jacket in the bicycle basket and grasped the handlebars again.

Wayne loosened his muscles, stiff from playing football, by jogging to the delicatessen. His grandfather had always told him that the best way to get unstiff was by doing what got you stiff in the first place. He bought some croissants and jogged home. Kate was in her room and her door was closed.

The telephone rang at eight-thirty. Mary Curtis was the caller.

'Have you heard anything from Juliet this morning?' she asked.

'No, should I?'

Wayne was aware that Mary knew about Juliet and him. All those meetings in Juliet's office with do-not-disturb instructions. It must have been obvious.

'She said she would be in at seven-thirty,' Mary said.

'Have you tried her mobile?'

'Yes, there's no reply. The voice mail is on. I've tried every other number I know.'

'Has she got meetings?'

'The first one is at nine.'

'She'll make that. Probably with a minute to spare before nine. Leave it for half an hour, Mary.'

Wayne had an image of Juliet sleeping. But Juliet never slept in. Surely she had not gone out again after Wayne had left.

Wayne made his last phone call about the executive Jim Bailey wanted to hire. He added two sentences to his report and emailed it to Bailey.

Then Mary Curtis was on the phone again, her anxiety raised.

'There's still no sign of Juliet,' she said.

Wayne looked at the clock. It was exactly nine o'clock.

'Still no sign?' Wayne asked.

'Nothing. I've tried everything I know. She would never come in this late.'

'I'll go round to her house.'

'Would you?'

'Yes.'

Wayne sprinted towards Juliet's home. Her house was in a select area of North Oxford where residents ate

quail's eggs and drove Volvos. When Wayne arrived he
saw that Juliet's car was still there.

Wayne lumbered towards the front door and rang the
bell. No reply. The curtains were closed. He walked
around as far as he could and saw her bicycle was also
there. He looked through a gap in the front-room
curtains. Her mobile phone was on charge. This did not
look good, but he had been in situations like this before
and there had been a logical explanation. Juliet was not
a person to worry about ordinarily, but Wayne was
worried now. Especially when he heard Juliet's cat speak
to him plaintively from inside the house.

Wow . . . wow . . . wow . . . wow . . .

Wayne remembered that the next-door neighbour
kept a spare key for Juliet's house. He ran there and rang
the bell. The woman opened the door as far as the chain
allowed.

'Yes?' she asked.

'My name's Shakespeare. We've met before – at
Juliet's. Next door.'

'Yes?'

'We're all very concerned about Juliet. She's not
answering her door and we're worried because she hasn't
shown up at work. It's unlike her. Do you still have a key
to her house?'

'She might be in the bath?'

'Did Juliet ask you to feed the cat this morning?'

'No.'

'Look, it may be easier if you phone the police and tell
them I'm breaking in. Just phone the police.'

'Wait,' she said. She opened the door. 'I have her keys. I'll get them.'

'Good.'

She was quick. She handed Wayne a set of keys and this time he went through a gap in the hedge he had spotted while waiting. The neighbour followed.

Yale to the left. Chubb to the right. Funny how you remember these things. Memories of late evenings came flooding back.

The door gave two inches and then stopped. Wayne shouted Juliet's name. No reply.

'The chain's on,' he told the neighbour. 'I'm going to break in. Can you witness what I'm doing?'

Wayne found a suitable tool on his multi-purpose knife and prised the chain bracket away from the doorframe. He walked in and felt the emptiness. He looked in the downstairs rooms. First the lounge, where they had made love for the first time, tumbling around on cushions tossed randomly from the couch to the carpet. Then the kitchen-diner where he had been seduced over salmon and champagne, and the cat had approved.

He called her name again. No answer. The cat came to Wayne and rubbed against his legs.

Wow . . . wow . . . wow . . . wow . . .

The cat led him to the stairs.

Wayne took them two at a time.

At the top of the stairs he sensed that she was close.

And then he found her – lying in a foetal position on the floor near the stairs that led to the attic room. At first he thought she was asleep. Her eyes were open, but that always happened when she was asleep. The eyes were without curiosity. Dull. Staring blindly at nothing. Wayne did what he had sometimes done in the morning. Moved a finger near her eye. This time her eye flickered. She was awake. Sort of. She pulled herself tighter into a ball.

He rested a hand on her hip and spoke gently to her.

'You're safe,' he said. 'It's going to be all right. We'll look after you.'

Her short-sleeve robe left her with decency, but her body was tight. Was she ill? Had she had a stroke? Was she injured? Had there been an intruder? Wayne's first thought was to phone Kate for help. But Kate would be teaching.

'What's happened, Juliet?' Wayne asked. 'Tell me what's wrong. What's hurting? Did you fall?'

Juliet didn't speak.

He touched parts of her body to see if she winced.

'Where does it hurt?'

Juliet stayed silent.

'Mister Shakespeeah? Mister Shakespeeah?'

The next-door neighbour's refined voice shook Wayne from his thoughts. He trod the stairs to ground level. The cat ran in front of him and tried to trip him up.

'She's upstairs, Mrs Owen. On the floor. I think she might have fallen. I'm going to make the emergency call.'

Mrs Owen sat on a chair in the hallway.

'Oh, dear,' she said. 'That happened to my friend. She fell downstairs. She was ever so lucky. She was black and blue for a month. The doctor wouldn't send her to hospital because they didn't have a radiologist on duty, so . . .'

'I'll phone from upstairs,' Wayne said. His voice hushed her nervous chatter. He phoned and gave all the necessary details.

He went upstairs and looked at Juliet again. He tried to remember what he knew about dealing with such scenes: don't make any assumptions; don't touch anything; was there a crime? Had someone else been there? Was it all connected to the threatening notes?

Wayne let his eyes record the scene for posterity – the position of the doors, whether the windows were open or closed, which lights were on. Any sign of activity? Any strong smells like smoke or gas?

Wayne went to the back door. Only one lock was on, there was no key in the lock and the bolts were off. Had she done that for Wayne, forgetting that he didn't have a key? No, wait a moment, there was no spare key on the hook where Juliet normally kept it.

Wayne studied more of the scene. There was no sign of a fight, no sign of a weapon, but he hadn't been up to the attic. Was this a crime scene?

Don't turn on the water. Don't drink. Don't smoke. Don't use towels. Don't touch anything.

Don't touch the phone.

Too late. He had forgotten about that one.

Wayne used his mobile phone to phone Jim Bailey's mobile. Wayne could hear the noise of traffic in the background when Bailey answered.

'Yeah?' Bailey said.

'Jim, it's Wayne Shakespeare.'

'Wayne, you've done a great job on that executive search.'

'Search?' Wayne was dazed.

'Richard is delighted. I've phoned him. He wants to congratulate you. I'll . . .'

'WAIT.' Wayne suddenly heard himself shouting. The coarse roar of a footballer on the field. 'Park the car, Jim. Go somewhere quieter.'

Go somewhere safer, Wayne thought.

Wayne held on while some of the white noise fell away.

'What's the matter?' Bailey asked.

'I'm at Juliet's house. I have some bad news. Juliet Bromage is injured or ill. She's at the foot of the top stairs and she's totally out of it. Something has happened during the night.'

Jim was silent.

'I'm serious, Jim,' Wayne said. 'I've called the paramedics. We have to deal with it.'

Then Wayne had thoughts about what Juliet meant to Jim. A surrogate daughter. A goddaughter.

'What happened?' Jim was struggling to talk. He was genuinely shocked.

'I don't know for sure. She didn't come in to work when expected. I came out to her house. I'm still here. The paramedics are on their way. Juliet is lying on the first floor at the bottom of the stairs to the attic. She looks bruised and catatonic. I'd rather not speculate. Do you want to tell Mister Richard, or shall I?'

Wayne heard Bailey exhale.

'I don't know,' said Bailey.

'I think you should do it, Jim,' Wayne continued. 'I

248

could be here for a while, and news could get back to Mister Richard from some other channel.'

'Yeah, I'll do it quickly.'

'Just tell him the bare details. I'll be in to explain more as soon as I can.'

'I'll go back and tell him now. I'm only five minutes away from the office.'

As Wayne hung up the phone he couldn't help but think of the irony of Richard Bromage's life. You find a former lover and your daughter has a setback. The game of life always ends in a draw. Birth puts you one up and death equalises.

Kate Park was laughing in front of her class. Most of the students were laughing too. They were laughing at things they were normally too professional to laugh at.

'I once said that contraceptives should be used on every conceivable occasion,' one student said, following up the other stories. 'It took me ages to work out why they were laughing.'

Kate was so pleased to be laughing. Her laughter muscles felt stiff and unused. She shouldn't have worried about not having enough examples of double meaning or misunderstanding. The class took over with their own stories and the room held camaraderie.

Yet she had spent a disturbed night. Wayne had come in loudly about midnight and she had woken for the first time. Then she had disturbed herself around dawn, feeling she was unprepared for the class.

'There are expressions that indicate impotence,' Kate said, 'such as "no toothpaste in the tube" or "no lead in your pencil". Occasionally you come across a new expression that you have to work out. Some may be obvious when you think about them, like "putting lipstick on his dipstick" but others may be harder . .'

'Harder,' someone said.

They all laughed.

'I remember one woman telling me that she was fed up of having oral sex rammed down her throat,' someone said.

'I've remembered one,' said someone else. 'The teacher explained to her young class that the man puts his seed in the woman and one girl thought it meant that he threw in some soil and planted it like you do in the garden.'

Kate was getting ready to summarise the key points about miscommunication and misunderstanding. She had also been thinking that she would like to know some of these women as friends, but she did not have enough energy to start friendships. It was a strange paradox. She really needed her friends, but she did not like bothering them. She hadn't yet told most of her friends where she was living. Everything about her life felt temporary.

Wayne entered the Bromage building and went straight to the third floor. He was in the elevator when the implications dawned. Life in the building would not be the same again. The whole organisation was in a state of flux. Richard Bromage was seriously ill, Jim Bailey was pulling out, and Juliet Bromage was seriously out of action.

On the third floor, Mary Curtis looked as though

she'd spent the night on a bus. Wayne debated whether her serious approach to life had been right after all. Maybe humour was misjudged, a lighthearted way of coping. Mary caught Wayne's eyes and stared through him. Her finishing school was too good for her to ask any questions.

'Mr Shakespeare is on his way in,' she said to someone out of sight as Wayne walked purposefully through. He knocked and walked in to Richard Bromage's office. The head man was ending a telephone conversation.

Bromage hung up and looked at Wayne. Wayne saw shock in Bromage's eyes. Jim Bailey, sitting on his left, showed similar bemusement.

The seriousness of the men's expressions told Wayne that he had better get this right. Wayne sat down, nodded clinically to Jim Bailey, and gave the details efficiently and effectively. No attempts at humour. No digressions. Wayne told Richard Bromage how Mary Curtis had been worried and how he had visited Juliet's home. He described the scene.

'I'm sorry to be the bearer of such bad news,' Wayne said. 'The paramedics asked me if there was any history or depression or self-harm. I told them I didn't think so. There was no sign that she had taken anything.' Wayne was feeling bad that he had not responded immediately to Mary's concern. He felt most guilty about not spending the whole of the night with Juliet.

'What do you think happened?' asked Jim Bailey.

'It's hard to say at the moment. I've sent Mackie to the hospital, so we should get to know as soon as possible.

She needs examining. She can't speak at present. It's like a trauma or a catatonia. But there was probably something to set it off. Either she fell downstairs or was knocked about.'

Wayne had lots of theories. There was no sign of forced entry but she could quite easily have disturbed an intruder. Or she could have let someone in and something might have happened between them. Most likely she got up in the night to do something, didn't switch on the light, missed the top step and fell headlong.

'We'll have to wait until she can tell us,' Wayne added.

They nodded. Wayne could see the frustration in Richard Bromage's face. He wanted an answer immediately.

'How had she seemed to you lately?' asked Jim Bailey.

'She was no different from normal most of the time. Excited about work. But something was troubling her. She had been receiving threatening notes.'

'Notes?' Jim Bailey asked.

'Three notes. Threatening her with death. I set up some protection for her. One of us – Mackie or I – would go round there or cruise by to see she wasn't being stalked. I saw her last night. She was in good form. She had things to look forward to. She seemed safe.'

But that was not all the story. Wayne wondered if it showed.

Richard Bromage shook his head from side to side. He looked distraught. Wayne suddenly remembered that Bromage would have spent a night with Claire (known to Wayne as Tracey) and now he had to face up to his daughter's problems. One had probably restored his zest for life, the other would reduce it.

'The cat will need looking after,' Wayne said, and he suddenly felt very emotional.

'It will be dealt with,' Jim Bailey said. 'We'll manage it from here.'

It was time for Wayne to slip away.

'Is there anything else, Wayne?' Jim asked.

'No.'

'Get out,' Richard Bromage said. 'Get out.'

The room was suddenly quiet. A layer of guilt rose from the floor like dry ice at a party. Wayne wasn't sure how much of it was his own.

He slipped away.

That evening Kate Park lay on her bed at Wayne's house. Her mind was buzzing. She was tired but excited because her teaching had gone well.

She heard Wayne come in. At first she was unsure it was him. He was much louder than usual, even louder than last night. Clumsier perhaps. Then she reassured herself that it really was him. But his entry disturbed her mood.

The door banged.

She looked at her clock.

21.00.

TWENTY-TWO

After slamming the door Wayne walked through to the lounge and ignored Rover. He picked up an ornament he'd always hated, juggled it a few times, stared hard at an image of himself in the mirror and threw the ornament at the wall. It missed the mirror by a foot.

'Wayne,' said a barely audible voice behind him.

It was Kate. She was wearing a dressing gown.

'Are you OK?' Kate asked.

'No, my aim's a bit off,' he said. He switched on a smile.

'Has something happened?' Kate asked.

'Yes. Juliet's in hospital.'

'Oh, no. I'm sorry. What's happened?'

They stood and looked at each other for a while.

'Come to the kitchen and tell me about it,' Kate said. 'I'll make tea. Then we can talk.'

'OK,' Wayne said. He patted the papier-mâché dog. 'Sorry to scare you, Rover.'

Over tea Wayne described the scene at Juliet's house. How she lay and where she was. He told Kate what he had felt at the time. Disbelief was followed by a tide of connection. Part of him wanted to hold Juliet. The rest was a vow to himself that this tortuous stop-start relationship was definitely over and he was free to continue his life.

He told Kate about the mixed emotions that had hit him during the day.

'I was with Juliet last night,' Wayne said. 'We had a row and I walked out. I think someone was coming to the house. She was meeting someone. I should have stayed.'

'Don't blame yourself.'

'It doesn't look very good. Me having a row with Juliet and her turning up at the foot of the stairs. I'm probably number one suspect. Richard Bromage and Jim Bailey have pushed me out of the loop.'

'I heard you come in last night. I remember the time.'

'That might be useful.'

'Not to my sleep.'

Wayne looked at his watch.

'Where's the day gone?' he said.

'What have you been doing?'

'I went to see Richard Bromage and Jim Bailey, did my day's work, and then I walked the streets. The city was vibrant. Young men and women in evening dress were rolling drunkenly on each other's shoulders.'

'Oxford,' said Kate.

'It's supposed to be princely and beautiful, but they don't tell you about the homelessness and the nurses and teachers in poverty.'

They sipped tea. Kate was alert now, tall, calm and attentive. Her face was fuller, her broad lips redder and her eyes wide-awake.

'Sorry to disturb your relaxation time,' he said.

She gave him an amused look.

'I don't have any relaxation time,' she said. 'I catch up on sleep later.'

'Are you all right?'

'Your story is bringing back my memories of Teddy's death.' She composed herself. 'Tell me about Juliet,' Kate said. Her voice was peaceful now.

'She feared for her life,' Wayne said. 'I didn't believe her.'

'But you took the threats seriously,' Kate said.

'Something disturbed me about the scene,' Wayne said. 'I can't work out what it was.'

'That you weren't with her? You are left wondering what had happened. And maybe that is like an extension of your relationship with her.'

'In what way?'

'There is never an ending to your relationship. I think that's why you kept going back. You had no clear account of the relationship.'

Wayne must have looked puzzled. Kate went on.

'I don't know Juliet – I only met her for five minutes – but I suspect nobody knew her well,' Kate said. 'She's attractive to men, dynamic, alive, independent, and she needed fathering. She desperately needed loving. But she was very elusive. Nothing about her was consistent. She was making it all up as she went along. Like we all do to some extent, I suppose.'

'Yeah, I know.'

'Well, you never knew what was happening to her when you weren't with her. That was true of her life. And it's certainly true now. You don't know what happened after you left last night.'

'So I need to find out what happened? I think someone was there. The back door key wasn't where it usually was. I went out the front door. Damn, damn, damn.'

'What's the matter?'

'I should have tried 1471 before I called the paramedics. To see who phoned her just before I left.'

'Or, instead of finding out what happened, just accept that you will never know what Juliet was doing when she wasn't with you,' Kate said.

'But why did she have to sabotage our relationship? Why did she have to sabotage other relationships? Why did she go for Buck Hanson when he clearly had a wife?'

'Maybe she has no faith in emotional security.'

'Juliet's not someone who is attuned to other people's emotional position.'

'People from her background have an inability to empathise, and executives daren't empathise, particularly with the people who have to implement their ideas.'

'You didn't like her either?'

'I don't know her well enough to judge.'

'You seem to know some of what I'm feeling at the moment.'

'I've been to a similar place.'

Wayne looked at Kate.

'A gentle sentence can seduce more than the fiercest of touches,' he said.

Kate turned her head away. She got up and walked over to reset the kettle.

'Your job is more important than mine,' Wayne said.

'Which job?'

'What you do. How would you describe it? What's the common theme with all that you do?'

Kate thought for a while.

'What I try to do and what I do may be two different things. I try to tinker gently with bodies and minds to bring some improvement in people's lives, improvements in health, emotion or sexual fulfillment, but the people have to want to make those changes. Sometimes I wonder if that is better achieved from outside the system than inside it.'

'I wonder that too.'

Kate shook her head.

'It's not just Juliet that's a mystery,' Kate said. 'The whole of modern-day life is a mystery story. The best we can do is make a bit of sense of our personal stuff.'

'How do I make sense of all this – Rachel Hanson missing presumed dead, Juliet Bromage mysteriously traumatized?'

'No word from the hospital?'

'Mackie phoned to say they were doing tests. There are no obvious broken bones. She is not speaking.' Wayne sighed. 'I was supposed to be looking after her last night.'

'She was used to looking after herself.'

'When I found her she looked so unbalanced and awkward. That was so unlike her. She was like a dancer. She was fit. She swam and did aerobics. What did you call it the other day – genital gymnastics?'

'Yes. Or coital choreography.'

'Yeah. She was never clumsy. But she looked awkward this morning. It was out of character.'

Wayne stared at the wall. He stayed like that for several minutes, until he felt Kate's hand on his shoulder.

'Relationships are funny things,' she said. 'Two people leap out of a plane and halfway down one asks the other if they've brought the parachutes along.'

Wayne looked at Kate.

'You're such a beautiful person,' he said. 'And I bet you carry a spare parachute.'

'Teddy carried one for me,' she said.

She squeezed his shoulder.

They were interrupted by the doorbell.

'It'll be for you,' Kate said.

'I don't want to see anyone.'

Kate went to the front door. She was still wearing her dressing gown.

Jeremy Spooner was on the doorstep. He took a stride into the house before she had thought about inviting him in.

Kate shepherded Spooner into the lounge and dared him to sit on a cushion. He chose to stand.

'I was expecting a report by now, Kate,' he said. 'And

I was hoping that you would get back to me about our other matter.'

Kate was aware that Spooner was talking loudly. Better to talk loudly here than in her room. She suspected that he'd been drinking.

'There's a loose end to tie up,' Kate said. 'I need to find out more.'

'I just wanted to see you again.' He looked around. 'Can we go to your room?'

'I'd rather stay in the lounge.'

'Come on, Kate.'

He reached for her hand. Kate stepped back. He held her by the arm. Roughly. She felt vulnerable, still in her dressing gown.

'Come on,' he said. 'Where's your room?'

'Please let go,' Kate said, more loudly.

Wayne arrived on the scene after taking the stairs two at a time. Spooner let go of Kate's arm.

'Perfect timing,' Wayne said. 'I've been looking for someone to hit all day. You look just right. Thanks for coming.'

Wayne stood with his hands on his hips.

'I'd have you in court as fast as God made the world,' Jeremy Spooner said.

'Is this your solicitor friend?' Wayne asked Kate.

'Teddy's solicitor,' Kate said.

'He won't be anyone's if he doesn't get out of my house now.'

'Hey, that's a threat,' Spooner said.

'Wayne,' said Kate.

'Out,' Wayne said. 'Before I count ten. Or you won't hear the next count to ten.'

Jeremy Spooner took two paces towards the door with vengeance on his face. Then he stopped and turned to Kate.

'I'm surprised at you, Kate,' Spooner said. 'You can do far better than him. I came to offer you a freelance job – as a sexology advisor on a film.'

Spooner slammed the front door as he left.

'I should send the front door to a refuge for abused doors,' Wayne said. He looked at Kate. 'What did he mean?'

'I'm not sure,' Kate said.

She walked towards her room.

'Kate,' Wayne said.

Kate turned calmly.

'I'm going to dress,' she said. 'Then we can talk.'

Five minutes later Wayne and Kate reconvened at the kitchen table.

'I apologise,' Wayne said. 'I hope I didn't mess up your evening.'

'No. Probably saved it. I just hope he pays me for the work I've done. He said he had another job for me, so I'll have to stay well in with him.'

'OK.'

'Thanks for trying to help with Spooner, but I would have dealt with it without you. I just need to be clear with him.'

'I know, I know. I've given the wrong impression to Spooner. He thinks you're with me, but you're not. I shouldn't have interfered.'

'Well, you meant well. I'll write him a note to say that I'm interested in any jobs.'

'How's the case you are working on for him?'

'I'm still working on it. It's much more complicated than I first thought. I've asked a friend to talk to someone who's crucial to the case. It might take her a day or two to get round to it. Something you said a while ago helped me construct a theory. I'll tell you the story of the case when I know it. But now I think we should talk about Claire, Rachel and Rachel's husband.'

'Let's decide on a name for Claire,' Wayne said. 'I think of her as Tracey Holroyd.'

'Let's call her Tracey as much as possible.'

'And that is how she presents herself at university – as Tracey,' Wayne said. 'You've started with three people – Tracey Holroyd, Rachel Hanson and Buck Hanson. Juliet is connected to those three too.'

'How is she connected to Tracey?'

'Through her father, who knew Tracey as Claire. Her father has just made contact with Tracey again. Are we talking in confidence here?'

'Of course.'

'Thanks.'

'And you are central, too, Wayne, because you met Tracey through the rag campaign.'

'And I found her again for Richard Bromage.'

'And you helped Tracey to fake-kidnap Buck Hanson.'

'And Rachel disappeared while Hanson was gone.'

'It must all be connected somehow,' Kate said.

Between them, over the next half an hour, they constructed a story. Tracey (known as Claire) was a high-class escort whose men had included Richard Bromage (a long time ago and then again this week). As Tracey she was building a more mainstream life as a psychologist. She was also a rag week organiser helping to raise money for local charities such as adult literacy, mental health and abused women. Tracey had lured away Buck Hanson on a kidnap stunt. Hanson was probably another of Tracey's clients, because he had heard of her as 'The Cat'. Other football club personnel might have come across Tracey in that guise.

Juliet Bromage had been threatened by notes. An androgynous figure, probably female, had hand-delivered the third note around 2am on Thursday.

'Buck Hanson is central,' Wayne said. 'He was with Tracey on Friday night and with either Tracey or Juliet on Saturday night. But Buck's not literate enough to send notes to Juliet. Not notes with colons in them. The notes are more likely to be from Robin Hookes, Juliet's ex-husband, who was embarrassed by her sacking him. If I was Hookes I would probably want to threaten Juliet.'

'I'd like to talk to Hookes,' Kate said.

'I'll give you his address.'

'Thanks. I need to go to bed now. You should get an early night too, Wayne.'

'No, I won't settle. I think I'll go out.' He looked at Kate. 'I want to go somewhere anonymous and think about things. What have you got planned for tomorrow?'

'Go and see Hookes. Meeting at the university. I'm meeting someone early evening. And I'll try to book a night shift with the Nurse Bank.'

'Best to see Hookes early. He's one for the pub once it gets to lunchtime.'

They said goodnight.

Half an hour later Wayne sat in a busy town centre pub and stared at the wall. He thought of a T-shirt he'd seen on a young man in Oxford: *No job. No money. No girlfriend. But I'm in a band.*

He remembered a place called No Man's Heath he'd been to with his grandfather. If he listened to his memory he could still hear his grandfather's voice: *Come on, lad. Show them what you can do. You can get through anything. It's just another challenge. All it needs is thought and strength.*

He focused for five minutes on how he had overcome all those setbacks of the past. The insecurity gradually evaporated and left in its place a rich array of choices. He was back in charge of his destiny. He could go in any direction from No Man's Heath – west to Staffordshire, east to Leicestershire, north to Derbyshire or south to Shakespeare's Warwickshire. As long as he went there in his mind, or to a place like it, he could touch his grandfather's roots and gather some extra strength.

Then Wayne heard a woman's voice next to him.

'You seem miles away,' the woman said.

'I was in No Man's Land,' Wayne said. 'Or, to be precise, No Man's Heath.' The woman looked puzzled. 'Or to be politically correct, No Person's Land.'

'Is there a place for me in No Person's Land?'

He examined her. Black hair. Very slim. Very close to him.

'That's the point about No Person's Land. There's only room for one at a time.'

'Let me take you someplace else,' the woman said. 'Where there's room for two. You look like you need cheering up.'

'My name's Wayne. What's yours?'

'Em,' she told him.

'For Emily, Emma, Emmanuelle or Emmerdale?'

'You're very funny. I can be your Emmanuelle if you want. I'd like to go to bed with you.'

Kate was drifting into sleep when the thought came to her.

Women.

She was fully awake inside a megasecond.

The fake-kidnap of Buck Hanson was organised by a woman.

The voice on the phone demanding money from Buck Hanson was a woman's.

The riders who collected the money were women.

The photographs of Rachel Hanson's death scene showed women.

The person delivering the third note to the Bromage building was probably a woman.

What if Buck Hanson had been deliberately taken away in order to allow Rachel time to leave?

Then, when Rachel had left, what had gone wrong?

Only Tracey could answer those questions.

Kate looked out Tracey's number, listed under Claire. Then she went to the landline, tapped the digits and left a message asking for a meeting.

Kate was too awake to sleep now. She felt anger swell up inside her. She felt she had been working every minute for months, and all she had to show for it was a sense of her life growing out of control. Even if she got a full-time job, it wouldn't necessarily help her to pay her way. She couldn't understand why Wayne could be so well-off after kicking a football around for a few years. He said it was because he entertained people. Was that the most important thing these days?

Oxford had some wondrous things – theatres, museums, cinemas, libraries – but only if you had time and money. When was the last time she did something special?

It was time to say 'at least' three times.

At least she had her work to fascinate her.

At least she had her health.

At least she had the prospect of a trip to the United States.

Slowly she settled down to become the restless filling in a sheet sandwich, needing a hug.

'I met a woman at a party recently, Em,' Wayne told the black-haired woman in the pub. 'Her name was Marie. She lived in Reading and worked two days a week in London, and was taking a course in Leamington Spa and her separated parents lived in Torquay and Paris. Her boyfriend was based in Banbury but worked in Warwick, and her ex-husband lived in Canterbury and covered the south-east region. Marie herself was born in Manchester and brought up in Birmingham and her two children were now at university in St Andrews and Nottingham.

She paid her tax to Glasgow and her national insurance to Newcastle. She renewed her passport at Liverpool and her driving licence at Swansea. She still had a bank in Aberystwyth from her student days, but her other bank had a head office in Edinburgh, and she paid her gas bill to an address in Southampton. I stopped her there and told her that she had too many places and didn't belong to any of them.'

Wayne's new friend held on to his arm. She was very familiar with him.

'I like being with you,' she said. 'I'd like to give you the best night of your night.'

'You're very thin,' Wayne said, stroking her arm. 'Are you anorexic?'

'I have a lithe body build. Don't I look like a gymnast? Feel my biceps.'

Wayne felt her biceps. Muscular.

'Feel my thighs,' the woman said. She took Wayne's right hand, placed it on her inner right thigh and kept looking into his eyes. She moved her face closer to his. 'I'd like to kiss you all over,' she said.

'Meet me at my house tomorrow night,' Wayne said. 'Eight-thirty.' He gave her his address.

'I'll look forward to that,' she said. 'And so should you.'

Wayne finished his drink and kissed her on the cheek.

'Tomorrow,' he told the black-haired woman.

Then he left the pub.

TWENTY-THREE

Kate rose at seven the next morning. She grabbed an apple for breakfast, gathered together all she needed for a university appointment at nine and then cycled out to see Robin Hookes.

The curtains were drawn at Hookes's flat. She would just have to wake him and risk an awkward male-female scene.

It took five minutes to rouse Hookes. Kate nervously subtracted the time from what remained before nine o'clock. She also deducted the time needed for the cycle ride to the university and composure time before her meeting. It left fifteen minutes.

'I need to talk to you,' Kate told Hookes. She introduced herself. 'This was the only time I had.'

'You're up with the lark,' Hookes said. He was wearing a dressing-gown and very little else.

'I need to talk with you about Juliet Bromage.'

Kate stood just inside the door.

'Poor Juliet,' Hookes said.

He looked very pained.

'You've heard that she is in hospital?' Kate asked.

'Yes, some sort of trauma,' Hookes said. 'I've lost my mother too,'

'I'm really sorry for your loss.'

Kate recognised the difficulties of his situation, but she was aware of her time.

'I won't trouble you for too long,' she said. 'Had you seen Juliet recently?'

'Not really. I was hoping to.'

'Did you send her any letters?'

'Texts and emails. I left a few messages with the dragon on the desk.'

'Mary?'

'Yes.'

Women, Kate thought.

'Are there any new women in your life?' she asked.

She saw Hookes smile.

'There is?' Kate prompted.

'Why do you ask?'

'You're involved in something complex. You may even be in danger yourself. Tell me about her.'

'About who?'

Hookes was still smiling.

'Wayne probably didn't tell you this, but Juliet had been receiving threatening notes from a woman.'

'Why would a woman threaten Juliet?'

'I don't know. Why do *you* think?'

'I have no idea.'

'Was your new woman a stranger to you, or someone you already knew?'

'A stranger. Not any more though.'

'Can you describe her?'

'An angel who was sent to cheer me up.'

'Sent by whom?'

'Sent by destiny, I think. To help me discover a sense of purpose.'

'Tall or short? Slim or well-built?'

'Tallish. Black hair. Very slim. Not an ounce of fat on her. She's a good listener. That's what I liked. She didn't have AIDS and wasn't HIV positive.'

'She told you that?'

'Yes. And she was very generous to me. She said I should go back to Juliet and get her pregnant.'

'Did she say that?'

'Yes.'

Did she indeed?

Wayne sat in his office at the Bromage building and stared at the wall. The atmosphere felt frosty. Even Mackie seemed quieter than usual.

A call from Bob Blazer came on Wayne's mobile phone at ten o'clock.

'Yup,' Wayne said. He was not at his most inventive.

'Wayne?'

'Any jobs in the offering, Bob?'

'Not yet. Bollards to the lot of em.'

Blazer laughed.

'Have you got a new budgie?' Wayne asked next.

'Flick off, Wayne, flick off.'

'Very restrained, Bob. Have you found a woman yet?'

'Woman?'

'Yes, woman. Shapely creature with intuition and insight.'

'Everyone who saw you on Sunday thought you could still be earning money playing football.'

'I might have to, Bob.'

'You free for a drink, Wayne?'

'Yeah, I can be for you.'

'Let's have a drink.'

'OK, can you come into Oxford?'

'Yeah. Get Mackie if he's around.'

'Good idea,' Wayne said. Then he remembered the black-haired woman. 'It'll have to be early this evening, Bob. I've got a date at eight. Make it the pub by the tennis courts off the Woodstock Road. I forget what it's called.'

Wayne gave him directions. He had chosen the pub carefully. He knew Robin Hookes might be there.

As Wayne Shakespeare approached the main university entrance, Kate Park was walking out. Kate wore tight-fitting blue jeans that tapered to casual white shoes. A smart navy-blue blazer sat snugly over a white T-shirt with black lettering that he could not read. If she took off the blazer her clothes might be provocative. With the blazer she was businesslike.

As Kate came nearer, Wayne tried harder to read the lettering on her T-shirt. She spotted his intention and opened her blazer.

If you think education is expensive, try ignorance.

Wayne looked up from the T-shirt and into her eyes.

'You have gorgeous eyes,' he said.

'Thank you.'

Kate self-consciously fastened the blazer buttons and backed away from him by a foot. A crowd of smoking students watched them.

'Were you looking for me, Wayne?' Kate asked.

'No. Yes. Always. I didn't realise you taught today.'

'I don't. I've just had a meeting.'

'Did that go well?'

'Not really. I want to apply for a research grant, but it is difficult to get sex research through the university system.'

'Why's that?' Wayne asked.

'Some people think sex should be personal and private. Others are worried about risqué publicity. How are you? You don't look rested.'

'I think I slept with Juliet's ghost.'

They stood awkwardly. Kate's hair flickered in the slight breeze.

'I'll see you through it,' Kate said. 'I've been there. It will get better.'

They shared the emptiness for a few moments.

'I have to meet someone,' Wayne said.

Kate nodded. She touched his arm lightly and walked away.

The psychology department administrator told Wayne where Tracey Holroyd would be – a seminar group on the psycholinguistic differences between twins. Wayne was expecting five or six students, but when he got to the room and peered through the glass rectangle he saw a crowd. He looked at his watch. He had about fifteen minutes to kill. Then it would be lunchtime. Unless Tracey was working over lunch.

Wayne read the notice boards and tried to calm himself down. Then he returned to the classroom and waited outside. The door opened and noises hit Wayne's face. Chairs shuffled and concentration disengaged. Tracey Holroyd was last out, talking with her tutor.

She saw Wayne and registered surprise. She ended her conversation abruptly. The tutor drifted away.

'I didn't expect to see you,' she told Wayne. 'Is something wrong?'

'Not at all. I just wanted to check that everything was all right with you. Do you have time to talk?'

'I guess I could make time. It may have to be here. I have to be at a meeting near here in ten minutes.'

'Can we use the room?'

'I think so.'

The setting was hardly romantic. The room had all the character of a home without furniture.

'Did the payment go through?' Wayne asked.

'Yes. Thank you.'

'It was the best way to do it. With the money laundering regulations these days it could have been a problem.'

They looked at each other.

'Has he been in touch since?' Wayne asked.

'No. I don't expect him to.'

'Do you feel safe?'

'Yes, thank you.'

'His daughter is in hospital.'

'Seriously ill?'

'Don't know. It's a real coincidence.'

'What is?'

'That's the second time you've taken a man away for the night and a woman has been affected.'

'A real coincidence. I'm sorry about his daughter. He was close to her, and I know that you were close to her too. He talked a lot about his wife and his daughter. Men always do, don't they?'

Her eyes were as big as Wayne had ever seen them. Her voice carried adrenaline and excitement. Something had lifted every part of her except her height. It may have been such a stimulating class. More likely, it was the value of extra money to her assets.

'I don't believe you about the coincidence,' Wayne said. 'I think you've had a part to play in both of these deaths. And I'm going to find out.'

'You came all this way to tell me this?' she asked.

'Yes,' he said, and then he thought of a question. 'Whose idea was the extra night? Yours or Buck Hanson's?'

'Ours is a confidential service.'

Tracey took up a combative stance.

Wayne took out the photographs of Rachel Hanson's death.

'It's the photographs again,' he said. 'Are you sure this scene isn't familiar to you?'

Tracey took the pictures without really looking at them.

'I am sure,' she said.

Wayne didn't believe her.

'I have a meeting,' she said, and walked away without another word.

Tracey Holroyd's meeting was with Kate Park. Their venue was a café in Headington where the confidentiality of their conversation was protected by background chatter and their own whispers.

'Are you ready for escort work?' Tracey asked.

'Not quite. My financial situation is not as bad as I thought it might be.'

'A windfall?'

'I have a generous landlord and the possibility of a job as a consultant on a film.'

'Things are working well for me, too,' said Tracey.

'I think I would need to create more time for escort work,' Kate said. 'At the moment I'm running around and working too hard. If I were to be an escort I'd also like the time to design a research project around my work.'

'Combine one work with another.'

'Yes.'

'What would you do – a study of the life?'

'No. I think I'd design a study that is to do with multiple partners. Something to do with sexual health. Escort work allows a condensed history of the effects of multiple partners. I haven't thought it through yet though. That's why I want more time. My mind has other confusions at the moment.'

'So why did you want to meet?'

'I'm intrigued by the rag stunt involving the professional footballer and Wayne Shakespeare.'

'Wayne Shakespeare?'

'Yes. I'm his lodger.'

'Oh.'

'Has he shown you his photographs of Rachel?'

'Several times.'

'The charity stunt was your idea?'

'Of course.'

Kate smiled.

'With an additional motive?' Kate said.

A pleasant silence passed.

'I may tell you the story,' Tracey said. 'Let me think about it for a moment or two.'

'I don't hold any position. I don't have to tell any authorities. I may have to tell Wayne if it affects his safety.'

'Can you trust him?'

'I think so.'

'It might be in my interests to tell you. He could keep bugging me otherwise.'

'I think he's the persistent type.'

'Yes,' said Tracey. 'I'd be interested in what you think about Rachel's story.'

'I'd be happy to listen.'

'I'll tell you the story in confidence and then we can decide whether we tell Wayne.'

'OK. I'd love to hear the story.'

'Let's get some drinks,' Tracey said.

They waved for coffees and then settled into their seats.

'Better do this now,' Tracey said. 'My recent earnings are such that I may be gone when the semester ends.'

Wayne went to a student café. He sat down with a latte and laid out the photographs of Rachel Hanson's death scene. Some students came and sat next to him. He felt crowded by them. He gathered up the more sensitive pictures and looked at them one by one.

'Where?' he said under his breath.

He looked up and caught the eyes of a female student who was sitting opposite him. She pointed to a picture that was still on the table. It was a photograph of a country scene, stretching to open woodland, but a very small part of a country-house garden was visible in the shot.

'That could be the Cat and Mouse House,' the student said. 'My parents took me there when I was young.'

You are still young, Wayne thought. She had blonde hair and was well spoken.

'Really?' Wayne said.

Wayne looked at her hands. She looked at his hands. He looked at her face. It had an openness that advertised naivety, while her eyes craved experience.

'How can you tell?' he asked her.

'That's the mouse. From behind. You'd only know if you'd been. I want to do my dissertation on topiary. I'm doing geography and psychology. I want to know why people commit themselves to topiary and what purpose it serves.'

'And this is a piece of topiary?'

'Yes. The pouncing cat and the running mouse. You

can only see a bit of it. It's not on a par with the deer at Blanchard in Northumbria. Birds are popular topiary. But you get all sorts in the international competitions. Camels. Cowboys on horseback. It's quite rare to get a Tom and Jerry scene though.'

'Is there a lecturer I could talk to about this?'

'Good luck. They're never there when I want one.'

'Do you know exactly where it is – the Cat and Mouse House?'

'Yes.'

She drew him a map. Wayne gave her his most appreciative smile.

'Thanks,' he said. 'Good luck with your dissertation.'

'Thanks. Not long for me to go now. Once I graduate you won't see me for landscape. Here's my mobile number in case you fancy a drink. My name's Rosie.'

'Wayne,' he said, holding out his hand.

Rachel had been nearly twenty-one when she'd met Buck Hanson, Tracey Holroyd told Kate when they had settled with their drinks, in a secluded corner of the café. Rachel had been working in a jewellery shop at the time. Then one day, apparently, Buck had walked into the shop as if he owned the place, smiled a rare smile and read Rachel's name tag.

'Are you doing anything Saturday evening, Rachel?' he asked.

'Can I help you?' she replied, aware that the shop owner was watching.

'Yeah, by coming out on Saturday evening.'

'OK.'

'Do you know who I am?'

'No.'

'You'll soon find out, so I'd better tell you.'

He'd told her he was Buck Hanson, famous footballer, taken her phone number and signed an autograph for a customer as he left.

Rachel loved the jewellery shop but hated the shopkeeper. He kept cornering her and telling her that she was a pretty young thing. Twice he put his hand on her bum and she had to be quick to escape. Another time he pressed her against the counter and kissed her. He kept staring at her. And he was married. Rachel wished she had been a witch. She would have put a spell on that man. Hated him.

Rachel kept her date with Buck Hanson on the Saturday evening, and they slept together on their fourth date, which was really fast for her and probably very slow for him. It happened in her bed in her parents' home, when her folks were away and her brother was out. But the time that sealed their relationship was one night at the shop when he met her at five-thirty and helped her lock up while her boss was away. She had just lowered the blinds when he pressed her up against the counter.

'Be careful of the merchandise,' she told him.

'You're the merchandise,' he said.

He didn't undress her. He pulled a few garments aside and then took her quickly. She thought it was passion rather than power and possession.

At first the bites were trophies. When they continued, after she had requested him to desist, she began to wonder. He called her his 'slave' and punished her if she annoyed him in some way she didn't understand. She noticed that it was worse after his team had lost.

She began studying at the local college, but she dared not tell him. He hated it when he saw her with a puzzled expression.

'Don't think,' he said. 'You're not paid to think. Now tell me what you did today. Everything.'

She found ways to conceal her studying hours.

In the college library, Rachel started reading about why men confuse sex with inflicting pain on women. Buck wanted to diminish her by making her powerless. Instead of him thinking that he was sexually afraid of her, he constructed it so that she would be afraid of him. He associated orgasm and sex with control. Maybe his father beat him or a brother hit him or he was sexually abused by someone in the family.

Then she realised that she didn't have to understand him. Instead she had to choose whether she stayed a pawn in his life or not. She could either participate or leave. She learned the meaning of empowerment. But she still had to find empowerment for herself.

She sensed that he was seeing other women. Did they allow him to go further than her or not as far? One of the other football wives had explained about the prostitutes on certain trips. That was the purpose of tours, Rachel was told. That was why the directors went. It was on such a trip that Buck Hanson had first met Tracey Holroyd.

When she realised that Buck would never phone home while he was away on the night before a match, she used certain evenings to read in a library. She learned the term algolagnia – the connection of sexual excitement and pain – and its division into sadism and masochism. She bided her time until she delivered her rehearsed line: 'You need a proper masochist.' Buck didn't understand. She sensed his powerlessness in that conversation and then felt his physical force the next time in bed.

Rachel learned that women could be taught sadomasochism by a sexual partner, and she realised that she could do that if she wanted. Of course it was unfair to categorise Buck alongside the Marquis de Sade and Leopold von Sacher-Masoch. For one thing Buck was not literary like them. For another he was not as extreme. She didn't like some of what Buck did to her – an unwanted bite, roughly squeezing her breasts, bruising her neck, making her vagina sore by not waiting, forcing her into anal sex – and she much preferred his charming and funny side. It was the suddenness of the assaults that shook her and made her nervous about sex. At least there were no whips in the house, although one time he had tied her up and held her chin tightly and . . . ugh . . . the memory was painful . . . and times when . . . Yes, she made excuses for him.

She knew that Buck would react violently if she went with another man, so, over the next few years, she retreated into avoidance. She dared not research where he went for sexual sustenance. She gave up her job in the shop, glad to see the back of that nasty owner, bought clothes, kept house, ate meals with Buck without speaking, slept apart without sleeping, saw less of her family and retreated into a world of fears. She broke her loneliness by studying. She went from an access course at the college to part-time study at a local university, where she took one course a term. She wanted to do more, but Buck might find out. He quizzed her about every greeting in the street. He scrutinised her mobile phone bills.

One day Buck left his mobile phone at home and Rachel redialled the last number.

'Cat,' answered a woman's voice. 'How may I help?'

Rachel hung up and made a note of Cat's number.

'I wouldn't have been unduly fazed,' Tracey Holroyd told Kate Park, sitting in the café. 'Escorts get a lot of hang-ups and I'd rather stick with established customers anyway.'

'Of course,' Kate said. 'What happened next?'

'One day, months later, I was in the university canteen queue and my work phone rang. I answered it in my usual way, but I've changed my greeting since then. I left the queue and went somewhere more private. I saw this woman watching me. A week later this woman approached me on campus.'

'This was Rachel?'

'Yes.'

'And you talked to her?'

'Yes.' She told the next bit of the story.

'You may be able to help me,' Rachel said. 'I'd like to talk to you about my husband.'

Tracey Holroyd took one look at Rachel and decided this vulnerable blonde woman was no threat.

'And who might that be?'

'Brian Hanson. He's also known as Buck. I'd like to know more about him.'

'What would you like to know?'

'Is he a sadist? Is he sick?'

'I'm no judge of that.'

'But you are having an affair with him?'

'No. He pays me for sex.'

'Oh.'

Rachel froze. She could not ask more. Tracey helped her out.

'He's rough,' Tracey said. 'I can handle him, but that may be me and my background.'

'What do you mean?'

'I'm used to a lot of punishment. I have a high pain threshold.'

'What?'

Tracey could have told Rachel about how her father, a professional wrestler, had taught her different ways to cut herself. She could have mentioned the black eyes from karate. She could also have explained to Rachel how she dealt with bruises, cuts and scratch-marks so that her next customers wouldn't notice. Or that she didn't always cover them up so that the next client would know what was allowed.

'He likes anal sex,' Tracey told Rachel. 'He knows he can't get that easily from you. He gets it from me.'

Rachel cried at the painful memory of Buck's attempts on her. She cried at the state of her marriage.

'Anal sex,' Rachel said. She looked shocked. 'Why?'

'I don't know why. He just wants it. I'm not the one to

analyse whether he's really gay or whether he was raped when he was a kid.'

'Don't you feel vulnerable and powerless?'

'I don't feel anything. I can handle myself. I give them trigger words. If I say the word they have to stop. Men know that if they don't follow my orders then I will hurt them. Or my security man will.'

'I don't think I want to go through that.'

'Why don't you fuck *him* rather than let him fuck you?' Tracey asked.

'I don't think I could do that. I want a gentle man.'

'Get rid of him then.'

'I don't know how to.'

'If you have to walk on eggshells around him, then it's time to do something about it,' Tracey told Rachel. 'Men who put pressure on women to have sex are showing warning signs of domestic abuse. I can put you in touch with a women's refuge. I staffed their phone line at one time. I know how their system works. I can be your intermediary. We can arrange a time when Buck is definitely away and I can send someone round to collect you. I can brief you on what to take. These people will take care of you.'

'Please tell me more,' Rachel Hanson had said.

TWENTY-FOUR

Wayne Shakespeare walked into his living-room purposefully.

'Where's the road atlas, Rover?' he asked the sculpture. 'Go get it, boy.'

Wayne took the road atlas from his bookshelf.

'Good dog,' Wayne said. 'That was quick.' He turned to the local pages. He found the village with the Cat and Mouse House.

Wayne went to his landline. It took a couple of calls to get through to Bob Blazer.

'Blazer,' he answered.

'Glory,' said Wayne.

'Is that you, Zany Wayney?'

'Do you fancy a jaunt?' Wayne asked.

'I don't smoke.'

'I'm setting off to find out what happened to Buck

Hanson's wife. I may need your help. I'm playing a cat-and-mouse game with a Cat and Mouse house.'

'Sounds interesting,' Blazer said, in a tone that suggested it wasn't at all interesting.

'Have you met Rachel Hanson?'

'Yeah. A couple of times. Nervous type. Buck kept her very quiet. One time I went round and she wouldn't answer the door.'

'Would you recognise her? Do you have a photograph of her?'

'Ooooh. I may have a photo. She came to a club social. Hardly said a word. It'll be a group picture.'

'If you send it to me, I can crop it and turn it into an individual shot.'

'I can do that, Wayne. I'll bring it to yours. I'll be at your house as soon as I can.'

Wayne hung up, phoned his friend about borrowing the car, and then wrote a note to Kate: *Gone to find a Cat and Mouse House. Don't forget to feed Rover.*

Kate Park looked at Tracey Holroyd.

'So, *your* people were responsible for rescuing her?' Kate said.

'That's what I thought would happen. They went round to collect her, but she wasn't there.'

'She wasn't there?'

'No. They waited for half an hour and then left and went back. Tried to phone her.'

'Where was she?'

'I don't know. Your guess is as good as mine. She had agreed to our arrangements and was motivated to do it.'

'Lots of possibilities,' Kate said.

'Buck Hanson might have found out that she was planning to leave.'

'Would she tell him?'

'Possibly. I think he was the type who wanted to know what his woman did with every minute of every day.'

'What did you think of Hanson?'

'Most women would see him as a brute,' said Tracey. 'He could be pretty mean. He liked to simulate rape with me. It could have been playful, but it felt perverted.'

Kate suddenly gave up on the idea of becoming an escort. There were times she liked Teddy to be spontaneous. But he would never have hurt her.

'You heard about the sadist who married a masochist and they lived happily ever after,' Tracey said.

'No,' Kate said, expecting a joke.

'No, I'm not surprised. It never happens like that.'

Kate nodded.

'Do you have other ideas about what happened to Rachel?' Kate asked.

'Yes. One other. When I checked with the refuge, they said they'd heard of another no-show.'

'Another no-show?'

'At another refuge. They had a woman who was going to leave her husband and come to them. She had to leave her teenage boy with another family because he was too old for her to take to the refuge. She delivered the boy and then never arrived at the refuge.'

'Did you speak with the woman?' asked Kate.

'The trail ran cold. I like my first theory better

though. I think Buck Hanson is mean enough to kill her.'

Kate sat back and reflected for a few minutes.

On their journey to the Cat and Mouse house, Bob Blazer and Wayne Shakespeare killed time by making their own fun. They tried to think of pop groups that fitted the 'cat and mouse' theme but didn't get much further than Curiosity Killed the Cat and The Mickey Mouse Club.

'You think there's something funny going on in this Cat and Mouse house?' Blazer asked.

'Yes. And it won't be our jokes.'

'Is it one of them houses where the man has a dozen wives?'

'I'll get you an application form, Bob.'

'No thanks. One wife was enough for me.'

Kate Park went to the jewellery shop and bought a battery for her watch. She checked the staff. A man in his fifties acted like the manager. Two attractive women in their twenties served the customers.

Kate waited outside the shop until the brown-haired woman – her name tag said Louise – came out and walked to a nearby sandwich shop. Louise was dressed for a night out at one of Oxford's better venues. She wore a dark trouser suit and a white blouse. Her hands were well-manicured and her shoes had two-inch heels. Kate watched her as she stood in a queue for sandwiches.

Louise came out of the shop and found a bench in a small public garden. She checked her watch, opened her paper bag and started eating.

Kate waited until she had nearly finished her sandwich. Then she walked up and sat on the bench.

'Are you from the jeweller's?' Kate asked.

'Yes,' the woman said, studying Kate. 'You bought the battery.'

'My name is Kate Park.' She handed over a card saying she taught at the university: Dr Kate Park. 'May I ask you a couple of questions?'

The woman nodded. Took her last mouthful. Seemed intrigued.

'Has there been anything odd happening at the jeweller's lately? Anybody asking for the owner?'

'No,' the woman said, now defensive.

'Any strange women appearing? Any signs of unusual activity?'

The woman gave off a sign of recall. Something had occurred to her.

'Shall I explain more about why I'm asking?' Kate said.

'Please do.'

'There was a complaint from a former member of staff against the owner. Suggestions that he was overstepping the mark. The complaint came to nothing. I was interested in whether you felt safe with him.'

'He tried to feel me up,' the woman said.

'Oh, really?'

'I stopped him. I told him if he did it again my brother would come down and sort him out.'

'Good for you.'

'He backed off. Just as well, because I haven't got a

brother. He's trying it on with others though. I think he brings women to the shop after hours.'

'What makes you say that?'

'One Sunday. Maybe the Sunday before last. We opened up. When I got there, the place reeked of stale sex, but you can't open windows in a jeweller's. There was a stain on the carpet that someone had tried to clean.'

'Do you think he's having a relationship with one of the staff?'

'No. I think it was a customer.'

'Did you see her?'

'She came in late on the Saturday.'

'Could you describe her for me, please.'

'Yes. Black hair. Very slim. She was wearing nice trousers. Will I have to go to an industrial tribunal over this?'

'No. I very much doubt it. What height was she?'

'Average height. Maybe a bit above average.'

'Do you think she was coerced into sex?'

'No. I think she was up for it.'

Yes, Kate thought. That fits part of my theory.

'Well,' said Wayne. 'That's the Cat and Mouse House.'

'And this is a cat-and-mouse chase,' said Bob Blazer.

They were sitting in the car observing the local hamlet. Wayne had knocked on the door of the Cat and Mouse House and no one had answered.

'I think we need to knock on more doors,' Wayne said.

'Good. I'll come with you to the first four houses and see how knocking on doors is done.'

'Bob, there's only four houses in this village.'

'Yeah.'

'Let's look for how they would get round the back of the Cat and Mouse House, and where the photo was taken from.'

They found a footpath that led round the back.

'How would they carry a coffin down here?' Blazer asked.

'Or why?'

It took a few more minutes to find the angle of the photograph. There was a lane wide enough for a car, and a quicker way of reaching the photographer's site. A mound of earth was present near the spot where the photograph was taken.

'Do you fancy having a look under that pile of earth, Bob?' Wayne asked.

'No, not really. Because it was there when the picture was taken.'

Wayne had a look.

'You're right,' Wayne said.

'Looks as though it has been there a while.'

'Let's knock on doors.'

'Yes, Boss.'

The Cat and Mouse House was still empty. The people at the second house had nothing to report. The old lady behind the twitching curtains at the third was probably too concerned about distraction burglaries to answer the door. A man of about sixty answered the door at the fourth house.

'My name is Wayne Shakespeare,' Wayne started. 'And this is Bob Blazer.'

'Have you come to sign me, lads?' the man said.

'Can I talk to your Dad?' Wayne said.

'Come in, lads,' the man said. 'I'm Dave Parish.'

'Pleased to meet you,' said Wayne.

'Likewise,' said Blazer.

'What can I do for you?' asked Dave Parish.

'This photo,' Wayne said, showing one of the seemingly innocuous pictures. 'It seems to have been taken at the back.'

Dave Parish looked at it.

'Yeah, definitely,' he said.

'About nine or ten days ago, I reckon,' Wayne said. 'Did you see anyone out there? Any of these people?'

'Not me. The wife mentioned something. When did you say it was?'

'A week or so back.'

'I'll get the wife. She's our neighbourhood watch.'

Parish left the room.

'If we show this guy the picture of Rachel, will he know that it's Buck Hanson's wife?' Wayne asked Bob Blazer. 'Will he go to the press?'

'No. Rachel's not a media WAG. He won't recognise her.'

'He recognised us.'

'We were better players than Rachel Hanson,' Blazer said. 'Good job I cropped the players and other wives out of the photo though.'

'Well done.'

'Do you still pay those old dears to watch the stadium?' Blazer asked.

'Yeah. We have a camera on their roof. We give them the option of a season-ticket or £500.

'Which do they take? On second thoughts, don't answer that. I might get depressed.'

The man returned with his wife.

'You're asking about the people with the box?' the woman said.

'Yeah,' said Wayne.

'They came early morning. About six. It was a Monday, I think, or a Tuesday. I suppose they thought they wouldn't be seen.'

'But they were?'

'Yes.'

Wayne gave her two of the photographs.

'This one looks dead here?' said Dave Parish's wife.

'Did you call the police?' asked Wayne.

'No,' said the woman.

'Even though she looked dead and it looked like a burial?'

'She didn't look very dead when she climbed into the box.'

'Oh,' said Wayne. 'Well well well. What happened then?'

'The milk was boiling over. Next time I looked they were gone.'

'How long after was that?'

'Five or ten minutes. Maybe less. Maybe more.'

Wayne thanked the couple. He showed them Bob Blazer's photograph of Rachel Hanson.

'Yes. She was the woman who climbed into the box,' said Mrs Parish.

'Had you seen her around before that?'

'No. She's not from round here.'

'I've never seen her before or since,' said Dave Parish. 'I've seen Bob play a few times though. Enjoyed watching you play, Bob. Always thought you were a great player. Hope you find a job soon.'

'I think this week will be "Job for Bob" week,' said Blazer.

They said goodbyes and walked back to the car.

'They must have killed her while she was in the box,' Wayne said.

'And carried her off in a coffin,' Blazer said.

They got into the car.

'Where are they now?' Wayne asked. 'The people in the photographs.'

'Anywhere in the country.'

'They pick a place that we could recognise, take the photographs, and then go back to where they really hang out?'

'Yeah,' said Blazer. 'But we've learned two things.'

'What are they?'

'She got into the coffin alive.'

'And the second?'

'That Dave Parish is a good judge of a player.'

'Hello?'

'It's Kate Park.'

'How are you doing, honey?'

'Not too bad. My sexology puzzle is distracting me from my bereavement.'

'You sound almost excited.'

'I wouldn't go that far,' Kate said. 'I was phoning you as someone who is an expert on HIV and AIDS.'

'I knew we'd get around to anal sex eventually,' said the woman in California, laughing.

'I hope I haven't disturbed you too early.'

'It's nine o'clock in California. I've been up for three hours. That was one of the things that bereavement did for me. It changed my sleep patterns.'

'I understand.'

'I think you do, honey. What's your puzzle?'

'I'm interested in people's responses to being told they are HIV positive. Is denial common?'

'Certainly is. Denial. Shame. Guilt. Fear. A lot of fear. Isolation. Hopelessness. Depression. Sadness. Questions about why it has happened to them. How long do I have? What will I have to face? Should I just kill myself now and get it over with?'

'Anger?'

'Yes. That too. Especially for the sexually inexperienced. It happens to some people at the first possibility, especially if they're scamming.'

'Scamming?'

'The idea that sex doesn't count if it's not vaginal sex, the idea that you can have anal sex and still say you're a virgin.'

'But it does count.'

'It certainly does if you're HIV positive. But it's like the Bill Clinton question: What actually counts as having sexual relations with someone?'

'Any other terms I need to know?'

'Do you understand terms like barebacking and bugchasing?' she asked.

'Go ahead.'

'Barebacking is where an HIV-positive man is intentionally having unprotected anal sex. Seroconcordant barebacking is intentional, unprotected anal intercourse with a partner of the same HIV status. And bugchasers are those people who try to catch the disease.'

'Why would they want to do that?'

'Maybe they falsely believe that it will improve their life. They're under the misconception that they can get benefits, attention, sympathy, whatever . . . then too late, they learn the reality.'

'Or maybe they are well-served with the victim mentality,' Kate added.

'That too.'

'Do some people get *more* sexually promiscuous after getting a diagnosis?'

'Some do. Manic sex. Hyperactivity. Spending sprees. Might as well spend if you think there's not much time left. Some people seek legal redress. That's very American, I suppose – sue, sue, sue.'

'Yes,' said Kate.

'Some people want someone else to be punished,' continued the woman in California. 'There was a man in Scotland who was incarcerated for five years for knowingly infecting a woman.'

Kate thought about the victim of one case where an HIV-positive man had committed grievous bodily harm by infecting a woman. As one witness said, *at least he can't infect anybody while he's in prison.*

'Thank you again,' Kate said. 'You're a treasure.'

'You sleep well tonight, honey.'

'I think I will. Especially if I solve my puzzle.'
Kate ended the call. Then she sat and reflected.

TWENTY-FIVE

Wayne Shakespeare returned the borrowed car and walked back to his house with Bob Blazer. Wayne found some sports kit for Bob to wear so that they could run along the canal to the pub where they were meeting Mackie and, possibly, Robin Hookes.

'I'm concerned about you, Bob,' Wayne told Blazer.

'About my drinking?'

'Yes.'

Bob Blazer said nothing.

Wayne changed from smart training shoes to an old pair because he knew the canal path was barely passable after recent flooding. Then he set off running with Bob, their heads down, noticing little except the next puddle and the safest mud. They took a few detours and wended their way under the railway lines and down to the river. They ran along the river for three miles and circled round to the main roads. They felt warmed up when they arrived at the pub. But Wayne didn't know what he was warmed up for.

'Mackie should be there,' Wayne told Blazer.

'Keep the conversation going,' Blazer said.

'Hey, Shakes,' someone called, as Wayne was waiting at the bar.

Wayne tried to remember the man's name. Nick Nicholas? Dick Dickenson? He had played football in his time.

'Hey, look who it isn't,' Wayne said to him.

'How are you doing?' the man retorted, and they were shaking hands.

'OK. How are you? How's the knee?'

'Knackered,' he said, and laughed.

'You and me both. It's my back this week.'

'You on your own?'

'No, I'm meeting Mackie.'

'I'd better get home and mind my kids.'

Wayne was reminded that Mackie had once kept the company of men who talked about glassings and baseball bats.

'Is that Bob Blazer over there?' the man asked.

'Certainly is,' said Wayne, excusing himself.

Wayne took his drinks and made a detour to where Robin Hookes sat on a bar stool.

'Ah, Chief Superintendent,' Hookes said. 'Bit close for a tail job, aren't we?'

Wayne pointed at the pint on the bar. 'Is that your sixth or your seventh?' he asked Hookes.

'Very droll,' Hookes said.

'Come and join us,' Wayne told him.

Hookes followed Wayne, and Wayne introduced Bob Blazer.

'Wayne once told me that there were only three types of pub,' Bob Blazer told Robin Hookes. 'The Spit and Sawdust, the Goalkeepers' Arms, and the Philosopher's Head. Was that right, Wayne?'

Wayne nodded.

'You drink and eat in the Spit and Sawdust,' Wayne said. 'Talk football in the Goalkeepers' Arms and solve the world's problems in the Philosopher's Head.'

'Are we here to solve the world's problems then?' Hookes asked Wayne.

'Or our own,' Wayne said.

'The future's bleak,' Hookes said. 'Beware the future.'

'Very cheery,' said Bob Blazer.

'I need to know about you and Juliet,' Wayne told Hookes.

'*I* want to know about you and Juliet,' Hookes said. His face reddened. 'You were the one who broke us up.'

'Juliet was the one who broke you up. Juliet broke up all her relationships.'

'Do not speak ill of the ill,' Hookes said.

'So it was said, in the Philosopher's Head,' said Wayne.

'Perfect Shakespeare,' said Hookes.

'Anyway, look at you,' Wayne added. He prodded Hookes in the stomach. 'When it comes to mattress athletics you don't even make the qualifying standards.'

'She came back to me, you know,' Hookes said. 'While you were seeing her. She kept coming back. She told me you were just a physical Neanderthal to her. She needed some conversation. She needed some intellect and some class.'

'You did write to her, didn't you? You did threaten her?'

'I met a woman in here the other evening,' Hookes continued, while Bob Blazer looked as baffled as Wayne had ever seen him look. 'She thought I needed cheering up.'

'Did she indeed?' Wayne asked. 'I can't think why.'

At that moment Mackie walked in. He looked at Wayne and nodded admonishingly.

'Yeah, I know,' Wayne said. 'I haven't been around much. Have there been problems?'

Wayne could see that there had.

'Bailey,' said Mackie. 'You need subservience.'

'Subservience? That's a good word, Mackie. That's your longest word this year. Where did you learn that?'

'The wife.'

Wayne laughed at that one.

'Let me get you a drink.'

Kate made two more phone calls. The first was to the Nurse Bank to cancel her night shift. The second was to Tracey Holroyd.

'I think I know what happened,' Kate said. 'Can I come and talk it over with you?'

'Yeah. Come to my flat.'

Tracey Holroyd gave Kate directions.

'What's the news on Juliet?' Bob Blazer asked the group.

Everyone looked towards Wayne.

'Much the same,' Wayne said. 'Jim Bailey is at her bedside. She's coming out of hospital. Jim's getting a nurse to look after her when she gets home.'

'What's wrong with her?' Blazer asked.

'It's not for me to say,' Wayne said.

'The doctors are wondering if someone molested her,' Hookes said. 'They've brought a counsellor in.'

The table went surprisingly quiet.

'Well, thanks for that,' said Bob Blazer eventually. 'Cheered us all up. Who did it?'

'One of Juliet's Neanderthals, eh, Robin?' Wayne said. He was thinking about Buck Hanson.

'Yes, she was seeing you that evening,' Hookes said to Wayne.

'Yes,' Wayne said, addressing Robin Hookes. 'I went to see her, but she was fine when I left. Did she tell you I'd been when you visited her later, when you molested her later?'

'She thought that if she fornicated with you then she could pay you less,' Hookes said.

'Fornicated with me?' Wayne looked at Blazer. 'That's a good word, eh?'

'What the fuck's going on?' Blazer said. 'Sorry, what the *heck* is going on here?'

'Just getting a guide on Juliet,' Wayne said. 'I think Robin here was writing threatening notes to her. I think he wants to kill her.'

'Is that right, son?' Blazer asked, turning towards Hookes.

'How about you, Mackie?' Wayne asked. 'Did you threaten her?'

Mackie looked at Wayne as if he was seeing a giraffe for the first time.

'You OK, Wayne?' Mackie asked.

'What's Mackie got to do with it?' Bob Blazer asked.

'He's been on the case,' Wayne said.

'He's got fornicate all to do with it,' Blazer said. 'Did you like that one, Wayne? Fornicate all?'

'What case?' Hookes asked.

'Julius Caesar,' Wayne said. 'All you can think of is language, Bob.'

'What are you two droning on about?' Robin Hookes asked. 'Could someone please translate from childspeak.'

'Who are you?' Blazer asked Robin Hookes.

'Let me explain,' Wayne said. 'Robin here is Juliet's ex-husband. He used to work for her, too, but Juliet laid him off to get rid of him. That was last year.'

'She did not lay me off to get rid of me,' Robin Hookes pleaded. 'She continued to reap some sustenance from me – intellectual sustenance, emotional sustenance and sexual sustenance.'

'So it was you who visited her late on Sunday night?'

'I'd arranged to see Juliet tomorrow evening at her house,' Robin Hookes said. His words were slurring. *Arranged to shee Shuliet ...*

'Don't push it,' Wayne said.

Wayne saw Bob Blazer looking at the ceiling.

'My turn?' Mackie said. Everyone looked at Mackie.

'Go ahead, Mackie,' said Bob Blazer. 'Best to speak before they get the handbags out.'

'Buck Hanson,' Mackie said. 'I reckon Buck.'

'Buck wouldn't type out notes,' Wayne said.

'No,' said Mackie. 'He visited Juliet midnight or later.'

'Well done, Mackie,' said Wayne.

'Poor Rachel Hanson,' said Bob Blazer.

'Good,' said Wayne. 'Now we've sorted that out, I can go and meet my date.'

'How might a rival group operate?' Kate asked.

'Your guess is as good as mine,' Tracey said.

'They would be operating illegally if they tried to extract money from Buck Hanson.'

'They may have people on the inside of the domestic abuse sector,' said Tracey. 'That's my concern.'

They were sitting in Tracey's flat. Kate had cycled the short distance to north Oxford. The two women had sat down and started talking immediately.

'Surely domestic abuse workers are ethical?' asked Kate.

'Most would be dedicated. Others would be simply employees. They took the job to earn money.'

'And they may be willing to accept money for mailing lists?'

'That's how the business world operates,' Tracey said. 'It buys mailing lists for likely clients.'

'I can't see it happening like that,' said Kate. 'I wondered if they checked newspapers and magazines for tales of domestic abuse among the wealthy and then they rescue the victims.'

'And target the wealthy husbands?'

'Possibly.'

'Where would they take Rachel?' Tracey asked.

'They must have a base.'

'Maybe they pull one job a year and that's enough money.'

'Maybe,' Kate said. 'Did you look at the work on cults?'

'Yes. They probably have a leader and there may be men in the group. The leader may be a man who is looking for acquiescent, vulnerable females. The followers may be dependent women who are sexually available to the men. A male leader might replicate the situation that the women are used to. He may abuse them. He might isolate them from their past. He may give them new names.'

'And a new life. Do you have a feel for whether Rachel is alive or dead?'

'I don't know,' Tracey said. 'I think she is still alive. I think that was their way of frightening Buck Hanson.'

'A way of hitting back.'

'Of course, it's possible that it's an all-woman group who are empowering these victims. Rachel may just turn up on Buck Hanson's doorstep one day to scare him as much as he scared her.'

'Or, in a few months' time, send an anonymous letter telling the police that Buck Hanson killed his wife,' Kate said.

Tracey Holroyd broke out into a big smile.

'Oh, that would be something,' she said.

Kate Park agreed.

Back home, in his kitchen, Wayne poured two glasses of red wine and gave one to the black-haired woman.

'Cheers,' the woman said, raising her glass. 'Here's to us.'

'Wayne and Em,' Wayne toasted. 'Wayne and Emmanuelle.'

They clinked glasses and exchanged glances. Wayne took a sip but noticed that Em put her glass down after hardly drinking anything.

'Nice kitchen' said the Mankiller. 'What are we eating?'

'Tuna casserole.'

'Shall I put my bag in your room?'

'If you wish. Just step through the scanner, please, Madam.'

'Ho ho.'

'What do you have in your bag?'

'A change of clothes. Toothpaste. Toothbrush. Oral contraceptive pills.'

'You're very forward,' Wayne said.

'Wait until you get me in bed,' she replied, smiling cheekily at him. She took two steps across the room. Put her arms around him and kissed him deeply. Searched for his tongue with hers. Pressed her chest against his.

'I didn't think you'd be the slow and modest type,' Wayne said, when he was able to breathe again.

'You make me feel so hot and lusty,' she said. 'The moment I saw you I knew I wanted you. Why don't you turn the casserole down low? Then we can go to bed before we eat.'

Kate Park met Jeremy Spooner in a hotel bar in the city centre. It was Tuesday night, but the city was simmering like a saucepan with a bouncing lid, bubbling and rattling, waiting to scold anyone who went too close to its centre. Kate was thrown in with the crowd. Oxford was the last place Kate wanted to be, and she wasn't sure she wanted to hear Jeremy Spooner's offer. But hear it she did.

'This actor-director is doing a film about six people,' Spooner told her. 'The six people had shared a squat many years ago and now they have a reunion in a country house. It's one of those films where the actors improvise and then they sharpen up the script.'

'Like a Mike Leigh film?'

'Sort of.'

Mary Curtis was working late in the Bromage building. She was thinking about a phone call that day. A persistent woman caller had been trying to reach Juliet, but Juliet was still recovering from her ordeal. This time Mary asked the caller if there was any message.

Yes, the woman said. *Remind Juliet that she has a fatal disease.*

Mary had seen two threatening notes and had passed them on to Juliet. She wondered what to say about the phone call.

Upstairs, on Wayne's bed, they kissed and touched and explored and enjoyed. They undressed each other a little and talked a while about films. They tickled each other and caressed some more. When they were both semi-undressed, naked from forehead to navel, Wayne told her he was going to get some water. He returned with two full glasses. He put them on the bedside table.

'Is that to drink?' she asked. 'Or to put out the fire?'

He poured the water over her breasts, stomach and trousers. He saw a dark veil of rage flutter into her face. The rage threatened to take hold, but she somehow fought it. She replaced the anger with theatrical giggles. Stood up. Took off her damp trousers and underwear, and dried herself with a towel that Wayne offered. Wayne covered the bed with a fresh sheet and she tucked in the corners. Then she walked around the room, tidying up here and there. Wayne sat on the bed, still wearing his trousers, and watched her parade nude in front of him. He watched her collect her glass of water and drink some while she was still standing. He watched her with great interest and fascination.

'The director worked with Teddy on a book project,' said Jeremy Spooner. 'She knew of you through him.'

'What's her name?'

'Bonnie.'

'I never heard him mention anyone called Bonnie.'

'I think it was a while ago. I think it was something to do with her autobiography. She's a sexologist, I think, very knowledgeable about sex . . . are you listening, Kate . . . Kate?'

Kate was thinking about two questions: Who would want to kill Juliet? How and why would someone try to kill Juliet?

She tried to put herself into the head of a woman who was clever, angry and impulsive. And when she did, Kate had a vision of a perfect murder, a case that could never go to trial. Kate shivered at the thought.

'Kate . . . are you all right?' said Jeremy Spooner.

'Oh, yes. I need to make two telephone calls. May I borrow your mobile, please?'

The first call was to Tracey Holroyd. The second was to Wayne Shakespeare.

Only one of the calls was answered.

The woman's pubic hairs were as black as the ones on her head. Wayne explored the detail as he sobered up. They continued hugging and kissing for ten more minutes and then she undid the zip of his trousers. Wayne reciprocated by pressing his fingers between her legs until a mottled rouge appeared on her chest and neck. Her availability was clear to him. When he pushed his fingers inside her, she buzzed histrionically like an electricity pylon in the rain, as if he were the most fabulous lover in the world. He was a little suspicious, but he was also aroused. Then an orgasmic noise rumbled up through her throat and across the room.

When she returned to him from her solo trip, she fumbled with his trousers. Peeled away the rest of his clothes. Tossed them aside. Lay back for him. He slowly stroked the tip of his erect penis along the inside of her left thigh, leaving a very thin trail of semen on her skin. Their bodies were moist with sweat and saliva and seeping juices. His left shoulder pushed against her right breast and his lips swallowed the skin on her neck. He was rougher than he should have been. She was startled. Her anger reared and then settled again.

Wayne reached in a bedside drawer.

'No,' said the black-haired woman. Her voice came from a long way away. 'No condoms. You're safe with me.'

'What was that?' Wayne asked.

'I want you. The real you. No condoms.'

'Is it safe?'

'Perfectly safe. Come on, come on.'

Then came a loud knock on Wayne's bedroom door.

'Fire in the kitchen,' shouted a woman loudly. He didn't recognise the voice.

'Wayne,' said a familiar voice. 'The clematis has toppled over. Come and give me a hand with it.'

'Ah, the clematis,' Wayne told the black-haired woman. He stepped out of bed, put on a dressing-gown and looked around the room. He waited until his erection had subsided. Then he picked up the woman's clothes, carried them out of the bedroom and locked the bedroom door from the outside.

TWENTY-SIX

'Where is she?' Tracey Holroyd asked Wayne when he appeared in the lounge.

'I've locked her in the bedroom,' Wayne said. 'She'll either break out and come past us this way, or she'll jump out of the window and break a leg or two.'

'Is that why you have that hook and eye *outside* the bedroom?' said Kate Park. 'To lock your women in?'

'The previous people put it on,' Wayne said. 'It was to stop the cat getting into the bedroom when they were out. I left it on. I thought it might come in handy one day.' He looked at Kate. 'And so it has. It's not strong enough to hold her, though.'

'Let's go in and get her,' Tracey said.

'Thanks for the clematis warning,' Wayne told Kate. 'You understood?'

'Indeed. Your code. A matter of life and death. Was she going to attack me?'

'Possibly in two ways,' Kate said. 'We thought we'd better err on the safe side.'

Wayne put his finger over his mouth. They hushed. Listened to light footsteps on the stairs. The black-haired woman, now dressed, suddenly took the last few stairs two at a time and tried to dart through the lounge towards the front door. Wayne moved out in front of her and Tracey Holroyd grabbed her from behind. Without showing any real exertion Tracey had the woman's arm behind her back and was forcing her to squeal.

'This is Em,' Wayne told the other women. 'I doubt if it's her real name.'

'Let me go,' said Em, 'You're hurting me.'

'I've not started yet,' said Tracey.

'I thought you were working tonight,' Wayne said to Kate.

'No. I cancelled. I needed to sort out a few things in my mind. Then I had a sudden fear for your safety.'

Em was wearing a pair of Wayne's old jogging trousers, rolled up at the bottom, and an even older sweat shirt. She was on the floor now, on her front, and Tracey was on top of her.

'She's wearing my clothes,' Wayne told Tracey. 'Don't spoil them.'

'Too late,' said Tracey, looking at the jogging pants. 'Years too late.'

'I need some backstory here,' Wayne said.

'Of course,' said Tracey, while effortlessly holding Em. 'My original plan was to distract Hanson so that women from a refuge could collect Rachel.' She looked at Wayne.

'Help me tie her to a chair and I'll tell you more.' She looked around the lounge. 'Do you have a chair?'

Wayne brought a chair from the kitchen and they wedged it into a corner of the room. Wayne and Tracey did the rope work. They sat the woman on the floor and tied her hands behind her back to the legs of a dining-room chair. Em was crying. Tracey leaned close to Em and whispered something that the others couldn't hear. Em looked frightened.

'Mackie collected Hanson from his house,' Wayne prompted, when they were ready.

'Yes,' said Tracey. 'Hanson was out of the way. Then something went wrong with our plan.' She turned to the tied-up woman. 'How did you find out about Rachel?'

'Who?' the woman said.

Tracey Holroyd hit Em on her left cheek with the palm of her right hand.

'Tracey,' said Kate, sternly. 'No.'

The black-haired woman was shaking now.

'She's not well,' Kate told the others. 'She's ill. We don't need to be as vindictive. We don't need to abuse her.'

Tracey Holroyd looked at her captive.

'Our main purpose is to find a way of stopping her doing more damage,' Kate said.

'She probably wants to be a martyr,' Tracey said.

'What's been going on?' Wayne asked.

'I think she has an infectious disease,' Kate said. 'Looking at her, I would guess hepatitis of some form. She has been sleeping without protection with a number of men in attempts to harm them. She picked up Robin Hookes in a pub and went back to his place to sleep with him.'

'Picked up me in a pub and came to my place with me,' said Wayne.

'Went after a jewellery shop owner who had wronged Rachel,' said Kate.

'I've an idea,' said Wayne. 'Let's get the men together here. Ask them if they appreciate what she's done for them.'

'Was Buck Hanson one of your men?' Tracey asked the black-haired woman. 'Oh, you recognise the name. Buck can be a brute in bed, can't he?'

'I've got Buck's number on my mobile,' Wayne said. 'Do you want to phone him, Tracey, get him round?'

Em was shaking again.

'Look,' Kate said. 'I'm concerned for her welfare. We need to take care of her. The best thing is to call the police and an ambulance.'

'The police can't do anything to me,' said the black-haired woman, suddenly feisty again.

'The problem here, Em,' said Wayne, 'is that you've got two bad cops and only one good cop.'

'She may be right,' Kate said. 'It may be impossible to have her arrested. We need to discuss this and think about it. We need to calm down too.'

'Has she got a mobile phone?' Tracey asked Wayne.

'No,' Wayne replied. 'I searched her bag and clothes when she was in the bathroom.'

'Let's calm down,' Kate repeated.

'Yeah, this place smells of revenge,' said Wayne. 'It's quite a sweet smell.'

'Let us not be vengeful,' added Kate. She looked at Wayne and continued the recap for him. 'We're guessing that Rachel Hanson left her husband on her own initiative, but she may have been coerced by a second organisation, perhaps some sort of cult. They tried to get money out of Buck Hanson and failed. So they staged photographs of Rachel's death. Rachel needs time to recover from her marriage. She needs a safe place until she knows what she is going to do. We need to think about Rachel too. We don't want to put her at risk from Buck Hanson.'

'Let's hope she's not under a patio,' said Tracey. 'Or down a well somewhere.'

'A kidnapping charge might be the easiest charge for the police to establish,' said Kate.

'But Hanson doesn't want that to happen,' Wayne said. 'He has something he wants to protect.'

'Maybe Rachel knows things about Buck Hanson that would make him drop charges,' said Em, more confident.

The other three looked at her.

'We know that Em delivered the third threatening note,' said Wayne.

'Did she tell you that?' asked Tracey.

'Her gait did. And her height.'

'She may have been trying to infect men so that Juliet could be infected as well,' said Kate. 'That's the threat.'

'Why don't we build a case for attempted murder against her?' Wayne asked.

'These cases are very complex,' Kate said. 'Especially if hepatitis B is involved.'

Em smiled.

'I think we should just beat a confession out of her,' said Tracey.

Em's smile disappeared.

'No,' said Kate. 'I'm not going to let that happen. We need to think about this. We need to consider what we can send to the police. Can we take a break? This could take a while.'

'Anybody for tuna casserole?' Wayne asked. 'There's enough for four. Are you hungry, Em, after all our exercise?'

'I thought the kitchen was on fire,' said Em.

'I lied about that,' said Tracey.

'Did you have time to, er?' Kate asked Wayne, nodding towards Em.

Wayne shook his head.

'Didn't get that far,' he said.

'I'm not hungry,' said Em.

'There's a bottle of wine opened and it's safe to drink,' said Wayne. 'I'll get dressed.'

The phone rang while they were still eating. Kate moved to the hallway when she learned that the call was from Deborah. She found a notepad and pen.

'I spoke with Holly Venn on the phone,' Deborah said. 'I think your theory fits. Well done for thinking about it. You may have a defence.'

'I think I will leave that conclusion to the solicitor,' Kate said. 'The problem is that he might have to put the young girl on the stand and interrogate her.'

'Surely they will drop the case.'

'If no one's career is at stake,' Kate said. 'But Fiona Coates would hate the charges to be dropped. She would like Bruce Venn to be hung, drawn, quartered and cut into sixteens. I understand her position.'

'Kate, you're doing your job. And doing it well.'

'So what did you learn?'

'Holly gave me a detailed description of Bruce's honking and bonking.'

'Honking and bonking. Was that what she called it?'

'What do you think?'

'I bet that's your summary, Deb.'

'Correct. I've put a transcription of my conversation with Holly in an email to you. I left off a private conversation that we had at the end.'

'Thanks. It's a pity we won't be able to discuss it openly and therapeutically with the fifteen-year-old. Why wasn't Olivia as angry and traumatised as the mother?'

'Maybe she'd come for the first time because he was inside her for so long.'

'Deb! Only you could think of that.'

'People have to learn how to seek therapy themselves,' Deborah said. 'Give them my card.'

'You come highly recommended.'

'Holly talked about him snorting while they were making love during the night. That was her word – snorting.'

'Snorting as in snorting cocaine?'

'No. Snorting as in making a snorting noise. I asked if the T could be silent.'

'And she said?'

'She said that she had often wondered about that, but she thought it impossible.'

'Oh, boy.'

'I asked her to mimic the noise. She snorted very well. It would make for a great stunt in court.'

'Thanks, Deborah. Send me your bill.'

'Thank *you*, Kate. It's opened me up to a new arena of sexual therapy.'

'I'll give Bruce Venn your details so he can contact you for therapy.'

'Sounds wonderful. I think I'll see him in person.'

'I have a list of remedies I can send to him first.'

'Can you send a copy to me too?'

'Of course.'

'Well done.'

'Yeah, sure,' said Kate. 'But I've got a much more difficult one to deal with now.'

'Tell me about that.'

'I will do – when I've got more time.'

They said their goodbyes. Then Kate made some notes on her pad in preparation for writing a report on Bruce Venn for Jeremy Spooner.

When Kate returned to the lounge, the situation was calmer. Tracey was reading a book and enjoying a glass of wine. Em was still tied to the chair, sitting on a cushion on the floor, but Wayne was sitting between her legs, pinning her thighs with his calves, feeding her tuna casserole with a spoon. Kate watched for a few moments. She found the scene surprisingly touching. Wayne held the woman's upper arm lightly and used his other hand to lift a spoonful of food to her mouth.

'I feel like a baby,' Em told Wayne.

'I felt just as helpless in the presence of your

lascivious beauty,' said Wayne.

Kate continued to watch. Eventually she decided on a way forward.

'Can we make one or two changes here?' Kate said. 'How about if we untie her and she sits on a chair while we talk. If she tries to make a break for it she risks getting seriously injured.'

'I need a wee,' Em said.

'I'll go with her,' said Tracey.

'Take anything dangerous out of the bathroom,' Wayne suggested.

'I'll stand over her,' said Tracey. 'She'll behave.'

Tracey untied Em. Wayne helped her to her feet, gave her a hug. Tracey and Em left the room and went downstairs to the toilet.

'You have a plan?' Wayne asked Kate.

'Not really. I'd like to talk through what might happen if we involve the police. First, I'd like to find out whether or not she did target Buck Hanson. Do you have a mobile phone with a number that Hanson won't recognise?'

'I can withhold the number on mine and I've got Hanson among my contacts. I'll get the phone for you.'

Kate waited until Em and Tracey had returned before making the call.

'Hello,' said Kate, speaking on Wayne's mobile, using a breathy voice that partially resembled Em's. 'Do you remember me, Buck? I'm the one with the black hair and athletic body.'

'Oh, yeah. The thin one.'

'I'd love to see you again, Buck.'

'Yeah, I suppose you would. But it was just a shag, darling.'

'Oh. There's a lot more I could do for you.'

'Yeah, I suppose there is,' Buck Hanson said. 'I'll be in the same bar tomorrow night.'

'Oh, thanks, Buck, I'll look forward to that.'

Kate disconnected.

'I just can't do this sex talk without it being a proper relationship,' Kate said, reverting to her normal voice.

'Stick to your day job, Kate,' Tracey said.

'Let's take this case to a hypothetical court,' said Kate. 'Let's examine the case for the prosecution and the case for the defence. Which do you want first?'

'Prosecution,' said Wayne.

'Defence,' said Em. 'There is no case.'

Ask a silly question, Kate thought.

'Prosecution,' said Tracey. 'There is no defence.'

'Oh, I think there is,' said Em.

Wayne picked up one of the spoons and banged on the hard floor.

'Order,' he said. 'Order in court. Or I'll set my dog on you.'

Everyone looked at Rover.

'Has he ever bitten anyone?' asked Em.

'No,' said Wayne. 'If he ever bit anyone I'd have him put down.'

'Right,' said Kate. 'The normal procedure is for the prosecution to go first. Let's say that Em has been accused of causing grievous bodily harm with multiple victims.'

'What's wrong with attempted murder?' asked Tracey.

'Some countries have introduced a new offence – having unprotected sex and knowingly infecting a lover with a fatal disease. In Britain the nearest offence has been the charge of causing grievous bodily harm.'

'Isn't it use of a deadly weapon?' Wayne asked.

'Thank you,' said Em.

'The governor of South Dakota once described a man deliberating infecting women with AIDS as no different to pointing a gun at someone and pointing the trigger,' said Kate.

'That's debatable,' said Tracey.

'Agreed,' said Kate. 'The victims in this case include the jeweller, Buck Hanson and Robin Hookes. I suspect there are a few more.'

'Objection,' said Em. 'Hearsay.'

'That's all we need, a barrack-room lawyer,' said Wayne. 'What about her attempt to kill me? What charge can I get her on?'

'I don't know,' said Kate. 'Attempted grievous bodily harm? I'm not sure that exists. There's also a charge of threatening behaviour, or whatever it's called, for her letters to Juliet. As regards Juliet it would surely be impossible to find a suitable charge. I can't imagine there's anything like criminal damage by coital cascade.' As she talked, Kate realised that she was too ignorant about police matters. 'I suppose we'd have to show that Rachel was Juliet's nemesis, Em was Rachel's accomplice and the men were Juliet's lovers. We also have to prove that Em had a disease capable of causing grievous bodily harm. What do you have, Em?'

'You'll have to find out for yourself.'

'Or we'll keep you here until you tell us,' said Tracey. She whispered something in Em's ear.

'I've got hepatitis B,' said Em. She looked at Kate and said, 'Clever girl.'

'How bad is that?' asked Wayne. Kate thought Wayne's voice sounded like that of a concerned new lover.

'Bad.'

'Cirrhosis?' Kate asked.

'Chronic active hep B with cirrhosis,' said Em.

'I'm sorry. Are you a carrier?'

Em looked away.

'There are several problems with our case,' Kate continued. 'One is the precedent that it's the victim's responsibility to protect themselves, especially on the first night. A first-time lover doesn't have to tell the other about their sexual history. Another is that most prosecutions have been brought against people who are causing grievous bodily harm because they are HIV-positive. Hepatitis B is very different. In a lot of cases it is difficult to determine the origins of the infection. Some people with the disease are carriers, but others are not. So we would have to wait until one of Em's victims clearly has the disease, while hoping that none of them do contract it. Symptoms of the disease may not appear for a few months. And by then the lineage may not be clear. It might have come from one of a number of sources if the victim has been sexually active with a number of lovers.'

'Why are you looking at me?' Wayne asked Kate.

Kate hadn't realised that she was.

'Another problem is that Em could plead that she was psychologically disturbed when she went on her rampage,' said Kate. 'She could argue that it was natural to feel angry and confused. And so on.'

'What counts as protecting yourself on the first night?' Wayne asked. 'Using condoms, I presume. How about asking your partner about her sexual health?'

'I suppose that may be evidence, depending on your partner's answer,' said Kate.

'Excuse me for a moment,' said Wayne. He went upstairs.

'We would have to prove that she consciously and deliberately set out to maim someone,' said Kate, looking at Tracey.

'This must have been discussed in front of other members of the group she belongs to,' said Tracey. 'Someone would be able to give evidence against her.'

'Unless she was a free spirit who didn't discuss anything with others,' interjected Em. 'A poor, disturbed, sick woman, suffering from post-traumatic shock and denial, taking her place in court in a wheelchair, a bag of bones who looks incapable of harming anyone.'

'Yeah, sure,' said Tracey.

'I'm sorry, Mr Judge, I didn't realise what I was doing,' said Em.

Kate thought Tracey might hit Em again, so she stepped between the two women.

'What are the symptoms of hepatitis B?' Tracey asked Kate.

'Forty per cent of hepatitis B cases have no symptoms. Hepatitis B is another silent infection. Early signs may be aching joints, a rash, abdominal pain, nausea, vomiting, dark urine. It eventually affects the liver. It's the leading cause of liver cancer.'

'And fatal, obviously?' Tracey asked.

'Yes,' Kate said. 'More than a million deaths every year. And that's only the deaths that the World Health Organisation knows about. It's very prominent in some parts of Asia, Africa and South America. Carriers may not become noticeably sick and may not realise they have the disease. A small percentage develop the acute form.'

Kate thought about her recent discussion with Tracey. Teddy Merlin had recommended the vaccination and Tracey had taken his advice. That conversation with Tracey seemed a long time ago now. Yet it was less than a fortnight ago.

'It's more likely to be transmitted during anal intercourse,' Kate continued. 'The incubation period is anything from forty-five to 180 days. In some cases it shows earlier. Basically, any time in the first nine months. The figures would be a big part of any court case. Tracing its roots. About one in twenty infected people are unable to eliminate the virus. The rest get rid of the infection and go on to have lifelong protection against being infected again.'

'Maybe I've got rid of it,' said Em.

Wayne returned. Carrying a tape-recorder.

'Better say that again for Wayne's benefit,' Tracey told Kate. 'About how it is transmitted.'

'Vaginal sex, anal sex, oral sex and perhaps even kissing,' Kate said. 'It can be passed from mother to child.'

'Kissing?' Wayne asked. He looked at Em, who turned her head away.

'Transmitted through blood or saliva,' Kate said. 'More of a problem when a woman carrier is bleeding.'

Kate thought Wayne looked concerned. She thought she saw him shudder.

'Exhibit one,' Wayne said. 'Tape of conversation between defendant and prey.'

He played the tape.

No. No condoms. You're safe with me.

What was that?

I want you. The real you. No condoms.

Is it safe?

Perfectly safe. Come on, come on.

They thought about Wayne's tape for a while.

'I don't know whether it's evidence or not,' said Kate.

'How about asking your solicitor friend?' Wayne asked.

'Good idea,' said Kate.

'What are we going to do with her?' said Wayne, pointing to Em.

'Can you put a security tag on her?' Tracey asked Wayne. 'So we know where she is at all times?'

'Can you tag wrestle with her?' Wayne asked Tracey. 'Use her as your opponent while you show me some useful holds.'

'Wayne,' said Kate.

'Shall I just put her over my knee and give her a good spanking?' Wayne said.

'Yes, please,' said Em.

'Enough,' said Kate. 'I could talk to Jeremy Spooner but I don't think he would be experienced in this sort of case. No one would be. I think we're all entering the unknown. I can't honestly see how she could be prosecuted. The case would be too complicated. She would evoke sympathy from a jury.'

Deep down Kate was doubtful about her own capacity to understand the complexities of this situation. Ideally she could agree a plan with Wayne and Tracey, but Kate had no idea what a peaceful solution was. What was the right thing to do?

'What can we do with her while we are thinking about it?' Kate asked.

'How about if you handcuff me to Wayne for the night?' asked Em.

'We need her real name,' said Wayne. 'Where are you staying?'

'Here,' said Em. 'Or so it seems. You're holding me against my will.'

'Were there no car keys in her possession?' asked Tracey.

'Kidnappers,' Em said. She went to scream.

Tracey was ready for it. She clasped a hand over Em's mouth and pressed her jaw.

'I am starting to feel like a kidnapper,' said Kate.

Tracey released her grip on Em.

'Let me check her clothes for car keys,' Wayne said. He disappeared upstairs.

'What about a kidnapping charge against *her*?' asked Tracey. 'Or we could introduce her to Buck Hanson. Tell Buck that she's the kidnapper who tried to infect him.'

'We're going round in circles,' said Kate.

'Nothing to identify her,' said Wayne, returning. 'No car keys.'

'I give up,' said Kate.

'How about if I get myself infected?' said Wayne.

'That's stupid Wayne,' said Kate. 'That's just bugchasing.'

'But think of the fun,' Em told Wayne.

'That would be your fault, not hers, Wayne,' said Tracey.

'We just need more time to think of something,' said Wayne.

'I have to go soon,' said Tracey. 'I've got to get changed and go to work.'

'I need to write a report,' said Kate.

'I think we should let her go,' said Wayne. He winked at Kate.

'Do what you want,' said Tracey. 'Thanks for the meal, Wayne.'

Tracey left.

'OK, set her free, Wayne,' said Kate. 'Return her clothes.'

'I'm happy to stay and use a condom, Wayne,' Em said.

'Chase her off, Rover, chase her off,' said Wayne.

Wayne watched Em change clothes and then showed her to the door.

TWENTY-SEVEN

'When did you decide that you would tape the pillow talk, Wayne?' Kate asked.

An hour and a half had passed. They were in the kitchen. Kate was working on her laptop at the table. She had nearly finished typing her report on the Venn case for Jeremy Spooner. Wayne was reading the report over her shoulder.

'I was suspicious of her at the start,' Wayne said. 'She bulldozed through my defences. I wanted to be alone in the pub and she intruded. Then when she came here I thought her gait and height resembled the woman in the CCTV footage. And I had very strong suspicions that she was interested in something more than my body and mind.'

'Well done. I thought Em was warming to your mind later, just before we set her free.'

'You're a very clever person.'

'Not really. I was clueless what to do with her and I couldn't think of anyone else who would know.'

'No, I mean your report for Spooner,' Wayne said, pointing to the laptop. 'On the screen here.'

'Could you fix the hook and eye on your bedroom door? Then I can lock you in.'

Wayne laughed.

'How did you know Mr Venn was suffering from sleepsex?' he asked.

'Several reasons. Holly and Bruce Venn gave different frequencies when asked how often they made love. Bruce couldn't remember anything about the incident with Olivia. He left the door open and made enough noise to disturb Olivia's mother. He was stressed at work. Disturbed sleep. And, when Holly Venn thought about it, she confirmed that on occasion he was snoring while they were making love.'

'I've never heard of sleepsex,' said Wayne.

'It's really a type of sleepwalking. About one per cent of the population may have direct experience with sleepsex. More men engage in it than women.'

'What's the sex like?'

'That's a typical Wayne question.'

'Can you give me a typical Kate answer?'

'The answer is that the sex is different from normal. The sleepsexer is often more adventurous. They moan more, bite more and are more vocal. It can be more exciting and playful for the other person, but it can be aggressive and frightening too. The other person may try to stop them but it's like talking to a brick wall. Afterwards the sleepsexer can't remember what happened. It's Jekyll and Hyde, Dr Awake and Mr Asleep.'

'I might worry so much about being a sleepsexer that I stay awake all night.'

'It's more likely to happen in the first two hours of sleep – the REM stage.'

'Great,' said Wayne. 'I just need to stay awake for the first hours of sleep.'

Kate smiled.

'You've done a great job for Mr Venn and Lawyer Spooner,' Wayne said.

'I guess.'

'You don't seem too elated.'

'It's complicated, isn't it? Sleepsex needs more publicity because it may be that men have been wrongly convicted in the past. But others might try to use it as an excuse or defence when they are actually guilty of sexual assault.'

Wayne read more of what Kate was typing. 'What do you think will happen now?' he asked.

'I think we will remain good friends,' Kate said.

'No, I mean with Em. You and me being friends is statutory in my law book.'

Wayne started massaging Kate's shoulders. Kate tensed slightly.

'It's OK,' Wayne said. 'I'm not trying to seduce you. I am just trying to show that I know you've been through a hard time.'

'I've also had a wonderful time. I had those years with Teddy and enjoyed every day. He was all I ever wanted in a man. We were very close. He was my intellectual mentor and he gave me a direction. I want to be a sexologist like him. I want to study in the United States.'

'Did you have a good physical relationship?'

Kate tensed her shoulders again and Wayne stopped massaging.

'Is that all that's important to you?' Kate asked.

'No. I'm just curious. You were two people who studied sex. I have a lot to learn. I'd like to inch towards your knowledge.'

A silence followed. Kate was thinking. Then she spoke.

'When we made love it was like he was doing it with a thousand years of experience,' she said. 'He was very gentle, very tender, very giving, and yet there were moments of pure passion. My body had years of that. My body is not yet ready for comparisons.'

'I'm sure you gave him a lot of happiness too,' Wayne said.

'I hope so.'

'Do you prefer older men?' Wayne asked her.

'I fell in love with Teddy because of who he was, not because he was an older man. But he was more relaxed than most men and he had less to prove. He had his career sorted out and he didn't need to be macho and selfish in bed.'

Wayne's mobile phone rang. Wayne looked at the caller ID.

'I have to take this,' he said. He hit the phone button.

'Listening,' he said.

'Fleur Rhodes-Jones,' said a male voice. 'Bed and breakfast. Car parked there. Number?'

'Please.'

Mackie gave Wayne the car number.

'Drove like a lunatic,' Mackie said.

'Of course. She probably drove like she didn't care if she lived or died. Sorry, I should have thought of that.'

'Mmm.'

'You did well, Mackie.'

'Safety first.'

'Yeah,' Wayne agreed.

'And, Mister er . . .'

'Has he asked to see you?'

'Mmm.'

'Do what Mister Richard asks. It's OK with me. I will bear no grudge, Mackie.'

Wayne disconnected.

'Em is now calling herself Fleur Rhodes-Jones,' he told Kate. 'Mackie lost contact with her because she drove like a woman who didn't care if she lived or died. Pity! I thought she might lead us straight to a cult. But he got her address. Strange thing about the address though.'

'What's that?'

'It's different from the one I got for her.'

'You got an address for her?'

'On a prescription packet that was in her pocket.'

'When did you find that?'

'When I slipped out to get the tape recorder.'

Kate turned round and looked at him.

'May I use your computer to send this to the solicitor?' Kate asked.

'Of course. It reads very well.'

'Sleep well, Wayne.'

'You too,' said Wayne. 'You deserve a good night's sleep. You've put in an excellent shift.'

'It was a bit different from the one I turned down at the hospital.'

Wayne woke very early on Wednesday morning. He lay in bed processing the events of the previous day, checking his mobile phone was alive, waiting for today to unfold. The phone rang at 7.43.

'Awake,' said Wayne.

'Come in to the office now,' said Richard Bromage, some venom in his voice as he despatched his words through thin lips. 'Come as you are.'

'I'll put some clothes on,' Wayne said, but he knew what Richard Bromage meant. Don't wear working clothes.

Wayne got to the Bromage building quickly. Mackie was on duty with the other security people. Keeping himself busy. Mackie didn't make eye contact. Wayne took the stairs to the third floor.

The third floor was funereal. No Juliet and no sign of Mary Curtis. It was like the middle of the night. Richard Bromage had his door open. He saw Wayne.

'Come straight through,' he called.

Wayne went through. Bromage seemed to have aged five years.

'Sit down, Wayne,' Bromage said.

Wayne sat down.

'I've been thinking about all this,' Bromage started. 'I think I see a solution.' Wayne kept quiet. He anticipated what was coming. 'I think it's time to come to an arrangement. I'd like to buy you out of your contract but keep a skeleton staff.'

'Of course.'

'Good.'

'How much?' Wayne asked.

Bromage told him and they haggled over money. Then they talked at length about Bromage's security staff. Wayne had trained the staff well and had given them freedom to act. Wayne suggested the name of another consultant to help if necessary, someone to provide what Juliet would have called a helicopter view. They discussed the advantages and disadvantages of in-house and contract staff, and the benefits of mixing the two. Wayne briefed Bromage on some details.

'I appreciate all you've done over the years,' Bromage said. 'You've done a good job for me, Wayne, but I'm going to have to change a few things around here. Split up the businesses. It's time for you to move on, and I'm looking after you.'

Wayne laughed. It was not the reaction Bromage had expected.

'Sorry. I was laughing at the idea of escorting myself off the premises.'

Bromage glowered. Then smiled slightly.

'Everything covered in the short term?' Wayne asked.

'Yes. I've spoken to Mackie. He'll take charge.'

'Yeah, he's a great bloke. I'll tell him where everything is. And he can phone me if he needs to know anything.'

Then Wayne looked closely at Bromage, who must

have felt Wayne's eyes assessing his body.

'It won't be long now,' Bromage said.

Wayne was a long time answering.

'I'm sorry,' Wayne said. 'I'm really sorry.'

What else can you say when someone knows they are dying.

'A few months, maybe longer,' he said. 'You can never tell with these things. You're best off out of the way.'

'I owe you a lot,' Wayne said. 'Thanks for all you've done for me.'

Richard Bromage looked embarrassed. Then he stood up and dismissed Wayne by offering his hand. Wayne shook it. Thin and bony.

'You always gave me a hundred per cent, Wayne,' Bromage continued. 'In your own way. That's all I ask for. Thanks.'

They shook hands again and Wayne walked out of the room.

Downstairs Mackie acknowledged Wayne's presence.

'Feel bad,' Mackie said.

'Don't you dare resign,' Wayne said. 'I'm being paid off. He wouldn't do that to you. Two out of work is worse than one.'

Mackie nodded.

'You know where everything is?' Wayne asked.

Mackie already understood the filing system. He knew all about patrolling, guarding, access control and the protection of cash in transit. Wayne told him all about the staff's salaries and made sure he knew about all the training courses available - IPSA, Group 4, SITO, universities, St John Ambulance, Fire Brigade - and the location of pressure pads. He told Mackie about the two old dears he paid to keep a lookout at key times.

Wayne and Mackie spent a couple of hours going through the details. Wayne was surprised by how relieved he was feeling. He was ready to move on. Juliet had become his main connection to the Bromage family and now that was all over. And doing it this way kept Mackie in a job until the empire disintegrated.

'Change all the door codes when I go out,' Wayne told Mackie, at the end. 'The computer stuff will give you the most trouble. But phone me any time, especially when you want to learn how to defend corner-kicks.'

Mackie nodded and smiled.

'No hard feelings,' Wayne added. 'You're well qualified to head a security operation. You'll probably do almost as well as me.'

They both laughed.

'Thanks for coming in,' said Jeremy Spooner. It was one o'clock at his office. Kate had had her best night's sleep since Teddy's death and had spent the morning organising her filing so that she could update sections of *Sex and Sexuality*. She had another hour before her late shift at the hospital.

'No problem,' said Kate.

'First of all, I still need to apologise for my behaviour at your house the other day. I was totally out of order. I think I was just bowled over by your beauty and intelligence. It happened again when I read your report.'

'I appreciate the apology,' Kate said. 'I'd like to make

it clear that I'd like to keep our relationship on a professional basis. I don't want any other form of relationship with you. But I feel that we can *work* together successfully.'

'Sure. Do I need to apologise to your minder?'

'Wayne?'

'Yes.'

'I don't think so. Wayne wasn't in a good mood that night either. He'd had some bad news. The apology could go both ways.'

'Just tell him that I know I was in the wrong with how I handled you. I'm afraid I had had a bit to drink.'

'Let's put that in the past and return to the case,' said Kate.

Jeremy Spooner opened the file.

'I'm going to see if I can get the case dropped,' he said. 'I phoned Bruce Venn and asked the questions you suggested - had it happened to him before? Had anyone diagnosed the problem? Had anyone even suggested what the problem might be?'

'And his answers?'

'He was shocked. Genuinely shocked. He didn't believe what I was trying to tell him. He answered no to all three questions.'

'There's nothing in his medical notes?'

'He says not. I believe him because he didn't believe me.'

'I'll speak with him,' Kate said. 'Tell him what he can do about it. If it happens again he will have no defence. He needs to get help. I'll explain how he can go about getting help.'

'This is very different to wet dreams, isn't it?'

'Yes,' Kate said. 'This is sleepsex, also known as sexsomnia. Nocturnal emissions are much more normal. About ninety per cent of men have nocturnal emissions, and thirty to forty per cent of women. People with sleepsex have a disturbed sexual identification. They are usually appalled when they find out what they've done.'

'You say in your report that people have used sleepsex as a defence against a rape charge.' Spooner read Kate's words aloud. '*Sleepwalkers can certainly have full-blown sex without realising it and without the other person wanting it; but their defence would have to be a legal test of what is consciousness, what is consent and what is evidence of force.*'

'Yes,' Kate said. 'It's difficult to fathom, like so much of sexuality.'

'There are precedents for acquittal,' Spooner said. 'Tell me more about how you see it.'

'We all have sleep activity,' Kate told Spooner. 'It usually consists of tossing and turning. Some people walk, talk or eat in their sleep. Others sit up in bed. It's much less common, but possible, for people to try – and succeed in – having sexual intercourse while asleep. Some people can be more sexually aggressive and dominant while asleep than when awake.'

'And you say it's difficult for those assaulted to prove that they have had sexual contact without their consent?'

'I've listed certain questions that you could ask Olivia.'

'And Holly Venn will verify that he made love with

her while he was asleep?'

'She heard him snoring and only later did she understand what was really happening.'

'She never told him?' Spooner asked.

'No.'

'She said that he lasted longer when asleep than when he was awake?'

'Yes,' Kate said. 'But the prosecution may try to say that he came more quickly in this case because he hadn't had sex for a while, or that he was excited as it was their first time together and Olivia was so young and beautiful.'

'What's ictal sexual hyperarousal? Under your list of identified sleep-related sexual behaviours you've listed ictal sexual hyperarousal, ictal orgasm and ictal automatism.'

'I think it means sudden and unexpected.'

'Can sleepsex affect women too?'

'Yes. Women can be the initiators in their sleep. Women can masturbate in their sleep.'

'Has that ever happened to you?'

'Thanks for involving me in the case,' said Kate, not rising to the bait. 'It's been helpful for me. I need to add something on sleepsex to Teddy's book.' Kate paused for a moment. 'May I ask you a question?'

'Of course,' said Spooner.

'It concerns another issue. It's a hypothetical case.'

'Go ahead.'

Kate told him about the black-haired woman with hepatitis B. She kept the characters anonymous and drew a diagram for Spooner as far as she could guess.

'So,' said Spooner. 'You're saying that she targeted a string of men and went on a spree deliberately trying to infect them.'

'Yes. She may have had anal sex with a few or maybe not. That's much more risky.'

'All consensual.'

'Yes. Seductive and consensual.'

'Only once with each one?'

'I don't know. Say it was.'

'I think it's the man's duty to protect himself for the first occasion.'

'Which side would you prefer to be on – prosecution or defence?'

'Oh, defence. Definitely. It would be a minefield for the prosecution without people hearing the woman say that she meant to kill the victims.'

The perfect serial killer, Kate thought. Surely there must be a way of exacting punishment.

'Is this an actual case?' Spooner asked. 'If it is, I wouldn't mind defending it. Especially with you on my team.'

'I'm not sure.'

'Let me know if it's one we can tout for.'

Kate nodded.

It was the next evening before Kate spoke with Bruce Venn on the telephone. They chatted for some time before they got down to the specifics of sleepsex. Then Kate quickly established that Bruce Venn had accepted his role as a sleepsexer.

'I've found a website about it,' Venn told her.

'Well done. Would you like me to summarise what I know about it?'

'Please.'

'The good side of sleepsex is when it occurs occasionally during an established sexual relationship, when both individuals enjoy it, accept it and view it with a sense of humour. The bad side of sleepsex is when it causes trauma and distress and the police get involved. A very bad side of sleepsex is if the trauma is suffered by someone with a history of being sexually assaulted or abused.'

'I'm still going to feel guilty.'

'You were very unlucky. It can happen when the sleepsexer goes to bed and falls asleep for an hour or two, and then the partner comes to bed and cuddles up to them. That can set off the sleepsexer.'

For the first time Kate wondered if Fiona had gone to bed next to Bruce at some time on that fateful night. Maybe that was why she had heard the rumpus.

'Let me give you a number to phone if you'd like some counselling,' Kate told Venn. 'I think it's important to show the court that you're doing something for this problem. This number is for a sex therapist called Deborah who does quite a lot of telephone counselling.'

She gave him Deborah's details.

'Thanks,' said Bruce Venn.

'I can give you a list of tips if that is any help.'

'Fire away.'

'Get plenty of rest so that you're not overtired. A

hypnotherapist might help. I'll ask around and see if I can find someone who might know about this subject.'

'Thanks. I do appreciate this.'

'Develop a calming mechanism for when you go to bed. I think it's a question of going back to basics. A warm bath. Soothing music. Meditation. A book that's not too exciting. Sleepwalkers are usually advised to stick to the ground floor, in case they go out of a window.'

'Gawd,' said Venn.

'Sorry, I don't mean to alarm you. I suspect that much of this will settle down as your life becomes more relaxed.'

'I should write and apologise to Fiona and Olivia.'

'Talk to Jeremy Spooner before you do that. He may see it as evidence of guilt.'

'Thanks for this, Kate. Anything else?'

'Oh, maybe find yourself a regular sexual partner.'

'Easier said than done.'

'I know. Good luck. You've got my number if there's anything you think of after we hang up.'

'Can I phone you to . . . er . . . you know . . . ask you out?'

'Thank you, but no. I'm recently widowed and not ready to date. I meant for you to phone me to ask questions about sleepsex.'

'Sorry.'

'I'll be in the rest of the evening.'

'Thanks again.'

TWENTY-EIGHT

'I was going to visit the United States but I think I'll stay and work on this film,' Kate told Wayne, as they sat on the floor of Wayne's lounge.

'What about that, Rover?' Wayne said. 'Our friend may be staying.'

'I'll have to stay on the film set for part of the project,' Kate said.

'I won't charge you rent while you're away.'

A fortnight had passed since Kate had submitted her report on the Venn case. Kate and Wayne had not seen each other much during those two weeks. Kate had been busy with as many nursing shifts as possible. Her teaching had ended and she was marking assignments. She had written a short section on sleepsex and a longer section on internet sex for *Sex and Sexuality*.

Wayne had been busy too. He had been visiting

universities in an attempt to win a campus security contract. But his football stadium contract had been renewed. Richard Bromage's health had deteriorated rapidly, Jim Bailey was planning retirement, and Juliet was back in her office trying to work out which parts of the business she wanted to keep. Nobody had explained what her trauma had been, but Kate had a theory about what Buck Hanson might have done to her.

'The place won't be the same without you,' Wayne told Kate. They had eaten together and were drinking whisky. Wayne was drinking most of it.

'So, you were going to tell me the Fleur Rhodes-Jones story,' Kate said. 'Go back to when you had two addresses for her.'

'Yes. Neither was much use. One was fictitious. The other was her parents' address. I went to see them, but they were distraught. Their daughter had been to see them a few weeks ago and told them that she was going away to die.'

'Oh, my,' said Kate.

'Going away to die like a cat. They had a few days together and then she left a note asking that they shouldn't think ill of her – it had been a short and sweet life.'

'That was my reason for letting her go,' Kate said. 'I didn't expect her to survive through a trial. She looked very ill.'

'I saw photographs of her in her younger days. I thought it was her sister. She looked much chunkier.'

'The poor parents. I hope you gave them comfort.'

'I told them Fleur was a heroic woman.'

'I'm glad the parents won't be put through any publicity or the shock of seeing their daughter in prison. The loss of a daughter is more than enough.'

'Yes. But she was on a callous crusade.'

'Maybe. There is a lesson there for you, Wayne. Protect yourself. Safety first, sex second.'

'My tests were negative. Well, apart from chlamydia.'

'Excellent news. You were fortunate.'

They sat quietly for a minute.

'Do you remember our walk near Stratford?' Kate asked.

'I'll never forget it.'

'It made me realise how much I needed to get away from Oxford. It would do me good to leave the country, but going down to Hampshire for this film will also be good for me, too.'

'Well, I'll certainly miss you. And Rover is looking particularly sad. Stop whining, Rover. She'll come back to us. Tell him, Kate.'

'I'll come back to you, Rover.'

'Thanks, Kate. Look how he's cheered up.'

They sipped their whisky.

'I visited Caprice yesterday,' Kate said.

'How was she?' Wayne asked. 'I've been meaning to call in.'

'She's just back from a trip. She's took the boat up the canal for a week. Towards Banbury.'

'A holiday?'

'Selling logs. Cutting hair. Quoting Shakespeare. Being Caprice.'

Wayne laughed and replied: 'Most people use

narrowboat holidays as a way of slowing down. Caprice probably had to quicken up.'

Kate smiled.

'My grandfather used to tell me that whenever I needed a sense of what is important in life I should walk into a hospital,' Wayne said.

'I go to hospitals all the time,' Kate said.

'Exactly – you know what's important.'

'There was a man the other day. He went down for an operation. He told me to tell his wife that he loved her and that she had been everything to him. Then he told me that he had spent too much of his life feeling frustrated.'

'Hospital experiences change people. Maybe he'll come out and do what he wants.'

'He didn't survive the operation.'

'Oh. Too late.'

'I think he knew he wouldn't.'

'Uh-huh.'

'I'm lucky,' Wayne said. 'It was time I walked away from my job, and I'm comfortably off. Others are not so lucky.'

'Most people hate their jobs. Their main work ambition is to win the lottery so they don't have to work. What are you going to do?'

'I think I'll write up the events of the last few weeks,' Wayne said.

'Don't you dare.'

'There's a guy I know who's a writer. I might tell him the story.'

Kate thought for a while.

'Change all the names,' she said. 'Change the locations. Change the details.'

'I'll phone the guy. He can write about our maelstrom.'

'My goodness, Wayne, if you know words like maelstrom you don't need to phone anyone. You could write it yourself.'

'Will you tell him your part of the story?'

'I would have to think long and hard about that. I don't make such decisions on the spur of the moment after drinking whisky. Especially when confidentiality is involved.'

They sipped more whisky. Wayne emptied the bottle into their glasses.

'Thanks for writing those letters,' Wayne said.

'They had to be done.'

Kate had written anonymously to three people – the man in the jewellery shop, Buck Hanson and Robin Hookes – to tell them that a black-haired lady had been diagnosed with hepatitis B and they should arrange for testing at a sexual health clinic. Kate had given them the relevant phone numbers.

'Any contact with Juliet?' Kate asked.

'No. She's back approaching full throttle according to Mackie. I haven't spoken to her since I went round to the house to apologise for not looking after her properly. I think she still blames me.'

'I wonder if she's been tested,' said Kate. 'Did you write to her to suggest that?'

'Yes, I did.'

They sipped more whisky.

'Our spell as housemates will soon be over,' Wayne said. 'Do you think we will ever be lovers?'

'I don't know,' she said. 'We certainly won't be before I leave, if that's what you're thinking.'

Wayne raised his glass to Kate and spoke: 'This could be the start of a beautiful friendship.'

Their glasses tinkled to the toast. They sipped and smiled. Finished off their whiskies without speaking.

'I've got an early start,' Kate said.

'Early shift?'

Kate nodded.

'Can I give you a hug?' Wayne asked.

'Sure,' said Kate.

'And can I say one more thing?'

'If you must.'

'This has clearly been one of the worst times of your life, Kate. Yet you've still been capable of making new friends and impressing people like me and Jeremy Spooner. And you've looked after people who are ill and in difficulties. You've given such a lot to us. That's a real testimony of what a wonderful person you are.'

Kate let out a sudden sob and clung to him.

'Come on, let it out,' Wayne said.

She howled for a few minutes.

'It's all right,' Wayne said.

His shirt grew damper and damper.

Eventually she pulled back. Reached for some tissues.

'It's a real problem being tall,' Wayne said.

'Why?' asked Kate.

'Our tears have to go so much further before they hit the floor.'

TWENTY-NINE

Some weeks later Wayne sat in a hospice in the south of England.

'Thanks for coming to my death bed,' said the black-haired woman.

'I had to come, Fleur,' Wayne told her.

'Call me Em,' she said. 'Call me Emmanuelle. I liked being your Emmanuelle.'

Wayne had responded to a short note: *Wayne: want to hear my confession? Em*

'So tell me what happened with Rachel Hanson,' Wayne said.

'We had contacts in three refuges. They would pick out the moneyed ones for us.'

'Why would they do that?'

'Because funding was under threat for certain long-standing refuges. Self-funding was a way to keep the work going. It's the free market. And we knew from Rachel that Hanson kept lots of money in the house.'

'OK. So you heard about Rachel wanting to leave Hanson?'

'The refuge people set it up for a Friday night. We called for her two hours earlier than the refuge had arranged. Freed her from the madman.'

'Did you enjoy your night with him?'

'What a bastard. It was just a sisterhood duty. A night with you would have been very different.'

'Were you riding one of the horses when the money was picked up?'

'I was in the truck. I wanted to do it but it would have taken up too much of my energy.'

'What about Robin Hookes? He didn't strike me as the type to treat women too badly. Why did you go for him?'

'He was a route to Juliet. She was Rachel's enemy. Juliet wasn't a sisterhood woman. We were looking to her for money. A kind donation to make me go away. But we couldn't ask her until the coast was clear.'

'The coast was clear?' Wayne asked.

'Until you left her unguarded.'

'That Sunday night.'

'Hanson went in after you. Didn't stay long.'

'Didn't he lock the back door after him?'

'No, he left it open. I locked the back door after me.'

'And you traumatised Juliet?'

'She was mostly gone. I don't think she had enjoyed her interlude with Hanson. You looked angry when you left.'

'I should have stayed.'

'I would have got to her some other way. But this worked out better than I would have hoped. It was a good time to make a pitch to her for some money. I broke the news that she may well have hepatitis B from Hookes, Hanson or Shakespeare.'

'But you hadn't been with me at that point.'

'She didn't know that. Especially after I had described Hookes and Hanson in the bedroom.'

'Did you injure her?'

'She was injured and in shock when I found her. Sitting at the bottom of the stairs to the top floor.'

Buck Hanson, Wayne thought. There's a score to settle.

'Are you going to tell me where your group is based?' Wayne asked.

'Of course not,' she smiled. 'Even if you brought your female muscle.'

Wayne presumed she meant Tracey Holroyd.

'Is the group based near here?'

'No, this is just where I wanted to be.'

'To go away and die like a cat.'

Em seemed surprised.

'I visited your parents,' Wayne said.

'Oh.'

Em looked thoughtful.

'Our group won't last forever, she said, after an uneasy silence. 'The straight refuges are on to us. It will be harder to infiltrate them. We will have to go directly to the victims. We do some of that already. We target the rich ones we find through newspaper articles, but we need to seek a balance of the wealthy and the really needy. The group will break up when the money runs out.'

'I don't understand why you went after Juliet. I thought you were pro-women, pro-sisterhood.'

'Only our sisters. Only the ones in our group.'

Wayne understood now. It was like that with football teams. You stuck up for your team mates and took on the opposition.'

'So Rachel was one of you?'

'Especially after she had told us her story on that first night. It fired me up.'

'For revenge?'

'For action.'

'What will happen to Rachel now?'

'I don't know. She is aware that she daren't go back to Buck Hanson. I offered to fix it for her so that she didn't go back. Now she has some thinking time and she will do some courses. She could just start a new life and apply for a divorce eventually. I think Rachel was shocked and hurt that Buck didn't come up with the money to save her.'

'He thinks she's dead.'

'That was the idea. What a bastard!'

'How many men did you try to infect?'

'Try to infect? Oh, you mean, how many men was I lovingly drawn to and seduced by? Handsome men like Wayne Shakespeare?'

'How many in your recent spree? There was the jeweller, Hookes, Hanson and me.'

'You know about the jeweller?'

'Kate did.'

'Amazing.'

'Any others?'

'An old boyfriend who treated me bad. He thought a minute of his time was worth a day of mine.'

'Can I inform him that he is at risk?'

'If you can find him.' She smiled. 'If you can get a minute of his time.'

'Are you proud of what you did?' Wayne asked.

'Proud?' Then her dull eyes brightened. 'I certainly felt empowered, Wayne, I felt so very empowered. I have never felt so strong and powerful, and yet my body was approaching its weakest.'

'Do your parents know where you are?'

'No. Don't tell them where I am.'

'Is that revenge on the abusers, too?

She gave a half smile.

'You don't miss much, do you?' she said.

Wayne shrugged.

'What does Em really stand for?' he asked.

'Em is for Emmanuelle.'

Wayne shook his head.

'I don't think so,' he said.

'That old boyfriend who treated me bad. He always kept me waiting. He once told me that I was a real mankiller.'

'Em is for Mankiller.'

'I was a real mankiller, wasn't I, Wayne? I would have had you eventually, wouldn't I?'

'You're irresistible, Em.'

'Publish my story, Wayne, if you can,' said Fleur Rhodes-Jones. 'Tell the world. Tell men what they have to fear if they don't treat women kindly. Help to stamp out abuse of all kinds.'

'Were you damaged when young?'

'An eye for an eye, a tooth for a tooth, a virus for a virus.' She looked at him. 'We could have been a couple, Wayne, you and me. I think you'd have looked after me, listened to me. Oh, we'd have had some rows, but we'd have made up properly and had great sex afterwards. I'd have taken you away from No Man's Land.'

We can but dream, Wayne thought. But he chose his words carefully.

'You're unforgettable, Em,' he said. 'You looked so beautiful in my bedroom.'

And felt so dangerous, Wayne thought.

'That Kate is too serious for you,' Fleur said.

Wayne nodded. Yes, she is too serious at the moment. But she won't always be.

'You may go down in history as my last lover, Wayne,' Fleur said. 'Hold my hand.'

Wayne obediently took her hand. As she drifted into sleep her hand seemed to grip his more tightly. He stayed there as she slept. Gradually she released her grip. Centimetre by centimetre, his hand detached from hers. He sat and looked at her for longer. He stood slowly, took a few steps to the door, turned back and studied her again. She seemed so peaceful and so terminally ill.

On his drive back to Oxford, Wayne turned off the A36 and visited a tiny place called Nomansland. He sat in the car and thought of the Mankiller. She would be in and out of the hospice for some time. Short spells of treatment. He planned to visit her again. Learn more of her story.

On leaving Nomansland it was Kate Park who entered his mind. He wondered how she was doing on the film set. He decided that he would phone her when he got home. Phone her at midnight. It would be so good to hear her voice at that late hour, even it was only the voicemail message on the mobile phone he had bought her.

A smile came to his face. Maybe he could visit Kate. He could use a holiday.

www.ingramcontent.com/pod-product-compliance
Lightning Source LLC
Chambersburg PA
CBHW070909260626
47162CB00007B/2609